STAR QUEST

BY PATRICIA LEE MACOMBER

Through his communicator, Tony heard everything that was happening on the bridge.

He heard Captain Hunter give the command for Mr. Parks to begin his maneuver.

He heard the furious yelling and threats of Benom.

He could not hear the thunk-clunk of the Oden-Khaar warrior as he made his way toward Tony's position.

The ship banked hard to starboard but Tony's boots held fast. The additional motion of the ship gaining speed worked against him, but he managed to keep his position steady. It was the first time he had ever been grateful that there was no air and no gravity in space.

His hand shook hard as it hovered over the portal generator's screen, awaiting further orders. Squatted down, half turned, he kept an eye on his would-be attacker.

And in turn, the bridge crew heard Tony's desperate prayers and panting.

"Now, Tony!" Hunter yelled into his com.

Tony's hand slammed down on the button and he held his frantic breath, awaiting the appearance of the portal. What seemed to take days and actually took only seconds was a personal triumph for Tony. He was rich and handsome and brilliant, but he was not brave. Yet, in the past five minutes, he had defeated a foe, clung to the hull of a ship that he, himself, had built, and activated the portal that would save the entire crew. The way he had it figured, if he died right then, all his arrogance would be vindicated. He would die a hero.

CHAPTER 1

Lieutenant-Commander Cara Bishop was excited. A new class of would-be pilots was headed her way. Green. Unformed. Blank slates. Half of them would wash out before ground school finished. All but the best five of them would wash out soon after. Never mind that, though. She had her lesson plan in place. This was not her first rodeo.

Even more excited than Cara were the recruits. They had the chance to be taught by the great Cara Bishop. She was legend. They were scared. If they washed out, they might as well just leave the Navy. Better that than have to face Commander Bishop for the rest of their lives.

Fifty young men and women sat in their seats, the room darkened, the chatter minimal, and when the door opened, the bright California sun flooded the room. A hundred feet hit the floor in unison, arms snapped to, and in walked Cara Bishop, her blonde hair bathed in sunlight, a halo shining brightly about her head. None of them turned; they didn't dare. They were at attention.

Cara ignored them, walked straight to her desk and turned on one heel. Her first words to them should carry weight, have meaning, stick with them forever. It should give them a clue as to her state of mind.

"At ease, you bums," she barked, stepping around her desk and coming to rest at the front of it. She folded her arms over her chest and crossed her ankles, glaring at them in the most severe manner. Several of them flinched and it almost made her smile. "How many of you have flown planes before?"

All hands went into the air. Some of them adopted a smug smile.

Cara nodded once. "Well, you haven't flown a Striker!" she yelled. "And most of you never will."

Hands went down, faces fell. Only one remained cock-sure and gloating. He would make it. He would be the class star. She knew it.

"Beneath your chairs are books. They will be your constant companions for the next twelve weeks, your best friends, your worst enemies. Know them, live them, eat, sleep and breathe them. Do not ever show up in my class without them. You will suffer."

She stepped back to the chalkboard behind the desk and pulled down a screen. It was old—pre-war—and showed it. The laptop on her desk was new, but that had been bought at her own expense. She got tired of using the beaten and battered Navy-issued piece of junk. She hit a few keys and stepped back, her eyes locked on the screen.

"This is the Striker-Z. It is capable of speeds three times the speed of light and its fuel cells will carry you over twelve hundred light years away before burning out. And this," she said, changing the picture, "is *my* Striker-Z. If you study hard and work even harder, you might one day be given a Striker of your own."

A hand went into the air. The arrogant one. Cara pointed at him and he came to attention at once. "Is that the Striker you flew in the Battle of Australia?"

"No, Mr. Powell. That is my first Striker. Veteran of four hundred and fifty-three kills, nineteen rescues, and over a hundred scouting missions. It is the first Striker ever built and sits now in the museum."

The door opened suddenly, and Cara turned, scowling. Surely, nobody would dare come late to her class. Nobody would dare interrupt her. A tall, thin lieutenant stepped inside and shut the door against the rising heat. His hat was tucked under his arm and he carried a clipboard. He came to attention before her, without blinking.

"Lieutenant," she sighed, casting him a perfunctory salute.

"Commander Bishop, the admiral wishes to see you in his office right away. He sent me to take over your class."

Behind them, a moan of disappointment rippled through the class.

Cara frowned and took the clipboard from him, scanned it quickly, and handed it back. "Very well. I'll try to be brief. Don't go easy on them. And if you have any trouble, I'll have them spend the next three classes running laps of my house."

"Ma'am, yes, ma'am." Another salute, which she ignored.

She would have loved to refuse but you can't refuse the admiral and he wouldn't have sent for her if it hadn't been important. She stepped through the door, cinched her hat onto her head at just the right angle, and unlocked her car.

The admiral's office was in the large complex just off the main road, after you passed the exchange, the bowling alley and the theater. She drove the speed limit, just as she always did. What would everyone say if the world's hottest hot-shot pilot got a ticket?

The car was scorching and the meager air conditioning did nothing to alleviate that. She circled the parking lot only once and slid her car into a space some four aisles from the main door. She felt sticky, in need of a shower. *Damn this summer heat, anyway.*

Commander Hansen and Captain Edmonds passed her on the sidewalk and she snapped to. The salute was returned immediately and she was on her way again.

The air conditioning in the main building worked better than any other place on the base. The air washed over her the second she pulled on the door handle, producing a sucking sound and a slight whistle. Inside, she removed her hat and made her way past the first two reception areas without incident. The admiral's office was at the far end of that long hall. Her shoes made tiny squeaking noises as she walked. That's what she got for cleaning the damn soles, after all.

Inside that office was a cramped reception area with not one but two aides. They sat on either side of the door and both smiled when Cara walked in. She stood, planted, between both desks and smiled.

"The admiral sent for me."

"He said you should go right in," the brunette said with a smile.

"Thank you."

She stepped past them quickly, eager to have done with whatever the admiral had in mind. He knew it was her first day with that class and he knew how she hated deviating from a schedule.

The admiral sat behind his massive walnut desk, hands folded on top of it. The desk was sparse, no clutter, no mess, nothing that wasn't essential. Cara stepped up to the desk and saluted. Only then did she notice the man sitting in the chair to her left.

"You wanted to see me, Admiral?"

He never returned her salute. "At ease, Bishop. Take a seat."

She dropped into the chair next to her, back board-straight, ankles crossed, hands folded in her lap. She was crisp and clean and squared-away, from the top of her regulation hair to the tips of her freshly shined shoes.

"This is Vice Director Benjamin Danforth. Mr. Danforth, this is Commander Cara Bishop."

"Pleased to finally meet you," the man said as he thrust out his hand.

His nails were freshly manicured, Cara noticed, his suit expensive and cleanly pressed. Whatever it was he was vice-director of, it must pay very well, indeed. "Likewise," she said, pumping his hand twice with a good, firm grip.

"Mr. Danforth has come to me with a request." The admiral smiled and nodded Danforth's way. "He's working on a special project and he's specifically requested you because of your... expertise."

Cara cocked her head to one side and eyed him. "My expertise lies in combat missions and flying the Strikers."

He smiled. His teeth were gleaming white, a counterpoint to his dark brown skin. It made his face a good deal softer and there was no duplicity in it. "I know. Which makes you perfect for this project."

She cast a quick sideward glance at the admiral, who showed nothing in his stoic face. "What sort of project did you say it was?"

"I didn't." Again, that smile. It was a salesman's smile, a

politician's smile, and anything but genuine. He sat back in his chair, finally at ease, and studied her.

"I'm confused. How can I agree to be assigned to a project if I don't know what it is?" She returned his infectious smile. It faltered quickly. "Unless command is changing my orders." She looked to the admiral but again, his face betrayed nothing.

"It would be far easier for me to show you the project than to tell you about it. The visual impact of such a thing is sure to sway you." He winked at her then, a very odd thing for him to do. "Of course, you'll have to sign a non-disclosure agreement…."

"I assure you. I have super-secret clearance. There's nothing you can show me…."

"Be that as it may, Commander, this is far more sensitive than anything you've ever worked on before. Nobody—and I mean nobody—can know about this. Ever."

Cara scowled right into his face and shook her head. "This is highly unusual."

"Give me four hours of your time, Commander. That's all I ask. Just take a little road trip with me and when we get back, if you still want to say no, I'll be on my way."

She stared at him for a moment longer, then nodded. "All right. I would like a word with the admiral first. In private."

Danforth stood and straightened his jacket. "I'll wait in the outer office, then. Whenever you're ready."

Cara spun on her heel and opened the door, letting the man pass through only barely before she closed it. Then she turned on the admiral.

"Permission to speak freely, Admiral?"

"Go ahead." His smile had taken over his face and his blue eyes sparkled with good humor and…was it a secret?

"What the hell's going on, Daddy?"

He laughed outright at that, his face reddening with the effort. "I was wondering how long you'd hold it in." He rose and stepped around the desk, placing his large hands on Cara's shoulders and giving them a little squeeze. "Look, princess, everything's going to be fine. I promise."

"Do you know what the project is?"

He nodded. "I do."

"Then why can't you tell me?" Her eyes darkened at that, her face slipped into a frown.

"You know why. Come on!" He chuckled a bit, then realized that his good humor had gone unappreciated. "Here's what happened. I got a call from the director of this project. He explained to me what it is and told me that they desperately needed you. He said that the project required only the best and he asked me if I thought you would be amenable to it. I told him that he would have to talk to you. And that's why Danforth is here."

"You know what it is. Would you do it?"

"Hell, yes! The only thing I can tell you is this: This is the most amazing, mind-bending thing you've ever set eyes on in your life. And you will never, ever get another chance like it."

She squinted at him through one eye and spoke in a low, deep voice. "Even more amazing than fighting aliens in one of their own space craft?"

"Lots more." He reeled her into a bear hug, stroking her blonde hair and staring over the top of her head into nothingness. "Go with him. See what he wants to show you, listen to what he has to say. You've got nothing to lose and everything to gain." He shoved her out to arm's length and smiled warmly. "We'll talk when you get back."

"Okay, Daddy. I'm trusting you."

"That's my girl." He kissed her forehead and tweaked her nose. "Come straight to my house when you get back. We'll have dinner and a nice talk."

She nodded and picked up her hat. She had worried at it without realizing it and there were fingerprints all over the brim. She buffed them out with her sleeve. "See you soon, Daddy."

When she opened the door to the outer office, Mr. Danforth was sitting in a metal chair against the wall, looking as calm as he could be. He rose upon seeing her and smiled that winning smile of his. "Shall we be off?"

"Let's." She followed him out the door, back into the heat, pressing her hat onto her head and snugging it down as she followed him to his car.

The car was government issue, she noticed; brand new and completely lacking in the normal cast-offs of everyday driving. She climbed into the shotgun position and adjusted the seat to accommodate her long legs. The car still had that new-car smell and she breathed deeply of it.

"So, where are we headed?" she asked as Danforth slid behind the wheel and started the car. The air conditioning blew hot for a moment before cooling off.

"Into the desert. There's an installation about an hour from here. We expanded it and repurposed most of the hangars and equipment. And now we call it home."

The conversation dissipated, leaving only the rush of air from the vents and the hum of the car's engine as background noise. Cara stared out the window, contentedly alone with her own thoughts. She hated mysteries and hated waiting for... anything. If she had to tolerate both, better it should be in silence.

"I'm afraid that being in the presence of greatness has stricken me speechless," Danforth said finally, startling Cara and eliciting a small sigh.

"Don't try to butter me up, sir. It won't work."

"Oh, I'm not, honest. But you have to admit, you are the most famous person on the planet. Single-handedly saving the human race from extinction."

"It was a concerted effort. That's what most people don't realize. I didn't do it alone at all."

"You saved the whole damn world. Ticker tape parades. A holiday in your honor. The whole shebang. If that isn't greatness, I don't know what is."

"It was my job."

"The way I hear it, you could have refused." When she said nothing more, he pressed on. "If I come out of this with nothing more, I'd be honored to hear you tell your story."

"I don't like to think about it. Ever." She turned her face to the window and stared. A shiver ran through her.

"Just one time. It's okay if you toot your own horn just this once. For posterity's sake."

She turned back to him. He wasn't going to let it go, not ever. They would be trapped together in that car for nearly an hour yet and he wasn't going to stop until she told him everything.

"Command was divided on whether I should be the one to fly the mission or not. Half of them said I was the only one who had a chance at pulling it off. The other half wanted me there in case it failed. They said they'd need me to beat back the retaliatory attacks."

"It was a suicide mission. You knew it?"

"Yes. The only way to destroy the mother ship was to drive a proton bomb right straight up the middle of it and detonate from the inside. They told me that I wouldn't come back, even if it wasn't successful."

"And you went anyway. But how did you...?"

"Come back?" She grunted, snorted, shook her head. "I got lucky. And I had a lot of good people on my six." Cara swallowed and looked at her hands. "Most of them didn't come back." Tears threatened, something she wasn't used to, something she hated.

"I know we lost a lot of good men and women. It was a dark day. But look at the millions of lives they saved thanks to their bravery."

"I couldn't have gotten close to the ship without all of them. They provided cover fire, distractions. They ran interference for me. The victory was as much theirs as mine."

"Yes." Danforth nodded somberly. "But how on earth did you make it out alive?"

"They gave me a new Striker. It was modified with the new payload system and weapons. The propulsion system was a good thirty percent faster than the previous models. But they painted it to look like my old Striker. I had a reputation. The aliens hated me and they wanted me bad. I had the proton bomb on board and the plan was for me to fly straight in through the hangar bay doors when they opened to release their fleet. Once inside, I was to detonate that bomb. 'Fly straight up their ass, burrow as deep into the ship as you can, then blow that fucker to bits.' That's what the joint chiefs said.

"Everything went beautifully. The rest of the fleet launched a huge attack on the mother ship, forcing them to open their hangar doors and take their shields down long enough to launch a defense. I was just about to push max speed when I got an idea. So, I cut my engines, and my life support. I used the emergency oxygen tank to stay alive. I was hoping they would want me alive bad enough to latch onto the Striker with a tractor beam. They could parade me through the streets, beaten and enslaved, demoralizing the rest of the citizens. And then they could hold my public execution. They needed me alive for that but they had to get me inside fast.

"They pulled me into the ship. Backward, which was lucky for me. The other ships had already launched, so it was just me, the Striker, and about two thousand fuel cells. As soon as I was in there, I dropped my payload on the deck. I set the detonation for sixty seconds, then I powered up my Striker and force-fed it every ounce of speed I could. I wasn't sure if I could get far enough away from the blast to save myself, but I gave it everything I had.

"I was halfway back to Earth when the bomb blew. I remember my headset filled up with chatter, from command, from the other pilots. They had no idea what I'd done. They just figured I'd chickened out. The first blast was spectacular. It blew out the after section of the hangar and tore a hole through the bottom. That destroyed their fuel cells. But the really amazing thing was the second blast. When all those fuel cells went off, it completely obliterated the ship. The splitting of the bomb's atoms set up a chain reaction. All that exotic matter went up like a supernova. I remember watching bits of the ship whiz past my windlass. And when I got back to base, there was an alien hand embedded in the left wing.

"People were cheering before I even climbed out of the Striker. And then I saw the joint staff marching on me. They were pissed that I'd changed the plan and told no one. They were pissed that I didn't follow orders to the letter." She laughed then and shook her head at the irony. "I saved the whole damn world and they were pissed that I hadn't died."

"That's military for you. Not a lot of room for creativity. Just rules."

"Yes, and then my father ran across the tarmac...."

"Your father, the admiral."

Her head whipped around and she stared at him suspiciously.

"You don't think I did my homework before coming to see you?" That infectious smile lit up his face again. "I know more about you than even you do."

"Good for you." She returned the smile. "Anyway, my father ran across the tarmac and grabbed me up in this big bear hug. And he literally told the joint chiefs of staff to go to hell. And I'm pretty sure we were both on the verge of being court-martialed, but the rest of the fleet began coming in and suddenly there were cheering men and women everywhere and the chiefs couldn't even get near me."

"Did they hoist you up on their shoulders and all that?" He was loving this story. It was the closest he'd ever get to true greatness and he was eating it up.

"Yeah, they hoisted me in the air and cheered. And people began pouring out of the buildings and cheering. We were free and the whole world rejoiced. Then we started counting how many ships didn't come back."

It overtook her in a flash. She never cried, not even on the day her mother died. There was no crying in war. She turned to the window and slapped her hand over her mouth, stared straight ahead so as not to spill the tears. She almost couldn't breathe, the lump in her throat was so big. It was a struggle to keep her shoulders from heaving.

Danforth knew. He took one look at the back of her head, the attitude of her back, and he knew. The way he saw it, there was no shame in shedding tears for the brave men and women who had died defending their planet. Even less shame if they were friends. He felt bad for her. She wouldn't accept his comfort, not even his words. So, he decided to prattle on and give her time to recover.

"And that's exactly what the president said in his speech. 'The selfless acts of many brave men and women have lifted us out of darkness and into the light. And never more shall we doubt that we, as a race, are one. We fought as one. We triumphed as one. And now we will rebuild as one.' I must have watched that speech a hundred times. He was the greatest president we've ever had. He served under the greatest adversity and he helped lead us out of darkness."

He paused and glanced over at her. She seemed a bit calmer.

"And then there were parties and ticker tape parades. They gave you your own holiday, the key to damn near every city on Earth. People had t-shirts made and everyone wanted to be just like our brave pilots. I swear, we almost destroyed a few cities while we were celebrating our victory."

She finally turned back to him, a smile threatening the corners of her mouth. "I think the other pilots and I actually did destroy a bar. But I was pretty much blacked out so I can't be sure."

They shared a laugh at that, the tension finally gone. Whatever pain had infected her, she'd pushed it back deep inside herself. Hopefully, she wouldn't have to let it out again.

"When we come up over the top of this next hill, you should be able to look down and see the installation."

Cara was surprised at how long they'd been talking. She was anxious to see any part of this base or the purported magnificent surprise that her father had alluded to. She leaned forward, eyes straining, her hands on the dashboard. Every muscle in her body was tensed.

When they finally crested that last small hill, the base came into view. There was a long dirt road leading down the hill and across the dustbowl toward it. She spotted several checkpoints and a security gate along the way but what was all the fuss about? There were a couple of small Quonset huts scattered about but nothing more. A larger concrete building stood at the center of it all, surrounded by a huge parking lot. There was nothing there to get excited about.

And then she saw it.

"Are those hangar doors? In the ground?"

"Correct, you are." Danforth grinned a bit.

"They're...huge." Her head spun in his direction, targeting him with her eyes. "What have you got down there?"

"You'll see." He was taunting her now...and enjoying it.

"Cryptic to the very end, huh?"

"Yep." He turned down the dirt road and slowed a bit as the car began to bump and bounce around. "We're coming up to Checkpoint Alpha."

He slowed even more, using one hand to rummage around in his pocket. He produced a small bi-fold wallet which he clutched along with the steering wheel. With his other hand, he rolled down the window and made ready to greet the two soldiers who came out to meet them. They were young, but not overly so. And they were armed. Heavily.

"Good afternoon, sir. Can we see your papers, please?"

Danforth flipped open the billfold and flashed some sort of badge at the man. His partner stood behind him and to the right, his rifle raised and his eyes dead-calm.

"Thank you, sir," said the first guard, shouldering his rifle. They both stepped back toward the guard house with a nod.

"On to Checkpoint Baker," said Danforth with a smile.

"Whatever you have here must be really important. You've got more security than the White House."

"We sure do. You have no idea."

The boys at Checkpoint Baker were a good deal more serious. They came out with rifles raised, three men ready to kill anyone who looked threatening. "ID please."

Cara produced her Navy ID, passing it to Danforth. The first soldier disappeared with it, Cara assumed, in order to validate it. When he returned, he had a sticker in his hand. This he slapped on the windshield of the car, then handed their IDs back to them.

Danforth rolled up his window, shutting out the hot air and sun. "Every car on this base has to have a new sticker every day. If they find a car without a sticker, they blow it up immediately. Don't ever forget your sticker."

"Duly noted."

Half a mile down the road was Checkpoint Charlie. Danforth stopped the car just under the canopy, cutting the engine before he climbed out. A soldier stepped forward and opened Cara's door for her, waving her out of the car. His eyes denoted recognition but he said nothing to her whatsoever.

One man scanned the car with one device while the other did a visual search of every square inch of it. Both Danforth and Cara were searched thoroughly, then made to stand away from the car. Finally, another man came in with a second device, which he used to search the engine compartment and the trunk. At long last, they were declared safe and allowed to return to the vehicle.

"I just wanted to say thank you, Commander Bishop. Your brave service not only saved us, but it made me join up, as well."

"Have you ever regretted it?"

He smirked. Cara marveled at how young his face was. "Not since basic training," he replied with a wink.

"Good man."

Danforth rolled up the window and pulled slowly away from the guards. "I'll bet you get a lot of that."

"I try to avoid it. It makes me uncomfortable."

He nodded slowly and turned left, toward the largest of the buildings and its adjacent parking. "Now, on to the main entrance," he said softly.

There wasn't much activity on the base. They never passed another car; no one was milling about outside. Even the smoking area was empty. As they walked up to the front doors of the building, Cara noticed a lack of signs. Each building was marked with a letter, nothing more.

The electric doors opened with a soft puff of air and inside was nearly as stagnant as the outside. Everything was military green and gray. The capacious building was quiet, despite an inherent echo, and the floors shone like mirrors. Two guards stood on either side of the front door; two more were on the far side, where the hallway began.

Danforth led her to a large desk to their right. There were two people there; one watched a monitor and the other idled at the middle of the desk, awaiting their arrival. This woman reminded Cara of herself, all neat and squared-away. Cara liked her instantly.

"How may I help you?" she asked without a smile.

"I need to sign in and get my guest here a visitor's badge." Danforth slid his own ID across the desk, then held out his hand for Cara's.

Cara presented the lady with her military ID, then waited patiently. It was so oddly quiet in that cavern of a building that she was hesitant to move, to make any noise. The computer printer presently broke the silence, whirring for a moment before it spat out a large paper badge. More noise as the woman behind the desk laminated it, then all was silent again.

"Please keep the badge on you at all times, Commander Bishop. And enjoy your visit."

"Thank you." Cara took the badge and slipped the lanyard over her neck.

Danforth took her arm and led her toward the hallway, their heels producing what amounted to thunder in the echoing room. For a moment, Cara thought about walking on her toes to minimize the noise. It made her self-conscious. And then they were through the opening and into the hallway.

"We have to undergo decontamination before we can enter," Danforth said in a low voice.

Cara shot him a confused look and blinked hard. "What the hell are you doing down here anyway?"

"Everything." The coy smile was back and this time, it unnerved Cara.

They stepped through another door and into a chamber which very much reminded Cara of a sunless tanning booth. There were sprayers all over the walls, ceiling and floors and a huge bank of sun lamps on the ceiling. Danforth stopped her in the center, pushed her over about six inches and then stood board-straight.

"Shut your eyes."

The air hit her with a suddenness that she hadn't thought possible. No wind-up. All pitch. It blew the security badge up into the air and whipped it about her neck. She flinched hard and held her breath. Then the lamps on the ceiling came on and they were pelted with a fine mist, followed by another blast of air. Finally, it was all over.

"A little extreme, don't you think?" she asked him as she fought to straighten her hair and fix her lanyard.

"You won't think so when you see what's down here. Come on."

The doors opposite them opened and Danforth stepped through, beckoning for her to follow. There was nothing to see in that hallway either and the echo was almost non-existent, so she walked quickly toward the next set of doors.

"More decontamination?" she asked snidely as they approached.

"Nope." He pulled out his card and slid it through the reader, then leaned forward for a retinal scan. The indicator light hesitated, then went from red to green and the doors slid open on an elevator. "Everything is underground here. Way underground."

She stepped into the elevator with him, not certain what to expect. There was no panel of buttons to indicate floors, only a phone for emergencies and a warning against ten separate violations. Cara read them all out of curiosity and boredom.

The elevator was fast. She couldn't tell how far down they dropped but judging by the speed, they must have gone about a hundred feet down or more. The thing was quiet, producing no more than a soft hum. Blissfully, the landing was soft and unexpected, and when the doors opened, Cara felt the air pressure change immeasurably. She popped her ears and stepped out to stand beside Danforth.

"How far down are we, exactly?"

"Three hundred feet."

"And those hangar doors? They're for whatever you keep down here, right?"

"Exactly. Come on. There's a lot to see." He took her arm and led her down a short hallway, to where it let out on a huge chamber. Off this chamber were a myriad of doors, each leading to something dark and mysterious, Cara assumed.

"Just what are you doing down here, anyway? Some sort of research?"

Danforth tried on his smile again, though this time it was decidedly disturbing and duplicitous. "We're doing all kinds of research. Bio-medical, bio-engineering, propulsion, you name it. But there's only one specific thing I want to show you. Come on."

She followed him, intrigued now. She had expected something lackluster, something completely banal. Now, she had hopes that the whole trip might well be worth it, if he would just get to the point.

They walked past several doors, a few glass walls, inside of which were various equipment and more than a few scientists. No one registered their passing or even glanced at them. Cara thought the presence of a stranger should produce somewhat more of a response than that. Perhaps they had more visitors than she had thought.

At the opposite side of the large room, there was a long, narrow hall. It was down this hall that Danforth next led her. Halfway to the end, he stopped her, turning to face her and flashing a smile that could only be described as that of a child on Christmas morning.

"I know this sounds silly, but close your eyes."

"What?"

"Close your eyes. I want you to have the full and stunning effect."

"Forgive me for saying so, Mr. Danforth, but this is just a little bit silly."

"Humor me. It'll be worth it. I promise." He watched as she shut her eyes. "Okay, I won't let you run into any walls or anything. Just come this way." He took both her hands, he walking backward, she forward.

She felt rather than saw the light of the next chamber as they stepped into it. There was more noise here, the sound of movement and of equipment operating. The air was different too, as though it were being cleaned every hour, warmed and sent back. She breathed deeply, waiting in her darkened world for the command to open her eyes.

Danforth positioned her just so, then stepped to her left. "Okay, open your eyes now."

Cara had no idea what she might see. During their trek down the hallway, she had imagined all sorts of things: aliens alive or dead, weapons of epic destruction, monsters even. Nothing she had conjured up in her imagination could have prepared her for that actual first sight of it.

CHAPTER 2

"That's…it's…it's a ship. A huge freaking ship."

Danforth nodded reverently.

Hovering about ten feet off the floor in the center of that huge man-made cave was a ship, contained by an electro-magnetic field of some sort. It was no ordinary ship, though, no Striker-Z. This ship was huge, easily a hundred times the size of a Striker. Cara blinked twice, rubbed her eyes. Only then did she realize that her mouth was agape. She stepped slowly to her right, thinking this vision to be nothing more than an illusion, a hologram. Staring, wordless, she walked several feet to her right, then to her left. Then her eyes targeted Danforth, who stood at the hallway opening, grinning like a madman.

"It could easily hold twenty Strikers."

"Thirty, actually," Danforth offered. "And that's just in the hangar bay."

"Where? How?" She swallowed hard and looked back to the ship. "Will it disturb the magnetic field if I walk under it?"

"No, no. By all means." He indicated the ship with a sweep of his hand. "Look to your heart's content."

Slowly, holding her breath even though she hadn't meant to, she stepped under the ship. She was suddenly taken with the insane idea that the field might fail, dropping the ship onto her and crushing her to death. She stepped to the side.

The thing was an elongated oval, over two hundred feet long and nearly a hundred feet across. Though she couldn't see the top of it, she was certain that it was at least six stories high. Lights flashed around the sides of it and the magnetic field produced a barely detectable vibration. The ship's lowest point was at its center, this being a mere two feet above her head.

She stood there, completely amazed and speechless. Slowly, she reached out one hand, fully expecting it to pass through the hull of the ship, to shatter the illusion. Then her fingers brushed against metal…or plastic…or something for which she had no name.

Her eyes shot to Danforth, still trapped behind his grin. "It's real."

"Of course it is," he laughed. "You think I'd bring you all the way here just to see a projection?" He laughed again.

"But where did it come from?"

"We made it."

"Made it? From what? How? Why?"

Danforth bent over, laughing. "We designed it from alien tech. But it's original. Nothing like anything they've seen before."

"And huge."

"Meant to carry a full complement of over a hundred crew members."

Cara shook her head slowly and finally smiled. "How fast? What are the weapons?"

From behind them came a man's voice, quite loud and almost bored-sounding. She wondered if she used the same tone when teaching her classes. Maybe that explained why her students suffered so much fatigue.

"The ship is capable of traveling at speeds in excess of fifteen times the speed of light and over a distance far enough to take us to the end of the universe. The weapons…well…that's why you're here."

Cara spun toward the voice and let her jaw drop again. A disheveled man in a white lab coat stood some ten feet from her, hands in his pockets, his face unreadable. His brown eyes were bright and large and bespoke intelligence and constant thought. His black hair, careless and untended, gave him a boyish appearance.

"You're–" She never got out another word.

"Tony Allen. Richest man on Earth. Genius engineer. Alien expert. And creator of all of this." He swept his arms around, finally offering a small grin.

"Creator of the Striker," she said with wonder, marching on him with her hand extended and her face stuck in a smile. "I've been waiting to meet you my whole life." She took his hand and pumped it hard. "It's such an honor. Without you…"

"Yeah, yeah. Without me, you could never have saved the world. Blah, blah, blah. Now, about the propulsion system…" He walked away from her as though he expected her to follow without question. "She's run on the same exotic matter that powered your bomb. But it's controlled. The explosions are smaller, shorter, of less power and more direction. And the fuel cells last virtually forever because the waste it produces is…you guessed it…more exotic matter."

Cara was star-struck. She gaped at him, only barely hearing anything he said. Her mind still hadn't wrapped itself around the events of the last fifteen minutes and her head felt numb. "You've actually flown it?" she asked at last.

"Oh God no!" Finally, Allen laughed. "They wouldn't even let me name it, much less take it out for a spin. Besides, it's not finished yet. We still have a lot of work to do."

"So how do you know the engines will even work?" It was an honest question, to which she expected an honest answer.

"Because I'm Tony Allen and everything I do works." He turned on his heels and walked away from the ship. "The models all say it will work."

Danforth crept up beside her, having been completely forgotten in Cara's shock over the ship and Allen. "And did he mention how modest he is?"

Cara turned to regard him with humor. "What about the weapons, Mr. Allen?"

"Tony."

"Tony. The weapons?"

Again, he spun on his heel to face her. "There's a proton canon mounted right here, and two disruptor beams, one on each fork at the front. Then…then there are the drones." He beamed at her then, his eyes shining and his face suddenly animated. "Come."

Cara and Danforth followed him to the far side of the huge chamber, affording them a look at the other side of the ship.

"Have you seen all of this before?" she asked Danforth softly.

"Not all of it, no."

"You see the eight ports on the sides of the ship? There's four on each side."

"Uh-huh." Cara craned her neck to look at the divots set into the sides of each fork arm.

"A drone docks with each one of them. They offer eight additional disruptors that can be used in battle. They can also be detached and flown separately. Over here. These are the pinnacle of human achievement, my proudest creation."

Cara followed him to a table against the wall where there sat a white ball about three feet in diameter. The smooth white surface was periodically broken up by a camera port, a disruptor barrel, and other sensors. Cara looked at it in wonder.

"As I said, they can be flown autonomously. You control them with this." Allen produced a glove. There were sensor pads in each finger and three on the palm. Allen slid it onto his hand and held it up for inspection. "Now, just watch."

He tapped a button on the back of the glove and the drone hummed to life, hovering about two inches off the table and awaiting further instructions. Allen smiled to himself and then raised his hand. The drone followed suit, lifting another few feet into the air. As the glove moved, so moved the drone, rising, falling, moving left and right. It passed without a sound, coming so close to Cara's head that she darted out of the way.

Allen made the big white ball spin, then right itself, flying about twenty feet from the ceiling and well away from anything that it might hit. Then it swooped under the ship, drawing a gasp from Danforth and Cara, and proceeded to pick up speed. Allen made it buzz one of the scientists working at another table, then circle the ship, all the while gaining speed.

"It hasn't even hit a tenth of its speed yet," Allen said.

Cara checked his face and noticed that he was smiling like a kid with a new toy. "Maybe you should keep the speed down while it's in close quarters."

"Don't worry. I got this," was Allen's reply.

He began making huge sweeping movements with his arm and hand, dodging, buzzing, doing loops. Cara watched with some amusement, but she couldn't escape the rising sense of doom that had come over her in the past few moments.

"Each of these finger pads controls a specific function," Allen announced, his voice rising, his eyes still locked on the drone. "Weapons, sensors, cameras, microphones."

"What about the fifth one?" Cara wanted to know.

A perplexed look came over Allen's face and he took his eyes off the drone long enough to look at Cara. By the time he looked back at the drone, it was headed straight for the wall at the far side of the hangar. He panicked then, going through a series of convulsion-like movements that were obviously meant to bring the drone back onto a safe path. But he had over-corrected and the drone spun and tilted, dropping toward the floor at an alarming rate.

"Crap!" Allen spat, making a few more spastic motions with his arm and hand.

"Oh!" Cara clapped her hand over her mouth and held her breath, watching as the drone careened toward them.

They ducked. All of them. The drone missed them by mere inches as it sped past, bound for the wall behind them. Clearly, Allen no longer had control over the thing. Its gyros had gone crazy and it tilted and spun, its path chaotic and random. Allen spat several curses and jerked back on his hand but it was too late. Momentum carried the thing straight into the concrete wall behind them, just to the left of a huge steel support beam. It crashed in a fiery blaze, raining parts onto the floor and dropping its shattered hull onto the cement where it sizzled for a moment before going dead.

Cara turned on him, her face caught between mocking and angry. "Your proudest achievement, huh?"

Allen chanced a look at Danforth and a cockeyed smile pulled back his cheeks. "I'll write a check for that in the morning."

"What the hell was that?" Another man in a white lab coat hurried toward them, his face pressed into service as an instrument of torture and his light brown hair wild. There were goggles perched atop his head and his hands were shaking. "I'm in my lab trying to introduce one DNA strand to another and all of a sudden the walls start shaking and I nearly spill the whole mess. What have you done this time, Allen?"

"He just crashed one of his drones. Not to worry. I don't think there was any structural damage." Danforth shot an amused look at Cara. "Commander Cara Bishop, may I introduce Dr. David Klein. Dr. Klein, this is Cara Bishop. Hopefully she will be our new weapons officer and we won't have to put up with Allen crashing things anymore."

Tony Allen should have looked contrite, embarrassed, any range of emotions denoting shame. He did not. He merely folded his arms over his chest and scowled like a petulant child.

"Yes, please come to work with us," Dr. Klein said. "My nerves really can't take any more of Allen's shenanigans."

Cara took Klein's hand and shook it. "It's a pleasure to meet you, Dr. Klein." She stepped back, looking confused. "Forgive my failing memory, but I'm sure I should know you from somewhere."

Klein shrugged and looked away, uncomfortable. "I was involved in the genetics end of the war. You know, autopsying aliens, studying their genetic make-up and what makes them tick, or rather, what makes them *stop* ticking...."

Allen stepped forward and grabbed Klein by the shoulders, giving him a hard squeeze and a shake. "Our good doctor is being modest here. He holds eight degrees in everything from medicine to bio-engineering and bio-mechanical reconstruction. His IQ is nearly as high as mine. And do you remember the SPARTA Project?"

"Genetically engineering super soldiers, right? Or something like that." Cara made a face. She hated being dragged into discussions on things which she knew nothing about.

"Exactly. Well, this is the guy who created the first...."

"And only...." Klein broke in, somewhat bitterly.

"He created the first and only super soldier. A total success, I might add, though the government later decided that hand-to-hand fighting was not the way to defeat the aliens and scrapped the whole project." At that, Allen cast a derisive glare at Klein.

"This is all lovely and you're quite the dream team," Cara laughed. "But what exactly is the point of all this?"

"The point, my dear, is to go out into space and find out if there are others…and if those others are friends or foes. The war proved that we're not alone. Now we have to find our neighbors and make sure that this never happens again." Danforth punctuated the statement with a decisive nod.

"And prove to them that, if it does, we are more than capable of defending ourselves." Allen never blinked.

"So, we're all going to climb aboard this magnificent ship and go looking for more aliens to attack us." She squinted at them, each in turn, and shook her head.

"No, we're going to go looking for friends. And knowledge." Allen finally remembered the glove on his hand. He removed it and slapped it down on the table. "Knowledge is the key to everything."

Klein nodded his head.

"Agreed. So, you want me to go along in case we meet some non-friends. I can see that." She thought for a moment, her forehead creasing deeply and her eyes glassing over a bit. "So, who's the captain of this motley crew?"

"That would be me," said the voice from behind her. "The aforementioned super soldier."

Cara spun to see who had addressed her, her eyes landing squarely on the chest of the giant who stood before her. He was easily seven feet tall, his sandy hair combed into perfect submission. His eyes were blue, sparkling, and full of warmth. Cara veritably swooned when she finally looked into them. He wore a grey t-shirt that barely contained his massive chest and shoulders. His biceps bulged out from the sleeves. He looked to be no more than twenty-five years old, though she knew that wasn't possible. He was, in every single way that she could find, the absolute perfect specimen of a man.

Cara's mouth had gone dry, her eyes unblinking. For many long seconds, she tried to shake herself back into the moment. Finally, she let go of a breath she hadn't even realized that she'd held and licked her lips. Then she cleared her throat and smiled feebly. "I'm Commander Cara Bishop."

He took her hand and some sort of electrical charge raced up her arm. She shuddered.

"Oh, I know exactly who you are. You saved the entire planet. Captain Steve Hunter at your service."

His hand completely engulfed hers, but his grip was so gentle that she didn't notice it at first. So enthralled by him was she that she failed to remember the other people around her. Thus, she started a bit when Danforth spoke.

"Captain Hunter, why don't you give Commander Bishop a tour of the ship?"

"My pleasure. This way...may I call you Cara?" His voice. God, his voice was like a warm fuzzy blanket.

For reasons completely unknown to her, she felt like a giggling little school girl every time she looked at him, every time he spoke. She had never reacted to anyone or anything that way before and it both perplexed and scared her. In an effort to save face, she reverted to her usual tactic of being cold and business-like. "Certainly, Captain."

Then he put his hand on her back to lead her away. Her knees started to quiver and she felt dizzy. She stepped ahead of him quickly, breaking the contact and saving herself from the most embarrassing moment of her life.

The ship was held aloft by a series of magnetic clamps that generated a false gravity field. A single, quite ordinary extension ladder led upward into the thing at the center of its main hull. Captain Hunter directed Cara in that direction, he taking long, easy strides, she chopping at the floor with her mincing steps.

"The elevators haven't been installed yet. I'm afraid it's ladders all the way." He looked at her, his blue eyes soft and warm, his smile apologetic.

"No problem, Captain." She smiled back at him but couldn't meet his gaze.

She bowed slightly when he waved her in front of him, then started up the ladder ahead of him. Her head was still foggy, trying to wrap itself around everything she'd seen and heard. Then there was the obvious effect that Captain Hunter had had on her. It had been as sudden as a twister, as unsettling as an earthquake. She hoped against hope that she could shake it off. And soon.

She emerged in a large section of the ship. It was the

bottom-most deck, a huge vacant place where every sound echoed and the floor vibrated from the effects of the magnetic clamps. Cara reached her full stature and smoothed out the creases of her pants.

"This is the hold," Hunter was saying as he cleared the ladder and stood with a little jump. "We'll have to carry all the supplies we need for the complete journey. Everything we'll need, in fact."

"How large will the crew be?"

"One hundred twenty-five people."

"And the length of our trip?" Always the pragmatist, Cara's forehead creased as she made the calculations.

"Three years."

Cara spun to stare at him, her eyes heavily hooded and her smile flat-lined. "Even at two pounds of food per person per day, that's two hundred seventy-three thousand, seven hundred and fifty pounds of food. How can this little cargo bay possibly hold all that? And keep it fresh?"

Hunter smiled and shook his head. "Obviously, you've mistaken me for one of the geniuses. I'm brawn, they're brains. You'll have to ask them about the food stores."

Cara nodded, still stuck in thought.

"There's really nothing more to see on this level. Let's go up to Deck Two." He led her to a ladder at the front of the cargo hold and waved her ahead. "After you."

When she had first gone into the Navy, a lot of the sailors would act like gentlemen and hold her door for her or invite her to climb a ladder first. She had thought them to be very gallant, when in all reality they were merely staring at her backside the whole time. She cast a suspicious glance at Hunter, decided that he simply wasn't the type to resort to such deception. Up the ladder she went, and if Hunter was in any way lascivious, he hid it well.

"Deck two is engineering and weapons. Forward, this way, on each side of the ship are the main weapon batteries. Aft is the cannon. I'm afraid they're restricted areas, so I'll show you the armory instead."

"I assume the ship's weapons are similar to the hand-held units we use?"

"Yes, only much, much more powerful." He opened the door and stepped through, propping it open with his foot as she stepped into the corridor. "This way."

The armory was large, with enough space to house hundreds of Rasters. The door was reinforced and had not only a keypad for security, but a large automatic bolt as well. Cara took a spin around the empty room and smiled.

"Not much to see yet, is there?" Her smile was casual. It lasted longer than she intended.

"No." That easy laugh echoed off the walls, making it seem almost menacing. "And of course, the armory will be under constant guard. Nobody in or out without authorization."

Cara nodded. "And that's all on Deck Two?"

"The elevator is all the way aft." Once more he held the door for her.

She followed him to the next level, their steps making an almost musical beat on the floor, his large, bass steps and her smaller, alto steps. This hallway was better lit, seemed more complete. Everything was clean and new and shiny. Cara smiled at the sight of it. When no one had spoken for several beats, she said, "So, Deck Three…."

"Deck Three houses the labs and the computer systems. The computer that powers the ship and oversees all the data input is about the size of a Buick. One of the challenges that Tony had was how to store the entire data dump from the alien ship in something that would actually fit inside the ship."

"Well, I'm guessing he knocked that one out of the park."

Hunter laughed again. "Yeah. And we have enough storage space left for another twenty data dumps." He walked down the hall slowly, pushing open a door here and a door there, letting her peer inside. "Nothing in any of the labs yet. But eventually, they'll offer space for all the sciences: Biology, botany, geology, sociology, everything."

"And on to Deck Number Four," Cara said without warning. She had become bored with looking at empty rooms and barren hallways.

"I'm sorry there isn't more to show you. It's only about half finished. But once the structure and the main systems are a go, they'll put in the rest of it pretty fast. This way."

Up another ladder to another empty deck. There were fewer doors on this deck and the hallway seemed a lot narrower. "I hope they put in the elevator next," Cara joked.

"Yeah, me too." He turned to smile at her, then waved his arm toward the forward section. "Deck Four is the sickbay, the mess hall, the hangar, a rec room, a theater, and two classrooms."

"Impressive. They really have thought of everything, haven't they?"

"Yes. And before you ask, no. There are no Strikers in the hangar." He flashed that smile at her again and she laughed outright. "Come on. There's actually something to see on Decks Five, Six and Seven."

Curious, she followed him up to Deck Five, hurrying up the ladder and jumping to the deck from the third step from the top. The deck did not disappoint. Stepping off the ladder—where the elevator car would normally be—Cara was immediately confronted with what appeared to be an enormous park. The smell of life reached her first, blotting out the smell of metal and heat and grease. There were trees two decks tall and the sound of running water took away the sound of the workers above and below. There were flowers and bushes, a pond full of fish and a large grassy area capable of holding a dozen picnics. Cara stared, her jaw hanging and her eyes sparkling.

"This is incredible. Simply incredible."

"My favorite part of the whole ship. Tony reasoned that people need a little piece of home wherever they go, especially if they're going into the cold, empty reaches of space. So, he put a little chunk of Earth right here for everyone to enjoy. It's an entire eco-system with fish in the pond, plants, running water. It will eventually have some birds and butterflies and fireflies."

"Amazing," she said softly, her head pivoting, trying to take it all in at once.

"But it's not just for looks. The plants help clean the air. The insects, fish and birds will allow them to study the effects of deep space on various life forms. And the water filtration system actually produces enough hydro-power to run the lights and the pump systems."

There was a small concrete bench amid a clump of rose bushes. Cara walked slowly over to it and lowered herself onto it. Her hands rubbed her arms and her smile seemed permanently etched on her face. "I love this." She felt rather than saw Hunter sit down next to her, felt his gaze burn into her face.

"I'm a little jealous, you know."

Her head whipped around, eyes locking on his. "What? Not of me?"

A little grin pushed his cheeks back into dimples and he looked down at his boots. "I was created for one simple purpose: to destroy the aliens and save the world."

Cara's jaw dropped and she felt a shiver run through her. "And then I came along, with my Striker and my bomb and I robbed you of that purpose." For just a moment, she felt profoundly sad for him. And a lot guilty. "I'm sorry."

He looked at her sideways. "It's not your fault. Besides, I have a new purpose now." He put his hand on her knee, realizing quickly that the gesture was too familiar, and pulled his hand back. "Let's go see the officers' quarters, huh?"

He led off and Cara rose slowly, catching up to him just as he reached the far side of the park and the door. She stepped through, leaving behind a room filled with life and entering the sterile, cold corridor. Even the light had a cold, antiseptic quality to it.

"These quarters are for the officers. You'll be staying here, too. Mine are at the end of the hall, directly under the bridge." He pushed open a door and she peeked her head inside. "Again, there's not much in here, but you can see they're quite roomy."

"I'm going to guess that Mr. Allen has already picked out his own quarters," she joked, turning to wink at him.

"Yeah. As a matter of fact, he built his quarters to his own specifications and he won't let anybody in there."

"I think I might just make it my mission to get inside. Know what I mean?" Her smile was a little wicked, a little taunting.

"You better take me with you."

"Deal." She leaned back into the corridor and put her hands on her hips. "So, I'm assuming Deck Six is just more crew quarters? Why don't we skip that and move right on to the bridge?"

"Okay, let's."

Up two more ladders and all the way forward was the bridge. It was an impressive sight...or would have been if not for the tangle of wires that protruded from literally everything. The captain's chair sat in the center, with stations fanning out in a horseshoe shape around it. A large screen would undoubtedly grace the front of the room, but it hadn't found its way home yet.

"I'm going to see if I remember this correctly. They've changed it all three times since they began construction. Of course, that's where I sit."

"Of course." She was at ease now, feet apart, arms locked behind her back, her eyes forward.

"This is where the computer and communications officer sits," he said, indicating a station to his right. "And next to that is chief engineer. Tony. On the other side is the helmsman and then the weapons officer. You. Or maybe it's the other way around."

Cara nearly burst out laughing at that, but she managed to hold it in check. "Do we have a communications officer yet? Or a helmsman?"

"Not as of yet. But we have high hopes." He turned toward the door and smiled. "And that concludes our tour of the ship. Care to see the simulator?"

"Is a frog's butt watertight?"

"I guess that's a yes. Come on."

Cara slid down each of the ladders, sailor style, walking briskly down each corridor and not even waiting for Hunter to catch up. His long strides out-matched hers anyway, so she wasn't too concerned.

Back on the ground, she straightened her clothes and looked up at Hunter as he descended the last few feet. "Which way, Captain?"

"Over here."

He struck off across the hangar, turning left down a short hallway, and emerging in a smaller hangar. In the center of this sat a huge ball that looked, more than anything, like an old diving bell. It was much bigger, though, taking up more than half the hangar. A lighted keypad next to the door indicated whether the simulator was in use or empty and allowed the entrant to input his key code. Hunter punched in a six-digit number and pulled the door open.

Inside, the thing looked exactly like the bridge. It was a perfect replica, except that there were no wires hanging everywhere. Cara smiled in spite of herself and looked over her shoulder at Captain Hunter.

"Welcome, Captain Hunter. Would you like to choose a scenario or shall I pick one?" It was the computer's voice, clear and human-sounding, without a hint of electronic timbre in it. The female voice was deep and all-business.

"Thank you. I'd like something short, just so I can demonstrate the simulator to a friend. I've brought a guest and she'll be standing right next to me but not participating."

"Very well, Captain. How about we take a lap around the moon and re-enter orbit? Will that do the trick?"

"That sounds good." He stepped around Cara and took his chair, watching with a smile as she edged up closer to him. "Begin."

The bridge suddenly came to life. The front screen lit up, showing the Earth beneath the ship, which was presumably in orbit. Beyond that lay the stars of space and…who knew what. One by one, bridge crewmembers glimmered into existence. Cara gasped as the first one appeared, marveling at the detail and realism. Tony appeared at the engineer's station, of course, but all the others were stand-ins, meant to fill in for the crew which hadn't been hired yet.

"This is amazing," Cara whispered to Hunter.

"Thank you, ma'am," answered the computer. "Captain, you may begin when ready."

"Helmsman, take us out of orbit. Orbit the moon once and then return us to orbit."

"Aye, Captain, leaving orbit." Buttons were pushed, entries were made. Cara had no idea what was being done but the faux helmsman seemed to know. The Earth below them was left behind and the moon appeared on the screen. "Engaging star drive…now."

From behind them, Tony spoke. "Sure you didn't strain

something giving that order, Hunter?"

Against her better judgment, Cara burst out laughing. "Man! The computer nailed Tony to a tee!"

"Yeah, well, he programmed the thing." Hunter wasn't nearly as amused as Cara had been.

Still smiling, Cara turned her eyes back to the screen. The moon spun beneath them, vibrant on the screen, and a slight vibration could be felt through the floor. Before she knew it, the ship was racing away from the moon, back toward Earth.

"Well done, Captain," the computer said. "Would you like to test another scenario?"

"No, thank you. End simulation."

The lights came up, the people shimmered away, and Cara was left standing on the bridge with Captain Hunter. She straightened, a silly smile stuck on her face. "That was awesome."

"There's just about any kind of scenario you can think of. You can even travel to one of the planets that we found in the Denarans' database after we defeated them. The computer fills in all the parts that aren't real: the view screen, crewmembers, etc."

"Remarkable. I can see I'll be spending a lot of time in here… if Tony ever comes up with a viable control for the drones, that is."

Hunter snorted and stood up. "If I were a betting man—and I'm not—I'd say he'll have something for you within a day. You challenged him. It's in his nature to answer that challenge."

Cara nodded and headed for the door. "Shall we go back and tell him how amazing he is for coming up with all this?"

"I guess we have to. Just tone it down a little. He gets a big head, we all suffer."

Hunter winked at her and she giggled, a ridiculous sound as she stepped into the open space of the hangar. One hand went to her mouth protectively, pushing back the sound and saving her from further embarrassment. She kept a few steps ahead of him as they walked back to the main hangar; she kept him from seeing the red that had painted her cheeks.

Tony had been tinkering with something on his workbench

and at the sound of their footsteps, he looked up. There was a micro-viewer perched on his head and covering one eye. He removed it and tossed it to the bench. "So," he called as he noticed their approached, "what did you think of the ship?"

"It's incredible!" Cara said, throwing her hands into the air. "I especially love the park. That was a stroke of genius, to be sure." She placed both hands on the bench. Her back remained stiff and straight but she tilted forward a bit at the hips to meet his gaze.

"Yeah, that's my favorite part. And what did you think of the simulator?"

"Oh, that is just brilliant. You didn't miss a single detail." She paused for two beats, then smiled at him. "You know what would make it even better, though?"

Tony leaned over and put his elbows on the bench, eyes sparkling as he drew in closer. "If you were in it." His eyebrows bobbed up and down and he smiled that billion-dollar smile of his.

That smile had won a thousand hearts, but it wouldn't win hers. "Why, Mr. Allen! Are you flirting with me?"

Tony straightened, looked severe once more. "Clearly, you can't tell the difference between flirting and recruiting."

"Oh, but I can. And neither one works on me in the least. Now, as I was saying, the simulator would be a lot better if there were controls for the drones in it."

"Oh, would it now?" He was mocking her now, his face nearly unreadable, though she thought she detected a touch of arrogance in it. He reached to his right and plucked something off the bench. "Here. Catch."

Cara's hands went out in the nick of time and she cupped the thing in her hands, turning it over and peering at it, confused. "It looks like an ancient game controller or something. What is it?"

"It's your drone control, silly."

"You made this? While we were on the tour?"

"Yes."

"Just now?"

"Yes." Tony stepped around the bench and pointed at the thing. "Think of the whole controller as the drone. You tilt it this way, the drone tilts this way. Tilt it nose-down, the drone dips. The rocker panel on the left is the speed and the big red button on the right is the firing trigger. So, yes, it basically is a game controller. And wherever the controller moves, the drone moves."

Cara frowned and turned it over in her hand. Then her eyes shot back to Tony. "But perhaps you don't understand the properties of space. There's not just backward, forward, left and right. There's up and down. Infinite up and down. If raising it like this makes the drone go up, then there's a limit because I can only raise it this far." She lifted the controller high over her head and stood on her toes. "See?"

He looked at her like she was an idiot and for a moment, her face grew hot and beads of sweat broke out on her forehead. "Tilt the front up, like this…" he jerked the controller upward at the front, scowling, "…and hit the gas."

Cara nodded. "Oh." She said no more, feeling suddenly awkward and stupid.

"Here. Try it out." Tony picked up what looked like an old-style computer chip from the bench and tossed it into the air. A screen appeared before them, spanning at least six feet of the work area. A drone appeared on the screen, motionless among the darkness and stars. "Run the drone test," he said.

Cara checked his face, then slowly pushed forward on the rocker panel. The drone on the screen began to move forward, slowly at first, then more quickly as she pushed the rocker forward. When she turned the controller to the left, the drone banked left, responding quickly. Up and down, spinning, moving deeper into space and finally rolling through loops, the drone answered her commands perfectly. When finally she brought it to a stop and passed the controller back to Tony, she was beaming.

"That works pretty damn well," she said happily.

"Of course it does." He reached through the holographic screen and plucked the chip out of mid-air. "Here," he said, taking her hand and slapping the chip into it. "You can practice any time you want. I'll get the new data transferred to the simulator as soon as I can."

"Thank you, Mr. Allen."

"Well, I see you're giving her toys. Nice move, Mr. Allen." Mr. Danforth had been watching, though none of them had noticed and even he wasn't sure quite how long he had stood there. "So, Commander Bishop, what do you think of our little operation here?"

"It's nothing short of amazing, Mr. Danforth. I can't believe you've managed to accomplish all this in such a short time."

"So, you'll be signing on, then?" Danforth's face looked hopeful, boyish.

She shot him a quick grin and shook her head. "If it's all right with you, I'd like to consult with a trusted advisor before I commit."

"Meaning…your father?"

"Yes. Of course."

He nodded. "It's a big decision. So, do you have any questions for us? Anything that would allay your fears?"

"Actually, I do." She turned to Dr. Klein, who had been working silently at his station the entire time. "Dr. Klein, how are you going to solve the food problem? Clearly, there's not enough room in the cargo hold to carry all the food that you'd need for such a long journey."

"Ah yes!" David removed his glasses and set them on the bench. His dark hair was crazy and his hazel eyes squinted from too much work. "I've been working hard on that. We've tried using the Denarans' food synthesizer but no luck. They have a very simple diet. No complicated ingredients, no complex proteins and the like. So, their synth machines simply won't work for human needs. We might as well be taking food pills, for God's sake.

"So, I decided to apply their algorithms to one of our 3D printers. And it worked perfectly." He stepped over to what looked like an over-blown microwave oven and punched a few numbers on the keypad. He waited a moment, whistling, and finally the door slid open, revealing a strawberry shortcake, perfect in every way. Gingerly, he removed it and carried it to Cara, into whose hands he delicately placed it.

Cara held the dish as if it were made of finest crystal, letting her gaze run quickly over it. "It looks right."

"And it smells right." He moved to her left, deliberately drawing her attention from the dish. "It feels right and if you were to eat it right now, it would even taste just right." He flashed the merest hint of a smile. "Go ahead. Give it a taste."

She nodded once and returned her gaze to the strawberry shortcake, only to see a pile of black goo coating her hands. "Oh my God!" She held her hands out, watching in horror as the goo drizzled through her fingers and spattered to the floor. The shortcake, the dish…everything was gone. "What the…?"

"Here." Dr. Klein leaned to one side, grabbing a towel from the workbench and handing it to her. "And now you see the problem. Stabilization. No matter what we make with it, it ends up like this within a few minutes."

"Yes," she sighed, wiping furiously at her hands and making a sick face, "that is definitely a problem."

"But I'm working on it. I'll get it. I always do."

She nodded and offered a tiny smile of most insincere encouragement. "I know you will."

"Any other questions, Commander?" Danforth was back at her elbow again, smiling hopefully at her.

"No more questions," Cara said with a shake of her head. "It was wonderful meeting all of you. And if I've seemed unimpressed, it's because I'm still in shock over everything I've seen today. Captain Hunter, thank you very much for the tour. It's been a pleasure." She stuck out her hand and smiled, feeling that electric-jerk reaction when he shook it.

"The pleasure was all mine, Commander Bishop. I hope to see you again."

She nodded. "Indeed." She turned on her heel and brought her gaze to bear on Mr. Danforth. "Shall we? Good day, gentlemen."

Once more she turned on her heel, marching toward the exit at a brisk pace, her steps measured and steady, almost a march.

Danforth scurried along after her, casting a wave as he slid through the door at the head of the hallway. They went through the sterilization procedure once more, then turned in Cara's badge at the front desk.

Once through the door and outside again, the sun and the

heat assaulted them, making them squint and bend their heads downward. By the time they had crossed the parking lot to the car, their eyes had almost adjusted. Danforth held the door for her, smiled as he shut it and rounded the car to climb behind the wheel.

They were required to stop at Checkpoint Charlie in order to have their persons and the car inspected for contraband. Once that was done, it was an easy drive to the main road.

"So, what are your thoughts? Concerns?"

Cara snorted softly and stared at the side of Danforth's head. "I have a million questions and even more thoughts. I just can't put them into words quite yet."

"Fair enough. I realize that this is all very daunting. It's a huge undertaking for everyone involved and not something that should be entered into lightly. You need to talk this over with someone whose judgment you trust but let me remind you that no one outside of this compound can be told of it, save for your father, the admiral."

"I know. And believe me, I will be speaking to him about this…in depth. And when I've reached a decision, you'll be the first to know."

Danforth nodded his appreciation without looking at her. "And if you don't mind me asking, what is your biggest concern?"

She turned to regard him then, studying the form and lines of his face. "That I might never come back."

He shot her a look, partly of shock, partly of concern, and for a moment, their eyes locked. "No. You might not."

CHAPTER 3

Danforth dropped Cara off in front of her father's house. She climbed out of the car and shut the door, only to lean in through the window. She was bone-tired and her head hurt from thinking through all possible scenarios in this. Still, she managed a smile for Danforth.

"You'll hear from me tomorrow either way, Mr. Danforth. I promise."

"I look forward to it. Thank you for having so much patience with me, Commander Bishop. Good night."

Cara stood up straight, feeling the now-familiar twinge of stress in her lower back. "Good night," she said with a wave, then turned and walked to the front door.

She rang the bell, an unspoken bit of formality between her and her father. She had her own place and so she didn't live with him. Besides, she didn't like to broadcast the fact that the admiral was her father. It's not that she wanted to keep it hidden, she just didn't like to give the appearance of throwing it in anyone's face.

"Cara!" shouted a spreading redhead with green eyes and a smile that could light a room. She threw herself at Cara and hugged her tightly. "Come in, child. It's late."

"Hello, Maggie. And yes, it is late." She took a deep sniff of the room and smiled. "Do I smell…?"

"You do indeed. When your father told me you were coming, I ran to the market. I've made all your favorites so you just come into the dining room and I'll call your dad."

Cara stepped into the dining room, pulling out a chair next to the head of the table and dropping uneasily into it. No matter where they had been in the world, Maggie had always been there with them, taking care of them both. They had hired her in Virginia, where they had been living when Cara's mother had passed. A long search had proved worthwhile, as they found Maggie. She had slid into her mother's shoes with ease, becoming a surrogate mother for Cara and a companion for Admiral Bishop. The three of them had been family ever since and, though Cara had never thought to call her "Mom," she always felt that Maggie was her second mother.

"There's my little princess," Admiral Bishop laughed. "Back from her big adventure." He moved in for a bear hug. "So, how was it?"

Cara smiled weakly and sighed. "It was interesting. But we'll talk about it after dinner."

"Lasagna, fresh baked garlic bread, a Caesar salad, and tiramisu for dessert." Maggie slid a plate in front of Cara and one in front of Admiral Bishop. In a blink, she was gone. When she reappeared, she held a large salad bowl in one hand and a plate of bread in the other.

"Maggie, you've outdone yourself. And I can't say how much I appreciate it." Cara wanted to stuff her face the second she had her plate in hand, but she deferred to her lifetime of training as a Navy brat.

"T'wernt nothin'," Maggie said with a wave, retrieving her own plate and sitting across from Cara. "Now eat. A lady needs her strength."

And eat Cara did. She was famished. She'd had a light breakfast and skipped lunch and this dinner was like a lifesaver to a drowning woman. "Oh, God, it's so good."

Maggie laughed. "You could eat like this every night if you moved home."

Cara shot her a stern glance. "I love you, Maggie. But I've been a big girl for a long time. We all need our privacy."

"I know, dear. I just miss you."

They ate in silence for a few moments, Maggie watching Cara and her father exchange glances, wondering what they were up to. She had endured a lot of secrecy in her time with them. She knew how to idle her way through it and to not push. Her deep Irish heritage made her want to pry but she didn't.

She knew they would tell her whatever she needed to know, whatever they could.

As if the conversation had never died, Cara said, "Besides, I'd have to let out my uniforms if I lived here." She leaned back and patted her belly, now delightfully full and with just enough room left for dessert.

"How about if I bring dessert and coffee into the study so that you and your dad can talk?"

"I'll help you clear the table," Cara offered.

Maggie waved her away. "You go. Sit in the study with your dad. I'll bring dessert in presently."

"Are you sure?"

Maggie simply thrust one pointing finger in the direction of the study and gave Cara a one-eyed sneer. Cara giggled and saluted, turning to walk with her father to the study. "After all these years, she still intimidates me."

"I heard that, missy!" said Maggie from the kitchen.

Admiral Bishop leaned in and whispered. "Me, too."

The study was lined with bookshelves, each full to exploding with books of all types. The admiral was an avid reader of all sorts of things and an accidental collector of rare books. There was an impressive walnut desk at the back of the room and a sitting area toward the front. Cara eased into one of the overstuffed arm chairs and sighed.

Within moments, Maggie appeared, bearing a silver tray with two plates of tiramisu and two cups of coffee. She set it on the table before them and stood straight. "Now, I'll close the doors on my way out and I'll be in the kitchen doing dishes, so you've no need to worry about me hearing anything you say. I'll turn away any visitors, 'cept for emergencies, of course."

"Maggie, you are a lifesaver," Cara said with a warm smile.

"You just don't forget to say goodbye before you leave, missy." Maggie shook a finger at Cara, then threw her a kiss and shut the door.

"So, now we talk." Admiral Bishop sipped at his coffee—too hot—and worked at his dessert instead. "How was it?"

"Well, since they already talked to you, I'm guessing you know everything I know. Why in the heck did they go to you first, anyway?" She stuffed a forkful of tiramisu into her mouth and moaned.

"I guess they wanted my help in persuading you. Or perhaps it was a matter of courtesy. Either way, they got squared away pretty quick once I told them that I had no intention of influencing your decision."

"They are…aggressive." She nodded once, considered licking her plate clean when she was done.

"You saw the ship…?"

"It's miraculous. Seriously, Daddy. The thing is the size of two football fields. Seven decks. There's a park inside, for God's sake."

The old man laughed and shook his head. "And the weapons?"

"Huge. They've got two Rasters fore and a cannon aft. Then they have these eight drones…I don't even know how to describe them. And you'll never believe who I met there." She watched her father's eyes, letting him stew a bit. "Tony Allen and Dr. David Klein. Oh, and you remember the SPARTA Project?"

"Some nasty business about super soldiers…a ridiculous play to win the ground war."

"Well, the only super soldier they ever produced is going to be our captain."

Admiral Bishop looked up, his eyes betraying his surprise at that. "I didn't know they'd actually had any successes."

"Just one. Captain Steve Hunter. You should see him. About seven feet tall, broad as a carrier and his muscles have muscles."

"And they chose him to be captain?" He picked up his coffee again and leaned back, let the chair swallow him.

"Yeah. I wondered about that, too. And then we talked…I think he's uniquely qualified."

The admiral eyed her peculiarly and shook his head. "All right, then. Why don't we get to the crux of the problem? You want me to tell you whether you should go or not."

Nail on the head. He had an uncanny way of getting inside her thoughts and yanking out the truth of things. She sighed and hung her head.

"Well, I won't do it. I can give you orders…as a father…as a commanding officer…but I won't tell you what to do personally.

That's all on you, princess." He took a long draw on his coffee and winced. "Okay, just like we've always done. What are the pros?"

She sat straight. Her voice never wavered; she stared straight ahead. "This is a unique opportunity. Nobody has ever had it and maybe nobody ever will again. The people behind this are genius and if such a thing is ever going to happen, they're the ones who can make it happen. The experience and the knowledge would be invaluable to me, to the world, to God knows who's out there."

"And the cons?"

She laughed a bit, ticking them off in her head before she spoke. "I might never come back. There is only one ship on the whole planet and if we get into trouble, nobody can come rescue us...at least not for a long time. I would be leaving you and Maggie and everyone I've ever known for three years. I have no idea what I'll find out there, if anything."

"So, to recap: The pro is experience and knowledge. The con is danger. Sounds like Monday to me."

She snorted and nodded. It was a thing they'd always said. Going out on a dangerous mission? Everything going to hell? Saved three men from certain death? Sounds like Monday.

"There's one more thing I haven't told you. I'm not sure I can."

He stared at her for a long moment, confused. "You've always been able to tell me everything, Cara. That shouldn't change now."

"This is embarrassing." Her voice was soft and shaky now and she wouldn't meet his gaze. "Personal."

The admiral leaned forward and put his hand on hers. "Whatever it is, you can tell me."

She finally looked up at him. "It's Hunter."

"The super soldier?"

"Yes, sir. He...affects me." She felt the sting of tears, the burning of shame in her face. "You know me, Daddy. I've only ever dated like three times. I never went boy-crazy. I just don't have time for that stuff. It's silly. But this man...this...I don't know. You know?"

He laughed, right in her face. "Oh, my sweet Cara. I do know. Now, why don't you tell me how this man affects you."

She moaned audibly and shook her head. "My knees shook the first time I looked at him. I thought it was fear at first but it wasn't. And when we shook hands...there was this...this... bolt of electricity, this current that went through me. I thought I might faint. *Faint!* Daddy, I've never fainted in my life!"

He laughed again, taking her hand and squeezing it for a moment. "Oh, my poor sweet little girl! God help you, you're in love!" And then he laughed again, adding to her pain.

The shock of it drained the color from her face, leaving her ashen and trembling for a moment. Then she shot up from the chair, her voice high-pitched and too loud. "That's absurd! I met the man one time. Spent maybe two hours with him. It's completely insane to think that I could have any feelings for him at all, much less be...in love!" She spat the last word out like a bitter apple, pulling a face for good measure.

"Happened that way with your mom. There I was working hard at my career. And one day, I'm just walking down the street and I see this face in the diner window. Bam! I was a goner. I went inside...."

"And you sat directly in front of her, folding origami roses until she was ready to go. Then you gave her the whole bouquet with your number attached."

"And she ran to catch up with me on the sidewalk to ask me why I would do such a thing. And when I kissed her hand, it was like I was hit with a Taser." He paused to reflect, his eyes taking on that far-away look and his smile faltering. "You're in love. Simple as that."

Cara moaned and threw herself against the back of the chair in abject misery. "Well, that settles it then. I simply can't go. I can't be trapped in space for three years with a man I might be tempted to fraternize with."

"You don't trust yourself?"

"No."

"Then you have to go."

"What?" Her head snapped around and she stared daggers at him.

"Listen, princess, the way I see it, you have to go. You have to prove to yourself that you can do it. Remember the obstacle course when you were thirteen?" He held her with his gaze, his face dark and severe. "You told me that you could run that obstacle course as well as any man under my command. And then you spent day and night practicing. You couldn't make it over that rappelling wall and so you spent the whole day out there, in the rain, trying and trying."

"You put my phone at the top. You told me that you'd believe I could do it if I brought you back that phone."

The admiral laughed and nodded. "Four o'clock in the morning, you show up in my bedroom, dripping mud, your spindly little legs shaking and bruised. And you took my hand and slapped that phone in my hand and you said, 'I can do anything, daddy. And don't you forget it.'"

"And then it took Maggie two hours and four shampoos to get the mud out of my hair." She laughed at that, her eyes tearing up at the effort. "And in three years, I was at Annapolis."

"Yes, you were. So, Cara, darling, you *can* do anything. You've proved it over and over. Prove it one more time."

She jolted forward and stared into his eyes. "Daddy, what if I don't come back? Who's going to look after you when…?"

"Don't you dare do that!"

"Do what?"

"Use me as an excuse not to live. I'm not ready for a wheelchair yet. And I have Maggie here with me." He stood up and began to pace. "Here's what it boils down to, Cara. Either you go into space and have the greatest adventure anyone has ever had. You see things that would curl most people's toes. And you return a hero…again. Or you stay here, babysit me, teach pilots for the rest of your life. The savior of the world rests on her laurels. She's done enough, after all. She's earned the chance to take it easy. No need to prove herself again."

"And what about Hunter?"

"What about him? Look, what's the worst that can happen? You find out that he's the one? You fall madly and deeply in love with him, get married, have a few babies…."

"Hey! Huh-uh. No you don't!"

"What?" He turned around, wearing a lopsided grin and a sparkle in his eye.

"You know damn well I'm not the settling down type. I'm thirty-five and way past the having-babies point. That's never been part of my plan. Besides, you said you weren't going to tell me what to do. It sounds an awful lot like you're telling me what to do."

"I know your heart. And your mind. I know you better than anyone else alive. And I've never known you to back down from anything, never known you to be afraid of anything. If you let them go without you, you'll hate yourself for the rest of your life."

She steepled her fingers under her chin and scrunched up her face. She thought hard and the admiral let her. When finally she stood up, her father held open his arms and let her hug him.

"I guess I'm going into space," she said into his chest.

CHAPTER 4

Cara's papers came through within hours of calling Mr. Danforth with her acceptance. She was relieved of all her Navy duties and attached to the space program's governing agency, Aegis, as an advisor. The thought of that gave her pangs of guilt. She'd spent most of her life in the Navy. The Navy had made her famous, had paid her bills, provided her health care, her training. Indirectly, the Navy was responsible for her entire life in that it had paid her father for most of *his* life. She felt disloyal leaving it. It was like giving up her best friend.

She spent two weeks cleaning out her barracks and spending time with her father and Maggie. She had called old friends, shipmates, former students…anyone she wanted to say goodbye to. Once all that was done, she had nothing left to do but wait. Cara wasn't good at waiting. It made her itch.

She called Danforth on his cell, desperate to move forward. She knew that the ship wouldn't be ready for quite some time. But surely there was something else she could do involving the project.

"We've got barracks here," Danforth had said. "You're welcome to move into one of them and maybe you can help out Hunter, Allen and Klein. Barring that, you can spend time in the simulator."

And so, she had packed up the few things that she wanted to take into space and had made the drive out to the base. She would return before lift-off to say a final goodbye to her father and Maggie but for now she was immersed in Aegis business.

By the end of the first week, she had logged over fifty hours in the simulator and then she helped Tony tweak the controls for the Zodiacs. The simulator was incredibly realistic, but she was still itching to see some real action, to let those Zodiacs fly for real.

The barracks they had assigned her to were on the east side of the compound, away from the machine shops and other noisy buildings. The only other building near it was the main office where she entered the elevator. Tony and David slept in the main building, close to their labs and work. The only other person sharing the barracks with Cara was Captain Hunter. Cara was used to sleeping in a barracks full of loud sailors and pilots. The noise soothed her somehow. Being in a totally silent building made her nervous. It kept her awake at night, staring at the ceiling and wondering what she would do the next day.

To make matters worse, she could see the Striker hangar to the west. Inside that hangar were six of the new eight-passenger Strikers. They were untested, untried, untouched by pilot hands. What she wouldn't give to just take off in one of them, fly around the world a few times, and slide it neatly back into its hangar.

On her sixth night there—her fourth night of insomnia—she found herself simply wandering. She took a walk around the barracks in the moonlight and finally found herself down in the hangar, looking for anyone at all to talk to. Failing that, she went into the mess hall to look for a snack. She found some peanut butter cookies in the vending machine, then spent her last dollar in quarters on a cup of cocoa. When she had been a little girl, her mother had given her cocoa to soothe her insomnia. When her mother had passed and Maggie had come to live with them, she had carried on the tradition.

She was seated at the table, remembering Maggie, those first days at the academy, and how Maggie had kept the secret of how awkward and ostracized Cara had felt. She had almost come to the conclusion that she was just feeling sorry for herself and needed a kick in the ass, when she heard a noise behind her. She spun in her chair, suddenly alert, and saw Hunter shuffling toward her.

"You couldn't sleep either, huh?" Cara mumbled.

"Comes with the territory. I never sleep." Hunter dropped into the chair across from her and ran one large hand through his hair.

"Never ever?"

"Nope. My body heals itself almost instantly, so I don't need to sleep."

"Wow." Cara didn't know what else to say. She couldn't even conceive of such a thing. "What do you do with all that extra time?"

"I read a lot." He offered up a thin smile and immediately looked away. "How about you?"

"I have insomnia. It's too quiet here. I'm used to a lot of people making a lot of noise. And I'm bored. There's not much for me to do around here except wait. And I'm not good at waiting."

Hunter nodded. "Tell me about it. I spent six years waiting for something to do."

"I thought someone said you were in the Army."

"Not anymore. I was honorably discharged. Once we destroyed the aliens, they had no more use for a super soldier."

"I don't know if you remember this, Hunter, but humans used to wage war against each other."

"Yeah, but the aliens put a stop to that. How about you, Bishop? What did you do after the war?"

"I was training pilots."

"Ah! At least you got to keep your hand in it."

"It was ground school. Not flight school. I haven't flown in a while."

"Do you miss it? Flying, I mean."

"Yeah, I do. Quite a lot actually." She got that sad, faraway look in her eye again and felt the past pulling at her. Cara took a sip of her cocoa and licked her lip. She was too old to be sporting a cocoa moustache. "How did you end up on this project anyway?"

"Well, let's see. After the government decided they had no real use for me, they started doing a series of tests to determine whether or not I was safe enough to be released into the general population. Physical tests, psyche evaluations, all sorts of assessments. When they finally realized that I wasn't a threat to John Q. Public, they gave me my release papers and all the back pay I'd earned from the Army. The day before I was supposed to leave, Tony Allen showed up. Tony knows everything that's worth knowing and he said he needed somebody just like me to help him test his new technology. Since there was nobody else like me, he offered me the job. He gave me a heck of a good salary and a place to live, so I jumped at the chance. Now, the most exciting thing I do is lift heavy things."

Cara laughed, too loudly in her opinion. "And I just sit here."

"Hey, at least you've been into space already. In your Striker."

"I never went into space. I wanted to, believe me. But I had my orders. Run the mission, kill the aliens, return to base. Day after day. My buddies and I would go up there and wipe out a whole squadron of Stingers. And we'd go have drinks. Remember what it was like when you first got your driver's license? You were just itching to drive…anywhere. And finally, your mom would ask you to drive down to the store for her and you felt such freedom. It was only two miles there and two miles back, but for those few minutes, you were a god. And you didn't want to stop. You wanted to drive past that store and keep going, see how far you could get. Anything just so the trip didn't have to end."

Hunter smiled and nodded.

"It was the same for me. I'd go up and shoot at the aliens. And when they were all gone, I'd just look up. There was all that sky and beyond it…everything. I longed to keep going, to just fly right on out of our atmosphere, circle the moon a few times. Just get out there, you know? But I didn't. I finished my mission and I returned to base."

"Because you always follow orders." Hunter nodded his understanding.

"Yeah. I always follow orders."

"Well, at least you made it up in a Striker. You have that."

"Yeah." She stared into her cocoa, feeling sad for everything she'd lost. Suddenly, she looked up at Hunter. "You've never been up in one?"

Hunter shook his head. "Never had a chance."

Cara tightened her grip on the cocoa and bit into her lip, thinking. "You want to ride in one?"

Hunter laughed. It was deep and resonant and warm. "Maybe once we're out in space I'll have the chance."

"Now."

"What?"

"Now. Right now. There are six of them in Hangar B, just waiting for their first test flight. And who better to test them than me?" Her grin was full of dark mischief and joy.

Hunter stared at her for a moment, his eyes slitted and his normally full lips pressed thin. "Are you cleared for that?"

Cara shrugged. "Maybe I am. Maybe I'm not. I never asked. And they never specifically said I couldn't." Her eyes sparkled as she thought about it. Flying again would be like an all-you-can-eat buffet for a starving man.

"We can't. If we get caught...."

"We claim innocence." Her smile widened.

Hunter sat back and crossed his arms over his too-broad chest. "You just don't strike me as a rule-breaker."

"Normally I'm not. But I'm gonna lose my mind if I have to sit here another day, doing nothing." She thought for a moment, then snapped her fingers. "What if I called Tony and asked him? If he says it's okay, I'll take you up. Deal?"

"Well...." Hunter grimaced at the thought of breaking regulations. He was the captain, after all, the one in charge of maintaining order and enforcing the rules. "Only if Tony says it's okay."

Cara whipped out her phone. Her face was filled with unrepentant joy and a six-year-old's innocence. Then she dialed Tony's number.

"Put it on the speaker," Hunter said.

And Cara did. Tony would be asleep at that hour. She was sure of it.

His voice was sleepy when he answered. "Allen."

"Tony. Bishop here. Is it okay if I test out one of those new Strikers?" She smiled and listened, hearing Tony yawn, and in the background, someone else yawned. A woman, she supposed.

"Sure, sure. Have fun, Bishop." He mumbled something to his companion and hung up.

Cara switched off the phone and turned her gigawatt smile on Hunter. "Let's go."

Hunter stared at her for several beats, unmoving. Then he

broke out in a huge smile and stood up. "Let's do this."

She was already through the door and into the night. She marched on Hangar B like her life depended on it and Hunter caught up in four strides of his long legs. Her face was stretched wide into a smile, her eyes nearly glazed over in joy. She hadn't felt this alive since the war had ended.

Cara reached the door and slid her keycard through the slot, then presented herself to the camera for facial recognition. The small side door slid open, revealing the treasures inside. Tony had shown her the hangar once before, pointing out the differences in the new Strikers. And then he had shut the door on them as though they were merely trinkets from the past.

"These Strikers are different. They're eight-seaters instead of one. And Tony says the engines are more powerful, quicker to respond." She hit a bank of switches, one after the other, and watched the ceiling lights come alive."

Instinctively, Hunter looked over his shoulder, just waiting to be assaulted by a guard. When none was forthcoming, he looked back to Cara. "And you're sure you can fly them?"

She dropped one side of her face and regarded him with squinted eyes and a lopsided grin. "I ran the simulator. They're exactly like my Striker, except a little less maneuverable because of the added length and breadth." She stepped quickly over to the back wall and grabbed a helmet from a hook. "You'll need this." Then she grabbed a helmet for herself. She tucked it under one arm and headed for the ship.

"Don't we need the keys or something?" Hunter asked in a hushed tone.

"No. They have a bio-ignition. And why are you whispering?" She was so amused by this that she almost giggled. She decided that would be a girly and immature thing to do.

"It just seemed appropriate, being that we're stealing a Striker and all."

"We're not stealing it. We're just borrowing it. And we do have permission, remember?"

"Right up until Tony realizes what he actually said."

She checked his expression, knew he was right. But it was too late to turn back now.

Cara pushed the huge button that opened the hangar doors and then made for the ship. There were handholds on the old Strikers, so the pilot could climb into it on his or her own power. This one was meant to be a passenger vehicle, so it had a ramp on the side instead. She lowered the ramp and stepped on, holding out a hand to Hunter.

"Come on up. From this point on, I think we should be a little faster."

He looked at her again, his expression disapproving. He climbed aboard anyway and settled into the seat behind Cara's. "Are there belts?"

"Yes. But you come up here. You're my co-pilot for this trip. I want you to get the full effect." She reached across and pulled out a harness. "Fasten this on and put on your helmet. In the event that we lose cabin pressure, it won't matter. We'll be dead." She checked his expression and laughed. "Sorry. Old pilot's joke. We'll be fine. Honest."

She fastened on her own helmet and harness, then placed her hand on the small screen at the center of the yoke. "Here we go."

If Hunter were scared, he never showed it. He sat, slightly braced for disaster, and looked straight ahead.

The engines were silent. Fusion drives produced no sound. Within seconds, the ship was rolling forward, out the door to the large patch of tarmac beyond. Then it stopped and Cara turned to Hunter.

"You ready?" she asked, checking his face.

"Yeah."

"Okay. Hold onto your lunch."

She eased back on the yoke and pressed down on the floor pedal. The ship rose steadily into the air, stopping when it was about twenty feet off the ground. Cara's face was caught in ecstasy, her eyes focused on the sky above. It was go time. She was back in the saddle, so to speak, and the thrill of it made her heart pound.

In a quick, decisive motion, she slammed down on the floor pedal and the ship, which had been steadily hovering just off the ground, leaped forward and upward. It plunged into the night, slicing the air with no more noise than a tennis racket during a backstroke. Hunter's head hit the back of the seat and stayed there.

"Yee-haw!" Cara yelled. She took the ship to thirty thousand feet and leveled off. "Damn! This thing is fast! You okay, Hunter?"

Hunter nodded, finally able to peel his head off the seat back. "I'm good. Where are we going anyway?"

"Out there." Cara shrugged. "You really good? Or are you just sorta good?" Her smile was wicked, threatening almost.

"I'm really good. Honest."

"Cool."

And then they were rolling. First to the left, then to the right, at almost a thousand miles an hour. She barrel-rolled over Los Angeles, then climbed to the very outer edge of the atmosphere. As the ship floated, frozen in place, Cara turned to Hunter again.

"You're gonna love this run. I used to make it all the time when I was logging hours and doing demos. But before we start, I want you to look down. This is our Earth, our home, and you'll never see it this way again."

Hunter leaned slightly toward the window, then realized that the Striker had tilted a bit, allowing him to see the ground more clearly. Actually, the thousands of miles between the Striker and the ground had obscured most of it. But he could see clouds and the lights of L.A. and off in the distance he saw the churning of a storm rolling in. It took his breath away and for a moment, he could hardly speak at all. When he did, his voice was shaky and low.

"It's incredible. Beautiful."

Cara nodded. "That's what we fought for. That and all the people who care for her. You ready?"

Hunter nodded again.

"Okay, then. Here we go."

Cara shoved the yoke forward until it was almost resting on the console and pushed the pedal to the floor. The Striker went into an instant dive, clocking nearly five hundred miles an hour before she leveled it off. By that time, they were over Utah. She banked hard to the south and suddenly they were in Arizona. Cara guided the ship to a mere twenty feet above the ground and increased her speed, zooming along the ground like some great predatory bird.

"The Grand Canyon is coming up," she said, adjusting her course. "You're gonna love this."

And love it he did. He had broken out in a huge smile, his eyes riveted on the windlass and what lay beyond. The Striker dipped down, easing into the canyon, close to the ground. Cara dropped her speed a bit, enjoying the view, the ride, the thrill of being airborne again. She flew straight toward the head of the river, waiting until the last possible second before pulling back on the yoke and putting the Striker into a climb.

"Whew!" Hunter said when she finally leveled off again. "You got me on that one." Then he laughed. It was an uneasy sound.

"I think we better head back now. No sense pushing our luck." She made a few adjustments on the console and then winked at Hunter. "But nothing says we can't enjoy the trip back."

She brought the ship up to ten thousand, then barrel-rolled toward Colorado. She looped over Nevada, then zipped in and out between the large cacti in the desert. She approached the base from the coast of California, taking a last spin over the ocean before she headed home. The ship was so low that it produced a three-mile wake as it passed and if she'd had a rearview mirror, she would have loved the sight.

Returning to the base, she jockeyed the Striker into position and set it softly on the ground, putting it in reverse in order to back into the hangar. It was still dark and there wasn't a soul around. The hangar was still silent when she climbed down from the Striker and pulled off her helmet.

"Well, what did you think?"

"It was awesome. Seriously, thank you for taking me up."

"Any time you want to go, you just let me know."

Everything about her had changed since she first climbed into that ship. Her posture, her expression, her very carriage and demeanor had been altered, all for the better. She replaced the helmets and shut the hangar doors, then signaled for Hunter to follow her out of the building.

By the time they reached the barracks, the sun had just begun to come up. A thin slit of light marked the horizon and reflected off the cloud cover above. Inside, Hunter went to the left and Cara to the right. They smiled at each other and winked, then headed off to bed.

Hunter didn't go right away. He lingered, watching Cara walk away and smiling.

Cara shut her door and threw herself on her bunk. She lay there for a while, on her back and staring at the ceiling, smiling as she remembered the flight. It was fifteen minutes before she fell asleep.

She awoke three hours later with a start. She couldn't remember the last time she had slept past five in the morning, much less nine. She shook off the sleep and stumbled to the shower, which only took off the edge. Then she dressed and headed for the mess hall, where she knew there would be coffee. It would be stale and bitter, but it was still coffee.

She nodded briefly to the man behind the counter, then poured a plastic mug full of Joe. She guzzled this first one, ignoring the heat, then poured a second. This second cup of coffee she drank on the way to The Hole, as she called it. By the time the elevator reached the bottom, the cup was empty. She sat it on a nearby railing and kept going toward Tony's lab area.

Halfway there, she was nearly run down by a man with a hand truck, bearing some sort of large equipment. She stood still for a moment, letting him pass, then stepped off. No sooner had her foot left the floor than another man with a huge cart came through. As she looked, she noted a flurry of activity: men going every which way with loads of equipment, moving it all into the ship.

A bit rattled now, she approached Tony with a lopsided grin. "What's with all the hubbub around here?"

Tony looked up as if he had just realized that there were other people on the planet. "They're setting up sickbay today. Tomorrow, the rec room and the mess hall get set up. I plan to have us moved into the ship by Friday next week."

"I see." She said no more. The coffee had managed to keep her eyes open, but little more than that. Her brain was still foggy.

"So, how was your flight last night?" Tony looked at her accusingly. It made Cara back up a step and, satisfied, Tony turned back to his work.

"It was great. So awesome. That Striker handles like a dream. I haven't felt so alive in months."

"Good." He paused for a second, fighting a smile. "And how did Hunter like it?"

Cara's head snapped around and she stared, wide-eyed. "What?"

Tony put down the instrument he'd been using and leaned against the table, beaming at her. "Oh, come on! Security cameras showed you and another person entering Hangar B. Unless you know another seven-foot-tall guy, it has to be Hunter."

Cara tried not to blush. It didn't work. She had nothing whatever to be embarrassed about, no reason to blush. But her face was lit up like the Christmas tree in Rockefeller Center.

"Oh, calm down." Tony laughed. "I'm just giving you a hard time. Any time you want to go flying, just feel free to take one of the Strikers."

"You mean it?" Cara's jaw dropped and her eyes sparkled. She truly hoped he wasn't messing with her again.

"Sure. My Strikers are your Strikers. Besides, you're the only one around here who can fly them."

"You can do that? I mean, won't you get in trouble with command?"

"What command? I'm Tony Allen. I do whatever I want. I created every single thing in here and if somebody doesn't like what I do, I'll just walk. Let's see them try to get into space without me."

Cara bit her lip for a second but only a second. "Arrogant much?" she chuckled.

Tony leaned forward and leered at her. "It ain't arrogance if you really are the smartest, richest person in the world." And then he winked.

With nothing more to say about that, Cara perused the items

spread out on the table. She wasn't a scientist, not even close. And the silence had grown awkward, so she asked, "What are you working on here?"

"It's a shield. Eventually, we're going to have to take the ship above ground to test the engines. This shield will keep anyone from seeing it. See, it works on the same principle as the shield we already have in place. Except, instead of instantly frying anything that comes in contact with it, this will project whatever view we want it to. So, no one will see anything but an empty desert."

"We have a shield around the base?"

"Uh-huh," he said absently.

"Wow. I better be careful if I decide to go out for a walk." Suddenly, she felt a little uneasy.

"Bishop!" came the call from across the hangar. "I've been looking for you."

Cara spun to see Danforth, his face lit with good humor as he crossed the huge room. "Mr. Danforth, what can I do for you, sir?"

"Get your gear. You're going on a little mission. And where's Hunter?"

For some reason she couldn't explain, Cara had come to attention. She imagined it was a Pavlovian reaction to an authority figure, but she found it odd just the same. "I'm not sure where Captain Hunter is, sir."

Danforth reached into his jacket pocket and fished out a stack of papers. "Here's your authorization, your passports, your orders. Get your gear, and get Hunter. You two are going to Pakistan to pick up a recruit."

"A recruit, sir? For our team?"

"Yes. Communication specialist Rakhi Mitra. Dozens of PhDs and a few special other things. It's all in the dossier right"—he fished around in his jacket some more, producing a pile of papers all folded together—"here. Have Hunter read it to you on the way. I need you to go right away. Take one of Tony's Strikers and leave ASAP."

"Yes, sir." Her lips twitched, wanting a smile. She merely licked them.

Rakhi Mitra moved across the sand at a steady, fast pace. Her dark eyes were locked on the man coming toward her and the sun shone off her black hair. She was wearing a tank top, shorts, a bottle of water gripped in her hand. Sweat covered her dark brown skin and soaked her clothes.

"No!" she shouted. "No, no, no!" She shook her finger back and forth, quickening her pace as she neared the man. On his shoulder, he held a bundle of wire a foot in diameter. His eyes questioned her. "You cannot use that cable. That cable will burn under the load. Get the S-7 cable."

She stopped then, one hand going to her hip, the other bringing the water bottle to her mouth. The man drooped, his shoulders sloping as he turned and began the journey back toward the massive warehouse.

Rakhi shook her head and drank three large gulps of water, then swiped her arm across her forehead. It was a hundred fifteen today. She'd spent a lifetime in Pakistan but she was getting older. The heat bothered her more now.

"Excuse me," said the voice behind her.

Rakhi spun and locked eyes with a very pale, very blonde woman. She was wearing a uniform of some sort, though Rakhi couldn't be sure what it was. American? She was fairly sure about that. But which branch? "Yes?" she said curtly, her face scrunching up as she shielded her eyes against the sun. There was a man with her and this man was huge. Rakhi took a step backward.

"I'm looking for Rakhi Mitra," the woman said again.

"You've found her. But I have no time." Rakhi turned and began walking toward the compound, her pace brisk, the muscles of her legs rippling as she went. "I'm on a tight deadline with this job."

"I only need five minutes of your time." The woman hurried to catch up, then fought to keep up. "My name is Cara Bishop and I work for Aegis." She whipped out her official badge in its official bi-fold.

Rakhi spun and took two steps toward Cara, effectively stopping her. "You're the one who saved the world. You took that bomb onto the mother ship." A tiny smile broke Rakhi's tight face.

"So, you'll talk to us?" Cara looked at her hopefully, her eyes wide.

"No!" Again, Rakhi spun and marched toward the compound. She went about thirty yards before she came upon a group of men who were preparing a huge satellite dish to be hoisted onto its supports. "When you are done with the connections, run a test before you put it up. It will save you from taking it down again if it fails."

"Miss Mitra, please," Cara called. "This is very important. It concerns a job that I think you will find very interesting."

Rakhi shouted back, over her shoulder and more loudly than she had intended. "The only job I care about is this one. I have thirty days left to get this communications system up and running. So far, I have no receiver, no servers, and my crew gets smaller by the day. If you'll excuse me, I have to have the entire server bank up and running by morning."

Cara took out her phone, thumbing through it until she found a picture of the ship. Then she trotted to catch up to Rakhi and shoved the phone in front of her face. "Would this change your mind?"

Rakhi froze in midstride, steadied herself as she glared at the picture. "What is this? What are you showing me?" Any disturbance in her work schedule irritated her but these games were enough to drive her to madness.

"This is a ship."

"Well, I can see that." Her glare was pointedly mocking. "What ship? Where? What are you doing with it?"

"Please understand that this is sensitive information and you cannot divulge it to anyone. Ever."

"Yes, yes! I have heard all this before." She waved her hand in front of her as though she were shooing a fly.

"This ship was built and designed by Tony Allen. The government agency that we work for, Aegis, intends to send it out into space to look for other signs of life."

"You mean more aliens to attack us? Are you mad?" Her irritation was clear. It blazed from her eyes like a flame thrower.

"We're looking for allies. Knowledge. And this ship needs a communication system. We want you to join our team."

"*Our* team? So, you are going into space, yes?"

"Yes. I'm the weapons officer."

"Of course." Rakhi jerked her thumb in Hunter's direction and frowned. "He is going too?"

"This is Captain Steve Hunter. He'll be captain of the vessel. Tony Allen will be the engineer. And we have Dr. David Klein coming along as our physician. There will be about a hundred more people on the crew. And...you, we hope."

"Well, I assume that since they sent you after me, you must have read my dossier. You know everything about me by now. I would like you to return the favor."

Cara shot a glance over at Hunter; he shrugged. "Of course."

"Give me your hand." Rakhi kept her eyes locked on Cara's, yielding nothing.

Cara shrugged and presented her hand, watched as Rakhi took it.

Rakhi's eyes closed, her face relaxed a bit, and then her head tilted to one side as though she were listening to a very quiet recording. After a few seconds of this, she released Cara's hand abruptly. "Now you, Mr. Hunter."

Hunter looked at Cara as he offered his huge hand, waiting as Rakhi took it. She shut her eyes, they fluttered for a moment, then she practically threw his hand away from her and stepped back. Her face was red and she was panting.

Cara grabbed the crook of her arm and put one steadying hand on her shoulder. "Are you all right, Miss Mitra?" She watched Rakhi's face, noted the tremble in her hand as she placed it on her forehead.

"I'm fine. Fine." She took a moment, her head spinning, her body suddenly weak. "They did not tell you everything about me, did they?"

Hunter and Cara exchanged confused glances. "What do you mean?" Hunter asked.

"Did they tell you about my abilities? My...affliction?" Rakhi felt vulnerable, weak. It was not something that she was used to. In fact, she hated it. "Walk with me."

She turned then and walked away without ceremony, her legs working hard, the back of her head toward them. She led them to the compound, to the building that housed her personal office.

Inside that building, the air conditioning cranked hard, producing a comfortable temperature, though just barely. At the back of the first huge room was a door and Rakhi headed straight for it. She wove her way around and through the many pallets and boxes until she finally reached the locked door. The key was on her belt and she pulled it out and unlocked the door, stepping inside. Then she froze in place, growling. She worked with about a hundred people on this job, some extremely skilled, others only barely qualified. Apparently, a barely qualified person had been put in charge of the server room coolers.

"Come in, come in. Shut the door." She went straight to the panel to her left and began adjusting the thermostats. "No matter how many times I speak to them, they never have this room cool enough. The servers must be kept very cool or they will overheat and die."

Cara and Hunter stepped inside, feeling the chill immediately. They stood out of her way, watching her move. She did everything quickly and with such economy of motion that it made one's head spin.

"You will forgive me if I work while we speak. I am on a very tight schedule and I have about six miles of network cables to install before I can begin uploading the software and preparing the servers." She pulled a stool across the room to a large rack of servers that spanned the entire back wall, floor to ceiling. "You'll find a few chairs and stools somewhere in here." Her hands were already busy, working as if they'd done that task a thousand times before. In fact, they had.

Cara and Hunter searched among the boxes, bundles of wires, carts of computer parts, and bottles of water until they found two wooden chairs, which they dragged across the room to sit a respectable distance behind Rakhi.

"I'm sure my dossier told you that I was the world's leading expert on communications, especially those used by the aliens, and that I developed this new system to be a sort of interstellar radio system, to put it simply."

"Yes, of course it mentioned all that. That's why we're here." Hunter narrowed his eyes, set his jaw. "But what happened back there? When you held my hand?"

"I was a young girl when the aliens arrived. I have lived in Pakistan all my life, except for the overseas jobs I have taken in the past ten years. I lived with my parents who were killed in the first wave of attacks."

"I'm so sorry," Cara said softly.

"After they were killed, I was left on my own. Pakistan was one of the first countries taken. I do not know why. But I lived on the streets, hiding, learning to survive by whatever means I could find. There were a lot of us like that.

"One day, as the aliens were fighting in our skies with the Earth Coalition forces, an alien craft was damaged. I stood in the street and watched it spiral toward the ground, cheering as it fell. We all did. I was only thirteen. It hit the ground and then spun out of control, crashing through buildings as it tore straight through our village. I ran but I was not fast enough. I ran toward a building, hoping to get around it but there wasn't time. The alien ship smashed into the building, with the nose sticking through the wall, right over my head and me curled into a little ball beneath it.

"When I finally found the courage to stand up and look around, I could see the ship, the alien inside, even the control panel. The side had been ripped away, the engine crushed. And the alien was dead. It was the first time I had ever seen an alien, and it was the most frightening thing I had ever seen in my life. There was fluid leaking from the ship…blood…fuel…I don't know. But whatever it was, I was drenched in it. People were yelling at me to get out of there, to come let them help me. But no one would come close enough to get me out. They were all scared.

"I was there for several moments before I came to my senses enough to walk. And when I walked around the side of the ship, to where the other people were standing, they all screamed and ran away. I did not know what made them scream. I couldn't imagine what had happened to me that would make them fear so. And when I finally found a mirror in an old bombed-out shop, I saw why.

"I was glowing slightly, a green aura all around my body. And my eyes...they were bright green and I had no pupils. My clothes were soaked with whatever had leaked out of the ship and I had to walk almost a mile to get to water that was not designated only for drinking. I washed up as best I could and hoped that the glow would go away. But when I finally checked, it had only gotten worse. I could still see, but my eyes were bright green.

"People avoided me whenever I walked in the street, people who had known me my whole life. No one would come near me. The other children stopped sharing their food with me and the shopkeepers chased me away with brooms when I came near. So, I walked three miles away to get to the only doctor I knew. And when I walked into his office, people turned away. They made me leave. He wouldn't see me. So, alone in the world, I just went back to my village, to the twisted piece of fuselage that I had turned into a shack. And I slept.

"The glow went away after a time, but the substance was in me. And it stayed in me. No one knows what it is or why it affected me the way it did. But ever since the moment it touched me, I could hear people's thoughts. All people's thoughts. I hear them all day and all night. Like a constant screaming in my head. I couldn't sleep for weeks after it happened. Not with the noise. And once I finally looked normal and people wouldn't run from me anymore, I discovered the rest of my power. Whenever I touch someone, I can see inside their mind. I can see their past, their thoughts, the events of their entire lives just as if I am living them myself."

Rakhi finally turned, abandoning the servers in deference to her guests. She targeted Hunter with her eyes, her sad, dark eyes. "When I touched you, Mr. Hunter, I saw it all." She paused, feeling the pain of his history burn at her eyes and constrict her throat. "Tell me, did you volunteer for the program? Or did they simply appropriate you for the experiment?"

Cara cast a glance at him. When she looked back at Rakhi, there was sadness in Cara's eyes.

"I volunteered. I wanted to do it. And I never regretted it."

Rakhi nodded solemnly, forcing herself to smile in spite of the pain she felt at her core. "I know. You are the only one of your kind in the world. Unique in all the universe, with all the pain and loneliness that comes with it. You are also honorable and kind and brave. You personify the very best that humankind can ever become. And you, Commander Cara Bishop, are selfless and courageous. You literally live to serve. You never thought twice about sacrificing your life for your fellow man. You are both good people."

Rakhi turned then, tending to her cables and servers once more, fighting to force back the flood of emotions that came with sharing the lifetime of memories that those two people had experienced. It always pained her. Even good memories came with pain because they were in the past, gone, never to return. Memories were just ghosts, dead things sent back to haunt us all. She was silent for several minutes but she could feel the stares of the two people behind her. She heard their questions, their impatience, their uncertainty.

At long last, she turned around on the stool, placing her hands on her knees and looking thoughtful. "When would I have to begin this assignment?"

"Ideally, as soon as possible," Hunter stated. "But you already knew that." He smiled that winning smile of his.

Rakhi smiled back. "Yes." She sighed deeply, wondering if she should even become involved in the whole thing. Being trapped in a semi-enclosed space with over a hundred thinking people could pose a threat to her sanity. "I must finish this job. I have thirty days to complete it but I could finish in as few as twenty. Why don't you email the papers you need for me to sign and I will sign them for you. And when I have finished here, I will contact you. If it is not too late, I will join your team."

Cara smiled broadly and nodded. She pulled out her phone, pecked at it a few times, then looked up. "The papers are in your inbox. I will caution you to read them completely before signing."

Rakhi laughed for the first time that day and the sound of it seemed alien even to her. "I read every contract I sign. Do not worry. I am an old cap at this."

"Hat," Cara said simply.

"Pardon?"

"Contracts are old hat to you. That's the saying."

"Yes. That is it." Rakhi stood, rubbing her hands on her shorts nervously and blinking too rapidly even for her comfort. "I will send these to you and contact you when I am ready."

"We're very glad to have you joining our team, Miss Mitra...." Cara began.

"Call me Rakhi, please."

"We're happy to have you on board, Rakhi." Cara smiled and shoved out her hand. When she saw Rakhi's face, she pulled back her hand. "I don't suppose you like shaking hands, do you?"

Rakhi shook her head.

"Well, thank you for speaking to us, Rakhi," Hunter said with a smile. "We'll let you get back to your work now."

"Good day to you. Please be careful going back to your car. The sun can sneak up on you. I'll see you soon."

Hunter opened and held the door for Cara, then pulled it quickly shut behind him. They remained silent throughout the trip through the building, even though they were both bursting with questions.

"Good morning, Mr. Allen," Bishop chirped as she crossed the huge hangar.

"Hey, good morning, Bishop. I didn't know you were back yet." Tony stretched his back and smiled in her general direction. Behind him, elbows on the table and his chin in his hands, was Dr. Klein. A burger sat on a plate before him, flanked by fries and a pickle.

"We got back late last night. Flying a Striker makes the trip very quick." She winked and smiled at him.

"It does at that. So, how did it go? Do we have a new communications specialist?"

"We do." She paused for a moment, glancing around Tony

to look at Klein. "I'm sorry. What is he doing?"

Tony regarded Klein over his shoulder and snorted. "It would appear that he's staring at food."

"Ah." Cara tipped her head to one side. "Why?"

"Beats me," was Tony's answer. He shrugged his shoulders. "The trip?"

"Ah. Yes, we have a new communications specialist. She has to stay in Pakistan until she's completed her current contract. But her papers have all been signed and faxed in."

"How long?"

"Two months at the outside."

"Good. I could really use the help around here. So, what did you think? Tell me about her."

"Multiple PhDs, really smart, dedicated, driven. I think she'll be quite the asset to our team."

Tony waved his hand in front of his face. "Yes, yes. But is she pretty? I need at least one pretty girl on board. You can't really expect me to spend three years in space without at least one lovely lady to heap my romantic gifts upon." He chuckled, then took a look at her disapproving glare and paled. "Relax, Bishop. You're most certainly qualified as beautiful, but somehow, I get the idea that I don't have a snowball's chance in hell with you. Am I right?"

"You're right about that."

"Like I said, we'll need *another* lovely lady on board."

"Has anyone ever told you you're a pig, Mr. Allen?"

"Every day of my life. Then I give them money and they call me 'sir.'"

She shook her head. She was about to say something bitter when Dr. Klein slammed his hands on the table, startling them both and drawing their complete attention.

"Damn!" he cursed, running one hand through his hair and sweeping the plate—now filled with black goo instead of a burger and trimmings—to the floor. "Back to the drawing board for me."

"Molecular cohesion problems?" Tony asked.

Dr. Klein shot Tony a look that told him *he* would be having molecular cohesion problems if he didn't shut up. Tony did.

"Have you been spending time in the simulator?" he asked Cara.

"Yea, quite a lot, actually. Especially since you installed the drone software."

Suddenly, Tony clapped his hands and rubbed them together, smirking mischievously at her. "Want to go topside and try it for real?"

"We can do that?"

"Haven't you been paying attention? We can do anything we want. So...you wanna?"

She laughed. He was arrogant and pushy and just about the biggest pig she'd ever met. For all of that, he made her laugh when she didn't want to and feel happy when she was blue. "Let's do it."

CHAPTER 5

"All that time in the simulator has really paid off for you, Bishop," Tony said as they guided the Zodiacs back into the elevator. "I never dreamed they could do those things. My God!"

She smiled for him, her eyes still on the Zodiac, her fingers working gently at the controls. "When I use the view screen on the controller, it's like I *am* the Zodiac. I can see everything so clearly. I can feel the tilt and pitch, all of it."

"Well, they certainly brought me the right girl for the job. Lady. Woman. Person. Damn it!"

Cara laughed then. She should have been pissed at him, but he was just so unabashed in his lack of social skills. Watching him try to bail himself out of tight situations had become her new hobby.

Tony pushed the buttons and the elevator began its descent.

They had spent the afternoon out at the test field. The Zodiacs had performed well, though Tony had claimed his was sluggish when she beat him in an all-out race. The only tests remaining to be done were the weapons tests, but it hadn't seemed like a good idea to send great silver balls out into the world to blow up cacti and jackrabbits. Still, it had been a great diversion and the fresh air had made her feel worlds better.

The elevator doors whooshed open and they stepped out, guiding the Zodiacs before them. They placed them in their docking stations, stowed the controls and sighed contentedly. The silence weighed heavily on them and in a sudden movement, Tony spun and plucked something off the workbench. He took three long strikes and slapped the thing in Cara's hand.

"Know what that is?" he asked, a sparkle in his eye and a smile twitching at his lips.

There was cool metal in her hand. It was smooth and simple, vaguely gun-shaped. "Some sort of a weapon, I'm guessing."

"You win the door prize. It's a fractal-energy-powered hand gun...weapon...never needs to be charged...massively destructive...tunable." He took a breath. Perhaps he simply ran out of words to spew. "I call it a Raster Blaster."

Cara looked at him from the corner of her eye and smirked. "Really?"

"I'm great at making things. I suck at naming them. If you have any better ideas, just let me know."

She nodded, lifted the weapon to eye level and sighted down her arm. "I'll give it some thought," she answered.

"Be careful. I honestly have no idea what that will do. It could take out the whole east wall in one blast." He smiled awkwardly and shrugged.

"You haven't tested it yet?" She removed her finger from the vicinity of the trigger and pointed the weapon at the floor.

"And when would I have time to do that?" He thought for a moment, pulling a face and staring into the dark laboratory behind Cara. "Wanna test it with me tomorrow? A little weapons check?"

"Where in hell are we going to test something like this?"

He didn't hesitate for a second. "My backyard."

"Your backyard?"

"Yea." His smile was broad and boyish. He emanated pure glee now. "You don't get it. My backyard is about five hundred acres. I own the whole mountain."

Cara turned the weapon over in her hands, contemplating everything that could go wrong in such a test. Then she thrust the weapon toward him and nodded. "You're on. Right after morning chow, okay?"

"Deal."

"There you two are!" Danforth came toward them at a good clip, papers clutched in his hands and a smile contorting his lips into something only remotely smile-like. "I've been looking for you everywhere."

"What do you need, Danforth?" Tony asked, sounding bored and annoyed.

Danforth stopped his forward motion and folded his arms over his chest. Rethinking, he put his hands on his hips, and then in his pockets. Body language was not second nature to him. "There's a meeting at 1600 hours in the conference room. All crew members are required to attend."

"What is the purpose of this meeting?" Cara wanted to know.

"Dissemination of information," Danforth stated simply.

"We'll be there," Cara said with a nod. She watched him go in silence, holding her tongue. Then she turned to Tony. "I'm going to go grab a shower and a cold drink before the meeting. I've been out in the blazing sun too long."

"Good call," Tony said. "I'll see you at the meeting."

Cara headed for the elevator, her footsteps echoing in the cavernous hangar, drowning out most other sounds.

"Need somebody to wash your back?" Tony hollered after her.

She, in turn, flipped him off.

"You did tell Klein about the meeting, right?" Tony asked Danforth.

"Of course." He looked at his watch. He was a stickler for punctuality and tardiness irritated him.

Holding the phone below the table so that Danforth couldn't see, Tony tapped out a hasty text. *Conference room. You're late. Get here. Now.*

After a few seconds, he looked down at his phone and snorted. "Klein is almost here."

A few seconds later, Klein burst through the door, stumbling into the room and dropping into a chair. "Sorry I'm late but you just can't walk off and leave a molecular compound unattended."

"I'm not going to pretend I know what you're talking about but we're all here now, so let's begin."

Everyone straightened in their seats, tried to look alert and attentive. The room was dimly lit, like a kindergarten classroom at naptime. Beneath the table, Tony still tapped out messages on his phone. Two seats down, Cara's phone binged. She flipped the screen toward her, scowled, and turned it off. Tony snickered.

"Now, we have a few things to discuss. It won't take long but they have to be ironed out. Not the least of which is a name for our beloved ship." Danforth shuffled a few papers. His eyes were busy; his hands were busy. He had lost his focus some time ago and he struggled visibly to regain it.

"I thought I would name the ship," Tony said. "I made it."

Danforth squinted at him in the half-light and shook his head. "Let's get real here, Mr. Allen. You engineered the tech. But you had one hell of a lot of help building it. And we are not sending the *USS Allen* out into space. Now then. This is a democracy. We shall take some suggestions, and then we shall vote on the best of them."

"I paid for it," Tony grumbled, pouting.

"Let it go, Tony," Hunter said, glaring at him. "Now, does anybody have any suggestions?"

There was silence for a few moments, then Klein said, "How about the *Intrepid*?"

There were nods all around.

"Or maybe the *Vengeance*," prompted Hunter.

"Too confrontational," Tony said. "This is a scientific mission, not a war."

"Okay, then, the *Odyssey*." Danforth put in his two cent's worth.

"I still think the *USS Tony Allen* has a ring to it." Allen put his feet on the table and crossed his arms over his chest, leaning dangerously far back in his chair.

"No!" they all yelled at once.

"We don't know whether we're just going to go exploring, or whether it might turn into a war," Cara said softly. "So, how about the *USS Endeavor*?"

She was met with stunned silence. Nothing moved, no one spoke, and even the fluorescent fixture seemed to have stopped humming. They turned to stare at her.

"That's it," Hunter said at last. "It's perfect."

They all agreed that it was. Back-slaps were shared all

around, as though they had actually acted as a team, then Danforth called the meeting back to order.

"Well, now," Danforth said, rubbing his hands together, "that wasn't so hard, was it? We managed to come together on a name. Now, let's see what we can do about uniforms."

Everyone sat forward, interested at last. Uniforms were something—like the ship—that they would spend most of their time in.

Danforth reached into a valise and pulled out several stacks of photos, neatly stapled together. They were mini catalogs of sorts, showing several views of each uniform type and offering up details. He passed the stack around so each person present could take one.

"Commander Bishop, as you'll see, we've offered several options for each of the ladies' uniforms. I have no personal frame of reference for this, obviously, so I'll let you decide."

Cara furrowed her brow and looked at the pictures carefully. They were simple uniforms, not much to them. Skirts vs slacks, high collars and low, plunging necklines and button-up. There weren't a lot of options.

"Slacks for uniform of the day. Skirts for dress uniforms." She nodded definitively.

"Why would we need dress uniforms?" Hunter wanted to know. "Do you think we'll get invited to a lot of alien parties?"

"Well, I don't know what's going to happen out there, do I?" She scowled at him and pursed his lips. "All branches of the military have two uniforms at least, not counting cammies. I just figured we would, too."

"I'll need scrubs, surgical gowns, hats, booties...." Klein began.

"You said booties," Tony snickered.

"Shut up." Clearly, Klein wasn't having any of Tony's childishness.

"All right, everyone. That's enough." Danforth leaned on the table and crossed his ankles. "Let's pick a color, at least."

"Ooh, red," Tony said.

"No, blue," Cara said quickly.

Danforth pinched the bridge of his nose between his right

index finger and thumb and groaned. "Okay, let's see a show of hands. For red?"

Tony and Klein raised their hands.

"And now for blue."

Cara and Hunter raised their hands. "Now we need a tie-breaker," Cara said. She immediately texted Rakhi. *Quick question. For uniforms, would you prefer red or blue?*

Definitely blue, came the answer.

"Rakhi says blue," Cara announced and Tony leaned in to look at her phone, hoping to catch her in a fib.

"Blue it is," he grumbled.

"There! That wasn't so hard, now was it?" Danforth chuckled, trying to lighten the mood. "Now, there will be another meeting in the near future, this time with our superiors. We are now in a tentative thirty-day countdown to our first test flight."

A nervous hush fell over the room. Stunned looks were exchanged. They had all known the day was coming. They had hoped for it, trained for it, craved it. Now that moment was upon them. Fantasy made real.

"Thirty days," Cara whispered to herself as much as anyone else.

"You all have your jobs," Danforth said. "If you have any concerns, needs, worries or problems, you should express them to me now. We're a team and, until the hierarchy presents itself, I'm your de facto leader. So, let me have it."

"I'm good," Tony said. "You good, Bishop?"

"I'm good. Hunter, you?"

"Fine."

Klein alone said nothing. He sat slumped in his chair, arms folded, his head bowed, face dark. He knew that the entire mission depended on him finding a solution to the food supply problem. He knew it. The crew knew it. Danforth knew it.

. Nobody even looked at him.

"All right then. Know that you can come to me at any time, for any reason. So, if nobody has anything to add...dismissed."

They filed out of the room in silence.

Cara sat opposite Hunter at breakfast. Next to her sat Tony, stuffing his mouth as fast as he could. He usually hated the food and had been quite vocal about how awful it was in the past. Not that morning. Hunter was already on his third plate of food. Surrounding them were half a dozen clusters of other people, equally immersed in their food.

Klein came through the door, his eyes sporting luggage and his hair spread out in all directions. He stopped at the first group of people he came to, clapping one man on the back and smiling.

"How's the food today? Good?" He received a heavy nod in answer and so moved on to the next group. "Chow good today? How are you liking those eggs?"

He was unusually happy that morning, a smile on his face, a slight skip in his step despite the hours of sleep he had missed. He approached Cara and the others, rubbing his hands together like the proverbial mad scientist and grinning madly.

"So, how are we enjoying our breakfast this morning? Is it good? How do you like those pancakes, huh? Nice and light and fluffy, are they?"

They all paused in their eating to study his peculiar expression.

"What's up with you anyway, Klein?" Tony asked around a bite of sausage.

"All I want to know is, do you like your food? Is it good?" He spoke slowly, overly patiently.

"Yeah, it's fine." Tony was clearly irritated now, his smile wilted and his eyes faded.

"Fine? It's fine?" Klein looked hurt. More than hurt, he looked crushed.

"It's really good, Dr. Klein," Bishop said finally. "I've never had food this good from the mess hall."

"Good! Because guess what?" He clasped his hands together tightly and bent at the waist, grinning. "I made it. All of it. I made it in my little magic food box."

They put down their forks at that and stared at him. For the first time, they noticed that the usual noise from the kitchen was absent. The line had only two servers on it, instead of the usual row of servers, cooks, and prep people. Gone also were the hot pans filled with food. They had been replaced with individual plates, already portioned out, waiting under the heat lamp.

Tony spoke first, his eyebrows shooting up and his eyes narrowing. "You mean you fixed it? Really fixed it?"

"I did!" Klein laughed and jumped in the air, throwing his hands up for Tony to slap. "I fixed the stabilization problems, tweaked the speed and spit out over a hundred breakfast plates in under an hour."

"Yeah!" Tony yelled, jumping out of his chair and slapping Klein's hands. Then he grabbed him in a big bear hug and whooped. "I knew you could do it. I *knew* it!"

"I don't mind telling you," Klein said as things finally calmed down, "I was really sweating it. I mean, if I hadn't straightened this out, then we wouldn't have had a mission. No pressure, right?" He laughed nervously.

"Well, you sure did a great job." Cara stuffed another forkful of food into her mouth and chewed hastily. "Everything tastes great. The texture is just right. And you finally solved the spoilage problem. How long did you have this in testing anyway?"

"Yeah, about that…" Klein began. Cara dropped her fork to her plate with a clang. "This…actually…is the test."

Cara's eyes went wide and she spit the rest of the food onto the plate. "You mean to tell me you have no idea how this food will react inside the human body?"

"Not really. But I should in…oh, say…about three hours."

"You bring a whole new meaning to the term 'mad scientist,'" Tony growled. "Come on, Bishop. Let's head out for that little test we had scheduled."

"Right behind you, Tony."

They scraped their chairs on the floor standing up and headed for the door in fast, measured steps.

Klein sighed and watched them go. He looked back at Hunter, who was still shoveling food into his mouth. He finished with his plate, then started on Cara's plate. Klein watched him for a few moments in fascination.

"So, how come you aren't all freaked out?"

Hunter shrugged and looked up. "I'm immortal. What do I care?"

Klein snorted. "Well, at least I have somebody on my side."

"Does your stomach feel kind of bubbly and gross?" Cara asked as they burst through the door and into the bright sunlight.

Tony put one hand on his stomach and frowned. "Now that you mention it, it sort of does."

"Do you think Klein made us all sick?"

"I sure hope not. For his sake."

They reached the junction of three sidewalks and Cara turned right.

"Where are you going?" Tony wanted to know.

"To the hangar, silly. We'll get to your house a lot faster if we take a Striker."

He took her arm and gently pulled her to the right. "Not today. I'm driving this time."

"You? Really?"

"Yeah. I got a brand-new custom Lamborghini and I'm itching to drive it." He winked at her so that she couldn't tell if he was kidding or not.

"A custom Lamborghini? Seriously? That's a thing?"

Tony laughed. "Yeah. I was driving to work one morning and this guy blows my doors off. So, I followed him and bought it off him. Now it's mine."

"Wow!" she laughed. "What must it be like to be you and be rich enough to have anything on the planet you want?"

"It's awesome. But mostly boring. Why do you think I come here and build space ships and ray guns?" He winked at her then.

Looming in the distance was a bright red Lamborghini, the sun flashing off the hood in a mosaic pattern of colors and lights. Cara nearly stopped in her tracks, her breath caught somewhere in her throat and her eyes bugging.

"Whoa! It's gorgeous! What did it set you back?"

"Nearly a million. The guy didn't want to part with it but... everybody has their price."

Cara trotted toward the car. She had never seen a car that expensive, must less ridden in one. Her first condo hadn't cost that much. Hand outstretched, she made ready to open the door as she ran forward.

"Stop!" Tony yelled and she froze. "She's got shielding. Anything gets within three feet of her from any direction, the shield goes up and it'll knock you back about ten feet."

Cara snatched back her hand, clutching it to her chest. "Well, that's a bit extreme, don't you think?"

"Yeah, but birds will never crap on my car, now will they?" He clicked the remote and shut off the system. "There. You're safe now."

She climbed into the car and ran her hands over the smooth leather, sighing audibly as her skin stroked the buttery, cool surface. Everything in the car screamed luxury, and when Tony turned over the engine, she nearly gasped. It never made a sound. Cara remembered the sports cars of old with their growling engines and the feeling of power rumbling through your bones. This car didn't produce so much as a hum and it glided out of the parking space as though it wasn't even making contact with the road.

"Buckle up. I mean it." Tony watched as she fastened the seatbelt around herself and cinched it tight. "Ready?"

"You bet," she said.

"No, you're not. You're really not."

The laugh he gave as he put the car in first gear would have inspired Satan. Then the car was moving. There still wasn't a sound, not a bit of vibration, but as they reached the front gate, they were doing over a hundred. By the time they reached the highway, they were nearing two hundred miles per hour.

Maybe Tony had expected her to be thrilled. Maybe he had thought she'd be scared. Nothing on earth could have prepared him for her response. Her fists were in the air and she was yelling like a teenager on a roller coaster. Her face was rapturous.

"Faster. Faster! Come on, Tony. Show me what she can *really* do!"

Tony punched it and the car leaped forward. Until that second, he hadn't been sure whether it had any more speed in it or not, but as he watched the speedometer reach two-fifty and past, he started to laugh.

"I thought maybe I'd paid too much for this thing," he said, the rushing wind nearly stealing his words. "Now I think I underpaid."

Sadly, it took only six minutes to reach the turn-off that led to his house. He slowed the car a mile before he reached it, taking the corner at almost fifty. The road up the mountain was winding, peppered with sharp turns and steep angles.

The house didn't come into view until the final turn was complete and they were facing east. It was a great box of a thing, all sleek surfaces and sharp angles. It was as if someone had taken a building block and shoved it into the side of the mountain. The side facing the vista was all glass, the back half of it disappearing into the side of the mountain. The garage was actually a good deal lower than the house itself. Cara looked at the whole thing in wonder.

"You know, it might have been a good idea to actually bring the weapons with us," she said as she stepped out of the car.

"Nah! I've got more of them here. My lab has almost everything. In fact, it's better than the lab back at the base."

She followed him to what appeared to be an elevator door, the only exit from the garage save for the large drive-through door. Along the way, they passed a dozen or so other expensive cars: Ferraris, Porsches, Jaguars, and, of course, the obligatory limo. Cara shook her head and smiled.

"For the record, that was the best ride I've ever had. And that does include quite a few flights in the Strikers."

"That's high praise coming from you." He pushed the button marked LIVING and watched the elevator doors slide shut.

"But why do you need so many cars? In fact, why do you need any other car?"

"I have a lot of cars at a lot of houses. So many that I can't remember where I left them all. That's not bragging, by the way. It's just a fact. I built this place quickly. I didn't want to stay at the base and the drive home, even in the helicopter, was becoming a pain."

"It really sucks to be you, doesn't it?" she said playfully.

"Yeah. It's awful."

The doors opened on a living room so large, Cara thought they might accidentally have come out in a meeting room of some kind. It overlooked the massive vista of neighboring mountains and desert. The place was tidy to the point that she wondered if anyone had ever set foot in there before.

"Let's grab a cold drink and then we'll go down to the lab and get some Rasters. That's what I decided to call them, by the way. It stands for Rapid Atomic Structure Energy Ray. Kind of catchy, don't you think?"

"It'll do until something better comes along."

"Anything you could want is in the fridge. Just grab something."

Cara looked around and, finding no recognizable refrigerator, frowned. "What fridge?"

"Oh, sorry. It's that room to your left." He was on his way to the bar, clearly in need of something stronger than pop.

"A room? Your refrigerator is a room?"

He shrugged and began pouring scotch into a monogrammed glass.

Cara opened the door to her left and stepped inside. It was literally a twelve-foot-square room, lined with insulation and stainless steel, wrapped in shelves, and cooled to the perfect temperature. She spotted several cases of soda to her right and grabbed a can of cola from one of them. The back wall was hung with sides of beef, chickens, and pigs, all dressed and ready to be sliced into ham, bacon, or whatever the master desired. She shook her head and closed the door.

"You really do like showing off, don't you?" she giggled.

Again, he shrugged. "Come on. Let's go down to the lab."

She followed him to a different elevator and watched as a panel on the wall scanned first his fingerprints and then his retina. A green light lit on the panel and the elevator door slid open.

"That's an awful lot of security for a private lab," she mocked.

"Yeah, well, the stuff I have in this lab could destroy the planet a dozen times over. Now, bear in mind, this is just my small lab. The real deal is back at my house in L.A. I hope you're not disappointed."

They descended to the base of the mountain and when the doors slid open, the air that met them was fresh and cool and only slightly humid. The lab stretched back for hundreds of yards and reached to the left and right further than she could see. There were all manner of scientific things in there; everything from robots and testing equipment to what looked like giant lasers and living things.

"This is your small lab?" she asked, gaping.

"Yeah. Sorry."

He moved away, bound for the west—or was it north?—wing. Cara followed, staring at everything she passed, trying to make sense of it all.

"Exactly what do you do down here, anyway?" she asked him.

"Whatever I want." He rummaged around inside a cabinet, finally pulling out a silver metal case and slapping it on the counter next to him. "Here it is!" He flipped up the lid and revealed two hand weapons. He plucked them from their foam resting place and shoved one of them into each pocket. "The testing room is this way."

Tony turned to his right and, side-stepping the benches and equipment, headed off in the opposite direction from the elevator. Cara followed dutifully, wondering how in the world she had ever gotten herself into such a bizarre situation. She couldn't have felt more ill at ease if she had been at a cotillion.

At the end of their trek was a sealed room. Tony threw a large bolt and switched on the lights inside. The walls of this chamber (for Cara could think of no more apt description) seemed to be lined with metal and the floor was nothing more than stone. It was a large room, maybe twenty feet wide and a good fifty feet long. At the far end of the room were two targets, the regulation type seen on every shooting range across the country.

"What do these things do, anyway?" Cara asked as she watched Tony fiddle with one of the Rasters.

"They kill people and destroy things, just like all other weapons." He finished his tweaking and set the Raster down on the bench to his left. Then he headed for the far wall.

"What I mean is, how do they do it?"

His voice came from an increasing distance away, his

swaggering form growing smaller as he walked. "They emit an electro-magnetic field, which disrupts the electrical field of the target, molecule by molecule. The process happens very quickly and it just sort of causes the molecules to lose cohesion."

She squinted at Tony, watching in confusion as he opened two panels near the targets and pulled something out of them. It wasn't until he had the second one almost in position that she realized they were mannequins. Then he started back toward her.

"This would all be automated if we were in the big lab back home," he explained as he came toward her.

She waited until he was standing in front of her to ask her next question, fearing the response. "So, if this thing makes molecules fly apart, to put it simply, then what's to stop it from having a chain reaction and causing the floor and walls to lose cohesion, then the mountain, the ground, the entire planet...?"

Tony smirked. "It's a limited reaction. Trust me. I could explain it to you, but you wouldn't understand." He paused for a second, then shook his head. "I don't mean that as a put-down. You're just not a physicist."

"No, certainly. I wouldn't understand a word of it."

Tony handed her a weapon and took up his place directly in line with the mannequin on the left. "Let's see how good your marksmanship is."

Cara adopted her shooter's stance and focused. "Don't worry about me. I've got medals and trophies going all the way back to age ten."

She drew a bead on the mannequin, breathing softly, wanting very much to show him up. When she was sure of her targeting, she gave the trigger one quick squeeze, not sure what to expect.

The was no sound, no kick, nothing at all to indicate that the weapon had actually fired. But when Cara blinked and checked the target, she found it sparkling. The thing shimmered for two seconds, then just sort of popped into nonexistence. She blinked again and squinted. Yes, the mannequin had completely disappeared and there wasn't a speck of debris.

She looked over at Tony, who had just fired his own shot. As she watched, his mannequin, too, shimmered into non-existence.

Tony snapped his head in her direction and smirked. "Well, that was fun."

"Yeah. It's just...gone." She checked his expression and then knit her brows. "Is there supposed to be a hole in the wall?"

"Huh?" He looked toward the end of the room and frowned, then turned back to her. "Huh?"

Already she was walking toward the wall, Tony in hot pursuit. In each space where a mannequin had stood, there was now a neat hole cut in the wall. It was about a foot in diameter and went as far back as either of them could see. Cara squatted down to peer more carefully at the hole.

"I see light."

"That's not possible." Tony squatted down as well, frowning as he looked inside the hole. "Damn." He looked up and over his shoulder at her. "I think it could use some tweaking."

"Ninety-eight point two...ninety-nine point five...one hundred six point three..." Klein prattled on as an assistant trailed behind him, noting the temperature of each patient on his or her respective chart.

"Doctor, aren't you concerned about a temperature that high?"

Klein shook his head and smirked. "Not at all. That's perfectly normal for Captain Hunter. Moving on...ninety-eight point eight...."

They had turned the mess hall into a makeshift examining room, running basic tests on everyone who had eaten breakfast that morning. Then he sent them all off with a clap on the back and a questionnaire. Exhausted but vindicated, he dropped into a nearby chair and clutched the clipboard to his chest.

"Well, short-term results are good. No ill effects that I can see."

"How long before we know for sure?" Hunter wanted to know.

"All our meals this week will be produced with the machines. I'd say by the end of the week, we should know beyond all doubt whether it will work or not. But I'm pretty safe in saying that we should celebrate this small victory." He winked at Hunter and smiled.

"What do you have in mind, Doc?"

"Remember what we used to do during the war when we needed to blow off steam?"

"Yeah."

There was a wicked gleam in Klein's eye when he said it. He could barely speak around the broad smile that had stretched his face. "Let's do that."

CHAPTER 6

Cara shuffled into the mess hall the next morning after only three hours' sleep. She had visions of the crew all screaming and running at the sight of her and, if she looked anything like she felt, they probably would.

"Forgive me for being insensitive," Hunter began, "but you look positively awful."

"Thanks," said Cara, dropping into a chair. "Nobody warned me about Tony."

Hunter looked stricken for a moment; that and worried. "What about Tony?"

"We went to his lab yesterday to test out the weapons. He said they needed a little tweaking and the next thing I knew, it was three in the morning and I was finally getting into bed."

"He's like that," Klein muttered. "Once he gets focused on something in the lab, the rest of the world might as well not exist. But the results are always amazing."

"I suppose." Cara hung her head for a moment, feeling the exhaustion at the base of her neck and in her shoulders. When she lifted her eyes, they targeted Klein. A smirk crept across her taut face. "What the hell happened to you, if you don't mind me asking?"

"We celebrated." Hunter said no more. He simply sat there, looking pained at Klein's very existence.

"Celebrated what?" Cara asked, trying not to laugh.

"The small victory of solving the food chain problem." Klein perked up a bit at that, though his face was still slack and slightly pale.

"I see. And exactly how did you celebrate? Getting hit by a truck?"

"We did what we used to do in the war," Klein said, almost proud. "First, we got a six-pack, see?"

Hunter leaned in, his voice low. "He got a six-pack."

"And then we went to the batting cages."

"A six-pack and the batting cages. Sounds reasonable to me," Cara said with a nod.

"We each hit a round of balls…." Klein continued.

"And everything would have been fine if we'd left right then," Hunter added.

Cara looked between them, sensing the tension, the guilt, the regret. "Go on."

"Then we ran out of beer…." Klein began.

"He ran out of beer." Hunter was not taking any heat on this one.

"So, we went for more."

"He went for more."

"And then we hit some more balls."

"By the second beer from that six-pack, he couldn't even see the balls coming at him."

"Oh, I could too! He exaggerates."

"I suggested we go home at that point but he refused. 'Not until the beer is gone,' he said. So, I poured the others out on the ground."

"Alcohol abuse, that's what that is," Klein grumbled.

"So, Klein said he wouldn't leave until I hit one over the fence like the good old days."

Cara pulled a face. "But those fences are like forty feet high."

"You should have seen it!" Klein bellowed, throwing his arms out wide. "It was magnificent!" At that point, he went back to holding his head and groaning.

"I didn't even put my full power behind it. I just hit it hard enough to get it over the fence. I thought." Hunter looked contrite and embarrassed.

"There was the crack of the bat," Klein said. "And that ball sailed a good ten feet over the top of the safety net. And it kept going and going until we couldn't see it anymore. And that's when it happened."

"A car alarm went off."

"And that's when I grabbed Klein by the arm and started hauling him toward the gate. We were almost out, too."

"Then this guy shows up. A big guy. Oh, not as big as Hunter here, but big enough."

"Bigger than you," Hunter added.

"He blocks our way," Klein chuckled, "and he says, 'Are you the moron who shattered my windshield with your ball?'"

"I was about to tell him that I would happily pay to have his car repaired when Klein stepped in."

"Yeah, I stepped right in close to him...."

"Staggered in close," Hunter amended.

"And I said...I said... 'So what if I am?'"

"And the guy took a swing at him. If Klein hadn't picked that exact moment to pass out, he'd be icing his jaw right now."

"I didn't pass out!" Klein roared with self-righteous indignation...and then went back to holding his head.

"He passed out. I told the guy I'd get his car fixed for him, but he just kept getting madder and madder."

Cara shook her head and frowned.

"I swear, all I wanted was to get Klein out of there in one piece."

"Oh no," Cara said softly, knowing what was coming next.

"He took a swing at me and I grabbed his fist in mid-air. I explained how he didn't really want to do that but he just took another swing at me and another. So, I put my hand on his head and tried to reason with him but he wasn't having any of it. That's when I picked the guy up and hung him on the fence. Then I threw Klein over my shoulder and left."

"And this is why we don't let Klein drink."

Everyone turned around to see Tony leaning against the doorway, his expensive sunglasses pushed down on his nose, and smiling.

"I was wondering what happened to you," Cara said. "And how dare you look so fresh after having only three hours' sleep."

"Oh, I haven't slept." He pushed off from the wall and walked toward them. "I went back to the lab after I dropped you off. I've got years of experience with sleep deprivation. Besides, I've done some of my best work after having not slept for several days." He pulled out a chair and sat backward on it, resting his chin on his arms and grinning. "I solved the weapon problem, by the way. You're welcome." He winked.

"Well, that's good to know. Now, when we battle evil aliens, we won't rip a hole in all of space and time." Cara pulled another face at him and giggled.

"Well, probably not, anyway." Tony winked. "Then again, we haven't tested the ship's weapons yet, now have we?"

Cara was about to say something sarcastic when her phone buzzed loudly. She looked at the text quickly and frowned. "Looks like my number is up. Time to make another trip to Pakistan."

"All right, all right!" Tony said, rubbing his hands together. "I'm finally going to get my communications officer. Let's go, Bishop."

Hunter's phone sang out next and he checked the message. "Sit down, Allen. I'm the co-pilot this time."

Tony got toe to toe with the larger man, his large, dark eyes pleading. "I'll give you a million dollars if you let me go."

"No can do, pal," said Hunter, clapping a large hand on Tony's shoulder. "We've got our orders."

"Oh fine!" Tony spat, slamming his backside on the chair. "Leave me here to babysit the lush."

"Hey! I'm sitting right here," Klein moaned.

"I know, I know," Tony laughed, grabbing his shoulders and giving the man a hard shake. "And I'm going to take great care of you, too, little buddy. Don't...you...worry."

Klein looked up in desperation and mouthed the words, *Help me.*

The round trip to pick up Rakhi took a little more than seven hours. Hunter and Cara were back in time for supper. By seven o'clock, Rakhi was settled into her new quarters, still gushing about her ride in the Striker and itching to get her hands on the ship's computers and bridge. Cara was exhausted and so she left Rakhi in the capable hands of Tony, with a stern warning for him to be a gentleman. Then she went off to bed.

"Your reputation precedes you, of course, Mr. Allen" Rakhi

said as soon as Cara had gone. "And I am amazed at how much you've accomplished."

"Actually, it's *Doctor* Allen," he said, somewhat bitterly.

"I beg your pardon?" Rakhi said absently. She'd been distracted by what she'd seen on the workbench.

"I said, call me Tony." He flashed his winning playboy smile.

My God! When did geniuses get so hot? Rakhi heard the words clearly in her head. *I wonder if she's got a boyfriend.*

"There is something you should know about me, Mr. Allen."

"Yes?" He stopped checking out her backside long enough to make eye contact and maintained that only by the sheer strength of will.

"I can hear the thoughts of every person within a one-hundred-yard radius. Clearly." She stared daggers through him then, waiting for his response.

Tony blinked, flashed a smile, blinked again. "Perhaps we should go to the bridge and I can brief you about the computer integration and communications station. We're using your near-space matrix, you know."

"Yes, I spotted this on the way in. I am honored."

Out of instinct, Tony waved Rakhi up the ladder ahead of him. His eyes were glued to her as she ascended and he was about to voice some unclean thoughts when he remembered that she would hear every one of them.

She's got the most perfect...damn it, Allen! She'll hear you. Baseball. Ferraris. That new yacht. Think of anything else...anything.

"You know, we might be able to come up with some sort of damper that would block out the thoughts for you." He tried to occupy his mind with anything but her.

"I have tried. Why do you think I went into the field of communications engineering and microelectronics?"

"Well, we have to keep trying, that's all."

"Certainly, it might be the only thing that keeps you alive." She was half joking, of course, but the way she targeted him with her eyes made him think that she was deadly serious.

Don't do it, Tony. She'll hear you.

"Yes, I will." She never bothered to turn and look at him. She couldn't have if she'd wanted to. She was smiling.

Damn it! I'm gonna need a tin foil hat.

Cara came upon Rakhi in the mess hall the next morning. She sat alone at the long table, surrounded by operating manuals, spec sheets, and a three-inch-tall stack of printouts. Cara grabbed a mug of coffee—the only thing not produced by Dr. Allen's machine—and sat next to her.

"Good morning, Commander Bishop," Rakhi said without looking up.

"Call me Cara, please. We're the only two women on the team so far. I could use a sister at arms."

Rakhi turned her head toward Cara and smiled. "It has been a very long time since I've had a real friend. I would like this very much."

Cara took a long draw on her coffee and set the mug down gently. "How are you settling in? Is there anything you need?"

"Everything is quite adequate, thank you." She said it curtly and without emotion.

"I'm sorry," Cara said. "Am I disturbing you?"

Rakhi turned and smiled at Cara. "No, it is I who am sorry. I am not accustomed to having other people around. I am, as you say, lacking in social graces."

"That's fine. But I do have a thick skin. If I'm ever bothering you, just say so. I won't be offended."

"I'm afraid the dynamic here confuses me. You and Captain Hunter are military, yes?"

"Yes."

"And Dr. Allen, myself and Dr. Klein are not?"

"No, they're not."

"I assume there will be a chain of command, though."

"Yes, there will be. The powers that be just haven't given us the playbook yet."

Rakhi made a face and tilted her head. "What is this playbook?"

"It's an expression. It means they haven't yet given us all the regulations."

"Ah. And I assume that one of the regulations will be no fraternization."

"I...don't know."

Rakhi looked at Cara as though she could see right through her and she smiled. "How long have you been in love with Captain Hunter?"

Cara nearly dropped her coffee mug. She juggled it for a few seconds, sloshing coffee out onto the table before setting it down carefully. "What do you mean?"

Rakhi laughed out loud, her cheeks dimpling and her eyes beginning to tear. "You cannot play dumb with me. I hear everything, remember? Oh, don't worry. I will not share your thoughts with anyone else. But I heard it twice now. First when we met and again just now. You are most certainly in love with him but you do not wish to admit it."

Cara shrugged it off and tried to make as though it wasn't important. "Doesn't matter. He is my commanding officer and we are on a mission together. Absolutely nothing can come of it. We're both military and even if the rules don't forbid it, it's incredibly stupid to have a personal relationship with someone on your crew...especially when you can't escape the ship for years. Case closed."

Rakhi studied her face with a smile. "I see."

"You're not hearing anything because I'm not thinking anything," Cara said, stabbing a finger in Rakhi's direction.

"He is a good man. You could do a lot worse." Her tone was half mocking.

"I'm still not thinking about it. Lalala. You won't get anything out of me."

"Even though he just walked in?" Rakhi said.

Cara spun in her chair and stared hopefully at the door. When she turned back, Rakhi was giggling like a school girl. "You tricked me."

"And it was very funny."

Cara was sound asleep, engaged in one of her oldest recurring dreams. In it, she was in a cardboard box, flying high above the houses and cars and people of her neighborhood. She had first had the dream when she was five years old and it had been the first spark of her love for flying. Tonight, the dream came to a frightening end when some noise in the real world broke into the dream, sending her cardboard flying machine plummeting toward the ground.

She scrambled to find the noise, her face pinched and her eyes searching the dark for the guilty party: her phone. It danced and buzzed on the dresser across the room and she made a dive for it, slamming her right shin against the desk chair as she snatched the thing off the bureau. Grimacing, she hopped backward and fell onto the bed, swiping through to the text message that had ended her flight.

Meeting tomorrow. 1300 hours. Dress uniform. Conference room. Joint Chiefs of Staff in attendance.

One by one, each of the crew members' phones vibrated and rang up and down the hall. Only Captain Hunter was awake to read the text.

Cara sighed loudly and let her phone hand fall to the bed, her eyes staring at the ceiling. For every thing that made her love the military, there was something that made her hate it. Meetings with higher ups ranked among those things she hated. Only inspections irritated her more.

After a few moments, she drifted back to sleep but the dream was not to be reclaimed and her sleep was short-lived. Two hours later, she was once more awakened by a loud and irritating noise. She lay there for a few minutes, hoping it would stop and trying to figure out the source of her irritation. There was the sound of grinding metal, of motors, and of heavy footsteps. Finally, in desperation, she threw back the covers and shoved off from the bed.

From inside the ship, deep in its cavernous home, there was no way to tell whether it was day or night. If Cara hadn't glanced at the desk clock on her way out, she would never have known it was not quite five in the morning. Feet slapping the deck, she left her quarters and peered down the hall, following the source of the noise with a sense of purpose that could only be described as obsessive.

"What the hell are you doing?" she bellowed as she came across a small group of men working on the elevator.

"Ma'am?" said the man closest to her, the one with the red curly hair and freckles.

"What are you doing working out here at five in the morning? Don't you know people are trying to sleep in here?"

"I'm sorry, ma'am. Mr. Allen told us to have the elevators working by ten or he'd fire us all."

She blinked at him and scowled. "Carry on."

She spun on one heel then, making for the ladder and the hangar outside. She was wearing a pair of regulation Navy boxers and her favorite tank top with the insignia of her last flight squad on it. She slid down the ladder and then marched on Tony, who was tinkering with something at his work bench, whistling as he did so.

"What the hell is wrong with you?" she yelled as she reached him. Most women couldn't pull off the fierce act while wearing their pajamas, but Cara actually backed Tony up a few steps.

"Whoa!" he said, laughing. "You are not pretty in the morning, honey. I think you could use a little coffee, too."

"Why? Why that? Why now? Just why?" Her hands were on her hips and she was frowning even more heavily now.

"Did you get a text this morning?"

"Yes."

"So, you know that the Joint Chiefs of Staff are coming today for a big powwow."

"Of course."

"Well, my text told me to be at the meeting and to make sure the elevators were fully functional by the time they arrived at ten. Apparently, Danforth wants to take them on a tour of the ship and also apparently, they don't like ladders."

"Well, they are a bunch of dinosaurs." Cara felt the steam seep out of her, let her muscles go slack by degrees. "I haven't slept. Usually, I'm good with noise. Can sleep right through it. I'm so tired."

Tony smiled weakly. "Again, it's not my fault, honey. I could still be in my expensive big bed with the silk sheets and the custom white-noise generator. It's crunch time. We've all got to make some sacrifices, put our shoulders to the wheel, you know?"

Cara nodded. "Okay. I'm sorry I yelled at you."

"No problem. We're all under a little pressure now. Go try to get some rest." She turned on her heel and stomped away. Tony watched her go, smiling. "You kinda remind me of my first wife when you're mad. But you're way hotter."

She kept walking as she flipped him off.

The crew gathered in the hallway outside the conference room that afternoon. Cara in her dress whites, Hunter in his dress uniform, and the others in lab coats and jeans. Dr. Klein clutched a stack of clipboards, file folders and reams of paper to his chest. His face was drawn and worried and for a moment, Cara thought he might actually pass out.

"Are they in there?" Klein wanted to know. "Should we go in?"

"They're in there," Hunter offered. "And we can go in when they escort us inside. Calm down."

Klein nodded rapidly and pushed his glasses up on his nose.

Tony leaned against the wall, the only one of the group not affected by the whims of the Joint Chiefs. He played with his phone and whistled. He looked for all the world like the school bully waiting to see the principal.

Suddenly, the doors were pushed open, startling the group, and two uniformed Marines stepped out. "You may come in now," said the one on the left. Both of them stepped aside and snapped to attention.

The conference room was huge and dimly lit. A long table sat against the back wall and this is where the Joint Chiefs sat, each with an assistant behind them. In front of that table and facing it was another, longer table and six chairs.

Board stiff and precise in every movement, Hunter stepped to the chair to his far left and stood at attention, mid-salute. Cara followed suit, her hand snapping into a salute and staying there, awaiting further orders. Rakhi, Tony and Dr. Klein went to their right. Tony pulled out a chair, letting it scrape the floor as he did so. Then he dropped into it, tilting it back slightly and putting his feet on the table.

"Sit up," Cara growled without moving a muscle.

"At ease, Commander Bishop," said the general. "It's all right. We're all well-aware of Mr. Allen's free spirit."

Tony never moved. "Hi, Mason, how are you? Mike, how's that daughter of yours? Adam, how's that Porsche working out for you? Was I right or what?"

"Best car I ever owned," said the admiral. "Now, let's get down to business, shall we? Dr. Klein, I hear that the food supply problem has been solved."

"Yes, Admiral."

"And the tests? Does it have any ill effects on the crew?"

"Negative, sir. A two-week testing period has shown no ill effects. They're in exactly the same shape as they were before, when they were eating regular food."

"Excellent." The admiral smiled and nodded. "I don't mind telling you, we were really sweating that food problem."

"I have to admit, I was sweating it too." Klein offered up a weak smile and pushed his glasses up once more. "I have all the data here if you'd like to see it."

"That's okay," the general said. "We'll take your word for it. Mr. Allen, I understand you have weapons in place and the engines are in place."

"Yep. Finished all that last week." Tony looked pleased with himself, his fingers laced over his belly, rocking gently in the chair.

"How often will you have to refuel?"

"Never."

"Never?" The general's face was caught between confused and impressed.

"We're using the same kind of ghost-matter propulsion that the aliens used. However, I've taken it several hundred steps further. I call it fractal power. You see, the splitting of each atom produces another, just as powerful bit of matter that can also be split, and so on and so forth into infinity. We'll never run out of power."

"And the weapons? Don't they produce a drain on the power system?" the general to the far left wanted to know.

"Nope. Actually, they provide power. Each time the weapon fires, it produces an explosion. In firearms, we call it a recoil, but it's the same thing. And that explosion, or recoil, is absorbed through a series of dampeners, which then transfer the power back into the grid. Voila! You can actually fire the weapons to produce power."

"Excellent." The admiral looked pleased. His face was softer now and full of good humor. It hardened when he looked at Rakhi, however. "Miss Mitra, I'd like to know some details about the communications systems. Delays, signal loss, etc."

Rakhi stood up and moved away from the table. "May I?" she asked, indicating the white board to her right.

"Of course."

"We're using the same sort of communications system that we used during the war," she began, drawing several small circles on the white board, each several feet apart. "This is our ship. This is Earth. And scattered throughout the known galaxy are various phenomena: quasars, ion storms, and so forth. The system utilizes a very advanced sort of fiber optic system, but without the fiber. Each signal will leave the ship here, carried on a tiny beam of light, then be bounced off one of these natural phenomena, off a satellite, and so on. Each time it is relayed, it will gain speed and strength until it finally reaches Earth."

"And how long of a delay can we expect in messages?" The admiral seemed fixated on the communications. He wasn't letting it go.

"In the beginning, I would estimate the delay would be no more than three seconds, plus or minus a nanosecond. We plan to drop our own buoys along the way, in order to boost communications. We have no idea what we may find beyond the limits of our own galaxy, however, so I am afraid I can make no guarantees as to the reliability of a signal beyond that point. I have theories, of course, and I do hope that they will be proved as we go along."

"Excellent." The general waved his hand and the two Marines at the back of the room moved to pick up a stack of books. As they passed them to each of the crew members, the general looked on with pride. "Now then…we are beginning a new enterprise here. Two of you are in the military. The rest of you are not. This new enterprise calls for a new system, a new branch of our military. For the moment at least, we're calling it the United Space Service. The person who saved the planet is an

American. The inventor of all this tech is an American. But this mission is really for the benefit of all the peoples of the Earth.

"Throughout history, mankind has always operated on an us-versus-them mentality. It took the arrival of the aliens to show us that the us part of that equation is all of humanity and that the them is someone out there. We very much wanted this to be an international mission and we plan on sharing the information we glean from it with all the nations of the world."

"And yet," Rakhi interrupted, "we are under the direct command of the American Joint Chiefs of Staff, not the United Nations or any other such international organization. Why?"

The admiral smirked. "A liberal to the very end, Miss Mitra? I like that. And you are correct. This is very much an American-funded, American-led endeavor. But not for the reasons you think. You see, most of the countries of the world were hit very hard by the war. Harder than the United States. Their populations dwindled, their resources exhausted, their economies crashed…they simply don't have anything left to give. We decided, unanimously, to absorb the burden and cost of launching this deployment in order to give the rest of the world's nations a chance to rebuild. And let's face it, without American courage and ingenuity, we'd all be bowing to our alien overlords right now."

"So, we are taking one for the team. Is that what you are saying?" Rakhi was suspicious, and rightfully so.

"Yes." The general smiled and for once, the smile seemed genuine. "And as soon as this mission proves successful, we will begin recruiting worldwide. We will put ships like the *Endeavor* into mass production, and all the nations of the world will reap the benefits of our risks."

"Now," began the admiral, "along with this new branch of the military come new rules. You have them before you now. And as soon as this deployment is completed, a seat will open up on the Joint Chiefs of Staff so that the Space Service is represented as well. We have streamlined the ranks, cutting out the sub-ranks. Therefore, Captain Hunter and Commander Bishop will retain their ranks. They will be paid on their respective pay rates and will be given USS pay as well. The rest of you will become lieutenants and will be paid commensurate with your risk. Suffice it to say that you will be well compensated."

"It's not about the money," Klein said softly.

"I know, Doctor." The general smiled and shook his head. "But we need order and discipline. In any event, the regs are all right there before you. Learn them. Know them. We are t-minus-fourteen days to our test flight. You must be ready."

"Now, we'd like a word alone with Captain Hunter and Commander Bishop. The rest of you are dismissed."

As the others filed out of the room, Hunter, flanked by Cara, stood at attention. The admiral motioned for the two Marine guards to leave as well and he watched as they shut the door, apparently guarding it from the outside. Then he turned his eyes to Hunter and Cara.

"At ease. Sit down." He watched as they sat uneasily in their chairs. No one could miss the deer-caught-in-headlights expressions on their faces. "Now, what I need from you is this: I would like to know of any special problems you've encountered, any hurdles that might get in our way. You've had a chance to work with these people and to live aboard the ship. What do we need to know that the non-military personnel won't tell us?"

Hunter folded his large hands on the table and looked directly at the general when he spoke. "The only thing that comes to mind is Mr. Allen. He's a brilliant scientist and I'm well-aware of the contributions he's made. But he shows a blatant lack of respect for those around him and a complete disregard for the rules."

The general laughed softly. "We're aware that Mr. Allen doesn't work and play well with others. And of his arrogance. It's who he is. We also know that he is not who he would have us believe he is. He presents himself as this super-rich science nerd who's only out for glory and the almighty dollar. But you should know that a lot of what you see here was done on his own dime. He nearly ran his own company into ruin when he abandoned it to work for the war effort and he continues to place himself at risk in order to keep this project going."

"That being said," the admiral broke in, "we also know that he is more accustomed to giving orders than following them.

We are tasking you with teaching him how a chain of command works. You can use whatever means you deem necessary, but he must be brought into line. It's one thing to put his own life in jeopardy to test an invention or prove a hypothesis, but he cannot put the lives of others in peril. So, you must impress upon him the team spirit. And if you have to discipline him in order to do it, then so be it. There's a brig on Deck One. Use it if necessary."

"Is there anything else?" the general asked. Cara looked at Hunter and shrugged. "Very well. Thank you for your candor. Dismissed."

They turned and walked toward the door. Neither looked at each other nor looked back at the Chiefs of Staff. They knocked twice on the door and it was opened. The two Marines stood aside to let them pass, then stepped into the room and shut the doors behind them. The sound of it played off the walls of the corridor and echoed into the large hangar.

"That went pretty well," Hunter said at last.

"Could have been worse." Still, they hadn't looked at each other. Their backs were stiff and they took strong, measured steps. "So, where are you off to now?"

"I think I'll go for a run. You?"

"I'll probably go to the gym and work out."

"You're not going to go hang out with Tony and play with his newest gizmos? You've been spending a lot of time with him lately."

Cara felt a little ripple of goosebumps race over her skin and fought off the shiver. "You jealous or something?"

"A little bit, yeah."

Oh my gosh! I was kidding. Is he serious?

She turned to look at him then, confused. If she hoped to find a hint of his real intent, she was disappointed. His face was soft and unreadable. It betrayed nothing of either humor or solemnity. "See ya around, Cap."

With that, she sped up, turning toward the ship as she entered the hangar. She never looked back, didn't listen for his footsteps following her. She went into the ship and straight to her quarters to change. The dress uniform was heavy and stifling and she couldn't wait to get out of it and into something a little more breathable.

Once in her quarters, Cara removed her uniform piece by piece and placed it on hangers. She finger-pressed the creases into place and adjusted everything just so. That might have been the last time she'd ever wear the uniform. At the very least, she should keep it in good shape even if just to be buried in it.

Once she was appropriately outfitted in her workout clothes, she went down to the gym. The place was empty, though she could tell that someone had been there earlier. They had forgotten to turn off the lights.

She went straight to the heavy bag and put on a pair of gloves. When she had first gone into the Navy, she had enjoyed kick boxing and mixed martial arts. There were a few trophies on her father's mantel that proved she was good at it. All that had fallen by the wayside with the coming of the war, however, but she still enjoyed it as a method of staying in shape.

She went through the steps of taping her hands and putting on the gloves, then started punishing the heavy bag. She had just started to work up a sweat when she heard someone behind her and spun to see who it was. Hunter stood in the doorway, one shoulder leaned against the frame and his ankles crossed.

"I thought you were going for a run," she said accusatorially.

"I was going to. But when I got outside, it was awfully hot and dry. I decided to work out instead." He pushed off from the door and walked slowly toward her. "You into MMA too?"

"Fleet champion two years running."

"Not bad…for a girl," he said.

"Oh, them's fighting words. Put 'em up, pal."

And he did. He displayed his open hands, waving them in mercy. "Oh no! I can't fight with you. I'd break you like a twig."

"You think." She moved toward him and punched one hand lightly. "Come on, big guy. Show me what you got."

"Seriously, Bishop. I can't. I'm enhanced, remember? I'd kill you."

"We'll just see about that." She hit him harder, this time in the chest. "Glove up. I can take it."

"Just remember, I warned you. And I'll try to go easy, being that you're unenhanced and all."

"Don't you dare go easy on me. Now, glove up. If I'm going to hit a superior officer, I want him ready to defend himself."

"I don't use gloves. They just get in the way."

"Fine by me."

She came at him then, with everything she had. Her entire body was behind the movement that pistoned her fist into his gut. It was like hitting the steel hull of a ship. Worse yet was the fact that it seemed to have zero effect on Hunter. He took it, still smiling, and deflected her next swing with ease.

She swung again, leading with a right toward the gut and following with a left to the jaw. He deflected both with a simple movement. It had no other effect than to make her mad. She came at him full force, leading with a right cross and following up with a spin kick to his head.

Hunter caught her ankle in one hand and, in a single blinding motion, swept her ankle up until she was dangling from his closed fist.

There was no saving face from that moment on. She was caught there, swinging from his grasp, unable to reach him, unable to struggle free. In a desperate attempt to save herself from further embarrassment, she merely crossed her free leg over her trapped one and folded her arms over her chest. With a heavy sigh, she adopted a bored expression.

"Okay, would you put me down now?"

He actually lifted her higher into the air until their eyes nearly met. "Would I put you down now...what?"

She pulled a face at him. "Would you put me down now, please, sir?"

He chuckled somewhere deep in his throat and lowered her gently to the floor.

She didn't struggle or thrash, she simply rolled over and pushed off from the floor, dusting herself off as she came to full height. "You have a size advantage. Duly noted."

"I have every advantage," he laughed. "You just don't want to admit it."

"We'll see, Hunter. We'll see."

She took a few more swings at him, noting the way he

backed up a bit each time not because he was afraid of being hit, but because he didn't want to show aggression. She continued her assault halfheartedly, letting him back up to within six feet of the back wall. Then she struck.

It might be true that she had no chance of beating him in a full-out assault, that she was no match for his strength. But she was more than a match for his cunning and she had agility on her side. She ran at him, knowing he would either back up further and take the hit, or he would step aside in the hopes that she would hit the wall. She knew how this all worked. He didn't want to hurt her but he couldn't lose face by letting her beat him.

At the last possible second, Cara leaped into the air and hit the wall, running two steps on it and flipping over. She landed square on Hunter's back, wrapping her legs around his torso and her arm around his throat. The motion was enough to throw off his balance and she took advantage of that by throwing her body to the side.

She had managed to bring the big man down on top of her. With the pressure still applied to his neck, she used her free arm to increase that pressure. There was little hope of overpowering him, but that didn't mean she couldn't bring him down. All she had to do was cut off the blood supply from his brain long enough for him to pass out.

His neck tightened beneath her grasp and the arm that was not pinned to the floor came up to wrap around her throat. It was large enough to encircle her neck completely and she felt him tighten his grip on her. She did the same, squeezing with one arm and applying pressure to his neck with the other, trying to redouble her efforts and gain a time advantage. She felt the sweat trickle from her face in slow motion, saw little flashes of light dance in her ever-narrowing field of vision. There were maybe twenty seconds left before she passed out.

Hunter's face was red, his eyelids drooping. He was slipping into unconsciousness. The only question was whether she could outlast him. Breath came hard and her arms shook. She feared she might release him in her oxygen-deprived state. And then it happened.

Hunter tapped out.

He slapped the floor with his free hand and she released him at once, rolling to the side as he let go of her throat. They lay crumpled on the floor, gasping for breath, watching the air sparkle before their eyes.

"You are one tough woman," Hunter said, not without a certain amount of awe.

"Thanks," she said, rubbing her throat. "You too."

They laughed at the joke and then Hunter stood and offered his hand to her, hauling her from the floor. His mistake was in holding on a little too long as he waited for her to steady herself.

"For the record, I gave in so I didn't have to hurt you," he said in all seriousness.

"For the record, I won." She grabbed a towel and began blotting the sweat from her face.

"Because I let you."

"Because I beat you."

"You didn't."

"I so did. Admit it, Hunter. A little girl just kicked your ass."

He laughed out loud and said no more.

She grabbed her water bottle and took a long swig, then looped the towel over her shoulders and made to leave. She turned when she reached the door, looking at him over her shoulder.

"Time to hit the showers," she said with a nod. "Oh, and also for the record, I get that you could have pulverized me."

She winked at him, smiled, and hurried down the corridor.

Chapter 7

A ctivity on the base increased tenfold over the next few days. More crew members arrived with each passing day and Danforth had taken up permanent residence in The Hole. It was all building up to their test launch and as the date grew closer, the tension grew nearly intolerable.

Cara had been cut off from the simulator, simply because there were so many crew members who needed to use it. Scheduled time was at a premium and so Cara took a step back and let the new crew members have their chance. As a result, there was very little for her to do with her days. She spent a lot of time reading and going to the gym, hoping against hope for a rematch with Hunter.

Her mind couldn't get past that day, those few minutes when they had grappled. Rakhi brought it to her attention on more than one occasion. Sadly, it was crunch time for Rakhi and she spent more and more time with her equipment and assistants. Tensions ran high all the way around as everyone struggled to be ready for launch date.

For Cara, that day couldn't come soon enough.

There were several hours during the night when there was little or no activity. Those few quiet hours restored peace to the ship and helped Cara regain her sanity. To that end, Cara slipped into the gardens and wandered among the flowers and butterflies. The koi pond had been filled and stocked by that time and the water lilies were in full bloom. It was so serene there with the trickling of water and the sweet soft scent of the roses and gardenias. She sat alone by the pond, watching the fish and basking in the silence. She had no idea that she wasn't alone until she heard footsteps grinding on the path. The bushes rustled and the branches parted and there stood Hunter.

"Oh, hey, Bishop. I didn't know anybody else was here. If you want to be alone, I can just…." Hunter jerked a thumb over his shoulder and raised his eyebrows.

"Oh, no, no. It's fine. Stay." Had she just cut him off too quickly? Did she sound desperate? "I was just enjoying the peace and quiet. And the fish."

Hunter took up a place on the cement bench across from hers. The physical space between them was slight but the distance seemed enormous. He looked down at the fish, swimming obliviously in their pond, drifting through the underwater plants like they hadn't a care in the world. "Fish, huh?"

"Yeah. I still can't get over the fact that we have a pond full of koi right here in the middle of a giant industrial space craft that we're about to launch into space. We have to take good care of them, otherwise, when we get out there, if they die, there won't be any more fish. I wonder if they know what's about to happen to them."

Hunter laughed. "You spend a lot of time contemplating the fish, don't you?"

Cara laughed in return. Her pinched face relaxed and lit up. "Actually, I do. That way, I can avoid thinking about other things."

"Like what?"

"Like…we're about to take our first test flight. And it could go really well and make us all heroes. Or it could completely fail and we'll crash back to Earth in a giant fiery ball. Not to mention the fact that I might be a total failure at being a weapons officer."

"Hey, at least you have that whole 'I saved the world' thing to fall back on." His smile was warm and genuine and it made Cara blush for reasons that would forever confound her. "Not like me. They keep me in the basement for years and then finally let me out. They put me in charge of an entire mission. Me. I've never been on a mission, much less led one."

Cara moved at once to sit beside him on the bench. She hadn't even made the conscious decision to do so; she just did it. "You've tested really well on the simulator. And you have great people skills. You're going to make a wonderful captain. Don't you ever doubt that. You're a natural born leader if ever I saw one. Heck, I'd follow you anywhere."

The words sounded weird the minute they spilled from her lips. To make matters worse, she suddenly realized that one of her hands was on his back, the other holding his arm. She pulled back immediately, turning so that he couldn't see her blush. She was too late.

Hunter stood then, clearing his throat as he took two steps away. "Well, I think I'm going to take one more pass at the simulator. If it's not in use, that is. Have a good night."

"You, too, Captain."

Stupid, Cara. Stupid, stupid, stupid. You had to get all touchy feely and you scared him off. Stupid!

She sat for a while longer, watching the koi and trying to calm herself. Then she shuffled off to her quarters for some shut-eye.

The entire crew gathered in the mess hall that morning, bent over their food and introspective. The launch weighed heavily on their minds and their tempers had reached a breaking point. Cara, Rakhi, Klein and Hunter sat together. There was no officers' mess or ward room, just one quiet corner set aside for the officers. Cara looked around and realized that she didn't know more than one or two of the crewmembers aside from the bridge crew.

Tony walked in, sporting an unfastened tunic and his usual bravado. "Good morning, *Endeavor* crew! Is everybody excited?" He threw open his arms and marched through the mess hall with a huge grin on his face. "Today, we make history!"

"Good morning, Tony," Hunter said softly. "Are you our new cheerleader now?"

"Sure! You're all so glum I thought I'd walked into a funeral. What's wrong with you anyway? We're about to do something nobody else has ever done. All our hard work comes down to this…this one moment in time. Savor it, my friends. It doesn't get any better than this."

"It's just a test flight, Tony," Cara muttered under her breath. "Besides, it might not even get off the ground."

Tony shook his head and frowned. "Well, fine, then. Be a

gloomy Gus. They're opening the bay doors and bringing the ship up now. I for one am going to go watch. But all of you just enjoy your breakfast. God knows, it might well be your last meal."

He turned and walked away then, taking large, purposeful strides toward the door.

"You're a lousy cheerleader, Tony!" Klein called after him.

Long moments of silence stretched out after that as each person focused on pushing their food around the plate. Suddenly, Hunter looked up, expressionless, and said, "They're bringing the ship up."

Each looked to the others in turn and suddenly, forks hit plates, chairs scraped the floor, and then they were off, running through the mess hall at full tilt, headed for the launch site.

By the time they reached the site, the ship was already halfway up the shaft. It sat on a platform, anchored by its magnetic tethers and rising slowly along the three-hundred-foot hole in the ground. The motors that accomplished this were amazingly quiet and the only sound they could hear clearly was the occasional creak of shifting metal.

The sun had begun to rise and was a mere red gash at the horizon. The buildings cast long shadows across the compound and off in the distance one could almost make out the mountains. As if timed for effect, the sun exploded into full bloom just as the top of the *Endeavor*'s hull reached ground level. In a burst of light and color, the hard earth gave birth to their ship. The ship gleamed with captured light as it cleared the hangar doors and came to a slow stop. An official photographer stepped forward, snapping pictures that would no doubt appear in history books until the end of time.

"She's beautiful," said a voice from behind Hunter's left shoulder. He turned to see who it was and there stood Tony, his lip quivering, his eyes brimming with tears.

Hunter put an arm over the man's shoulders and gave him a shake. "Yes, she is. You done good, Tony. Real good."

Tony cleared his throat and stepped away, smiling. Behind those carefully lowered lids, the tears threatened to spill.

"She really is magnificent, isn't she?" Cara said. "I mean, she was impressive down in the hole, but seeing her like this, out here…" She broke off, shaking her head in awe.

Tony hurried toward the ship, waving in the attendants and maintenance people. He pointed and gestured, talking nonstop the whole time. The *Endeavor* was his baby, the pinnacle of his career, and everyone understood how he felt. He had every right to be proud. By the same token, if it all came crashing down, the blame would fall solely on his shoulders.

Having completed his instructions to the ground crew, Tony made for the group again in his short, clipped gait. He was rubbing his hands together and smiling. "Everybody suit up. If we're gonna do this, we're gonna do this right."

Everyone turned, eager to get on with it. Somehow, the *Endeavor* had taken on a totally different personality since its emergence from the dark. It was almost a living thing, a three-dimensional representation of the human experience. It made her crew desperate to live up to her ideals.

They rushed into the ship to put on their uniforms. Within ten minutes, all were assembled save for Rakhi. Of all of them, Rakhi was the biggest stickler for punctuality. So far as any of them could remember, she had never been anything less than fifteen minutes early for anything.

"Where's Rakhi? Tony asked.

"Where indeed?" Hunter wanted to know.

"I'm right here," Rakhi said as she rushed down the gangway. "Sorry I'm late. But I wanted to look great in case there were photographers or something." She primped her hair a bit and smiled feebly.

The others were stunned to silence, all except for Tony, who said, "Oh, there won't be any photographers. This is a secret project…meaning nobody knows about it."

"Oh." Rakhi's shoulders slumped and she looked at the ground. "Okay, then." She let loose the pin in her hair, letting it fall about her shoulders in a disheveled mass.

Danforth had drawn a bead on them. He marched their way, his expensive loafers hammering the ground and his face stretched into a huge smile. "Good morning, my friends, good morning! How are we all feeling?"

"I don't know about these guys, but I feel like a million

bucks." Tony pumped the man's hand and moved in for a hug and a back-slap. "Hey, everybody move in. Come on. Rakhi, you stand next to me. Keep all the looks at one end of the line."

Rakhi pulled a face at him but followed his direction anyway. "What are we doing?"

"Oh! My goodness! What could that be?" Tony grinned and flipped his expensive shades down over his eyes. "Oh, yes! That's a photographer."

Rakhi spun and looked over her shoulder, horrified. "You said there wouldn't *be* any photographers coming."

"And there aren't. He's *my* photographer. He's here to take pictures for my own private archives. Oh, and Sid? I'll be wanting a nice eight-by-ten glossy of that one you just took. The look on Rakhi's face was priceless."

Rakhi slapped Tony hard in the chest with the back of her hand and growled at him. "I'll get you for this, Tony."

"Okay, baby. You do that. Say cheese now."

"Cheeeeeeese!" Rakhi said, leaning in close to Tony. His arm was around her waist but she didn't care just then.

The flash went off, Tony let his practiced smile fade, and he sighed dramatically. "She just made rabbit ears behind my head, didn't she?"

"Yep!" Cara said, popping the "p."

"Ah, whatever! I'm in such a good mood today that I don't even care."

Danforth was closing on them again. He stopped several feet shy of them and squinted into the bright morning light. "I want you all to know how much we appreciate your service. And I'm being very serious now when I say that you have one last chance to walk out. No one will think any less of you. But please know the risk you're about to take and ask yourself if you're ready to pay the ultimate price for glory. If the answer is 'no,' then you should go home."

No one moved an inch. Hunter waited a few beats and then, with total self-assurance, he said, "No one's going anywhere, Mr. Danforth."

Danforth bowed. "Very well, then. Godspeed to you all. When you get back, the drinks are on me."

He shook everyone's hand in turn, then turned on his heel and marched back to the shade—and safety—of the observation deck.

"Shall we?" Hunter said, smiling and sweeping his arm in the direction of the gang plank.

They walked in single file, no one speaking, no one looking at another. It was a solemn moment. They were about to make history, to realize dreams, but the moment lacked the luster due such a momentous occasion.

Into the elevator they went, still in silence. It was awkward and unusual, especially for Tony, who hadn't passed a single silent moment since the team had been assembled. When the door slipped open and they stepped onto the bridge, the tension immediately broke. An energy came into them all, lighting up their faces and animating them.

"Everyone to your stations," Tony chirped, rubbing his hands together and smiling. "We're going to go through this one step at a time…."

"Lieutenant Allen," Hunter said with some degree of force.

"First the boosters, then the engines…" Tony went on as if he hadn't heard Hunter at all.

"Lieutenant Allen," Hunter said, louder and with more urgency.

"…then the weapons and support systems…."

The newly baptized Captain Hunter stepped up to where Tony stood, placing himself mere inches behind the man and staring down at him from his two-foot height advantage. "Lieutenant Allen!" Tony spun, his eyebrows raised. "The minute we stepped onto this ship, everything changed. I am the captain of this ship now. She is my ship. Not yours. Now, I want you tending to the engines while we start up her systems. Not on the bridge."

"Oh, but I have all the controls and sensors on this tablet here, see?" Tony's face had taken on a boyish, contrite, and pleading quality.

"That was an order."

Tony stared at him. He blinked. His face twitched and a definite tic developed in his left eye. "Aye, Captain," he said, taking a step back. He spun on his heel and headed for the elevator.

The others watched in silence, watched Hunter watch Tony leave. They were watching still, their faces frozen in concentration and tension as he made his way to his chair at the center of the bridge. He eased into that chair like a little boy testing out his father's recliner and finding it big enough to engulf him. Then he exhaled loudly and relaxed into it.

"So, who wants to go into space?" he asked with a broad smile.

Hands went up around the bridge, faces beamed back at him.

CHAPTER 8

"Very good. Shall we begin?"

"At your command, sir," Bishop said and smiled.

"Commander Bishop, since we have no need of weapons, you'll be at the helm this time. You'll get a chance to test the Zodiacs later, but for now, we need your expertise at the controls."

"Aye, Captain." Bishop stood and moved from the console at his right to the console at his left.

"Very good. Boosters at one quarter," Hunter said.

"Boosters at one quarter," she echoed, throwing the switch that ignited the boosters and moving the slide bar to one quarter. "Tether strength decreasing."

"Excellent. Boosters to one half."

"Boosters one half."

"Ready when you are, Lieutenant Allen."

Tony's soft voice came over the com. "Beginning initial sequence."

The ship lurched and a gentle vibration rippled through them as the engines fired up.

"Yes!" Tony said softly, hoping not to be heard. Everyone smiled in sympathy. "Engines now at full power, all readings normal, no special interference."

"Excellent. Commander Bishop, please increase boosters to full power." Into his radio he said, "Ground crew, prepare for untethering."

The radio squawked and then a strong voice said, "Ready for untethering, Captain Hunter."

Hunter smiled and gripped his chair arms more tightly. "Boosters to full power."

"Boosters, full power," Cara said. The tendons in her arms

and neck stood out. Her teeth were gritted. This was the moment of truth. Either this bird would fly or they were about to destroy over a trillion dollars' worth of ship.

"Ground crew, cut power to tethers."

"Tethers released," said the disembodied voice on the radio.

"Take us to one thousand feet."

Cara felt her hand trembled as she engaged the fractal drive and leveled out the ship at one thousand feet. "At one thousand feet, sir."

"Lieutenant Allen, how's she look?"

"Hey, my engines are perfect." There was a smile implied in that response, that and arrogance.

"How are your readings?" Hunter fought a smile. It was just Tony being Tony, after all.

"All readings well within normal parameters."

"Bishop, take us to thirty thousand."

"Aye, sir. Thirty thousand."

"Engines holding fine."

"Forward one quarter."

"Forward one quarter."

Hunter smiled. "Come up to the bridge, Lieutenant Allen."

"I'm right here."

Hunter turned his chair and spotted Tony standing right behind him, smiling and waving his fingertips. "I told you...."

"You told me to tend to the engines and I did. From this," he said, shaking the tablet at him.

"I told you to go to the engine room."

"No. You told me to go tend to the engines and get off the bridge. That's what I did. I stepped into the elevator which, the last time I checked, is *not* the bridge. And I tended to the engines." Tony smiled again and cocked his head. "See? I can follow your orders to the letter."

Hunter stared at him for a long time. He had to pick his battles with Tony. This was not one of them. He spun his chair around to face the viewing screen. "All systems report."

"Engines looking goooood," Tony said, pumping his fist.

"Life support has full power," said a voice through the intercom.

"Weapons fully charged, Zodiacs fully charged," Cara chimed in.

"Communications, scanners and computer banks fully operational," Rakhi said.

"Excellent. What's say we burst the bubble?" Hunter said with a grin.

"Oh yea! Let's blow this popsicle stand," Tony said, looking at Hunter and thinking better of it. "Sir."

"All right, Commander Bishop. Let's begin our ascent. Half speed, fifty degrees." He stared at the view screen intently, so focused that nothing else seemed to exist. There was a soft buzz inside his head but he wasn't sure if it was from the equipment or simply a product of deep concentration.

"Half speed, sir," Cara repeated. "Fifty degrees."

A few beats passed. "Increase speed to three-quarters. Level her out."

"Speed to three-quarters. Leveling now."

The tip of the ship slipped into the upper atmosphere. Cara bit into her lip and held her breath. This was the moment when so many things could go wrong. So many things.

"Punch it," Hunter said.

The order made no sense to her at first. The term was alien. It had no relation to what they were doing. Then its true meaning occurred to her and she slapped the speed control to its number two position. The *Endeavor* leaped forward and pierced the outer atmosphere, the ship's hull taking on a slightly pinkish hue from the heat and friction.

And then she was free. The Earth grew smaller behind her and her hull lost its discoloration. Breath held was released and they all looked at each other.

"That…was…awesome!" Tony yelled.

"I made it," Cara whispered, so low that no one heard. Then she turned and, in a louder voice, said, "We did it. We're in space."

"Yes, we are, Commander," Hunter said with a smile. "Slow speed to one quarter."

"One quarter speed."

"Time for you to test those Zodiacs," he said with a grin.

Cara's head snapped around and she stared at him, her eyes wide and her lips trembling a bit. "Now? Before we even leave the solar system?"

He shrugged. "I figured you should have a chance to test them before we engage the Light Drive and possibly blow ourselves up."

"But who's going to...?"

"I'll take the helm." She looked frightened at that but he smiled into that fear. "A captain should be able to perform all the duties on the bridge in order to understand those under him. I spent a lot of time in the simulator learning each of them. Now, stand down, Commander."

Cara nodded and stood up, relinquishing her station to him. She took two steps to her right and took over the weapons station with a smile. Tony was at her elbow, nearly as excited as she.

"There are two things I really need to know," he began. "First, I need you to take the Zodiac to the far side of the planet so I can see how it interferes with the telemetry. Second, I need to know the range of the telemetry in an atmosphere-free section of space."

Cara nodded. "Okay. So, take her to the far side of Jupiter, then in a lateral line through open space."

"Now you're getting it."

She picked up the control. She knew how the Zodiac responded in the thick air of Earth but she had no idea how well it maneuvered in the vacuum of space. She powered up the controller, then made the connection to the Zodiac. So far so good.

Separation was automatic. A single button-push sent the orb sailing out of its port and around the starboard side of the *Endeavor*. She stopped it in front of the view screen and then played with the controls. The Zodiac spun, went left and right, up and down, back and forth. A smile split her face and she nodded with satisfaction.

"Lieutenant Mitra, please put the Zodiac's camera on the view screen."

"On the view screen, Commander."

"Thank you." She shook out her right hand, looked at Tony and winked. "Let the games begin."

Before she had turned her head back toward the screen, the Zodiac sped away. It made for Jupiter at top speed, drawing an awed nod and chuckle from Tony. Then it made its turn, following the curvature of the planet on its path to the far side. Looking at the screen, it was like viewing the journey firsthand. The images were crisp and clear, in full color.

"Can we get some sensor readings on this, please, Lieutenant Mitra?" Cara asked.

"We have atmosphere readings, temperature readings, life form readings…."

Cara jerked her head in Rakhi's direction. "Life forms? It's detecting life forms on Jupiter?" There was more than a little shock in her voice and her face had become drawn.

"Sorry, Commander. The Zodiac provides life forms readings. Currently, it is detecting zero life forms on the planet."

"I understand." Cara chuckled a bit and shook her head. "Had me going there for a second, though." She looked at Tony. "Okay, we've got her all the way on the far side of the planet. Camera, sensors, controls…all are responding well."

"That's what I like to see." He made a few notations on his tablet and studied a few charts. "Let's take her out as far as she'll go. When she stops responding, we'll go get her."

"All right then."

Cara spun the thumb wheel on the control and in two minutes, the Zodiac reappeared over Jupiter's horizon. Its trajectory changed then and it shot off in a straight line, unobstructed, headed for the far reaches of the solar system.

They waited for half an hour, watching the images and scanner readings scroll across Tony's tablet while the Zodiac streaked through space. Every now and again, Tony would look at his watch and smile.

"Velocity times duration equals distance," he said, staring at the screen. "I think I can safely say that the Zodiac has exceeded all my expectations for distance. Bring it back and we'll do a weapons check."

"All right!" Cara said with a smile, and turned the thumb

wheel, bringing the Zodiac in a half circle, directing it toward the *Endeavor.* "But we have eight of these things, I'm gonna have to start naming them if I have any hope of telling them apart."

"Never name your weapons, Bishop. It personalizes them, humanizes them. It makes it easier to kill and easier to place the blame on the weapon instead of where it belongs."

She cast a sideward glance at him and frowned. "Tony, I've been in the military my whole life. They trained me and taught me to kill and I'm damn good at it. I've killed humans and aliens and a few things I wasn't sure what they were. They call me The Savior but what I really am is The Murderer. Believe me when I say that no one has ever held human lives in higher regard than someone who has taken so many of them."

Without warning, without ceremony, without saying a word, Tony flung his arms around her and squeezed her tight.

"Okay, what are we doing?" She stood motionless, unblinking. The control hung loosely in her hand.

"You looked like you could use a hug." He withdrew, hesitantly, and blinked at her. "Did I read that wrong?"

She cocked a half-smile at him, then forced her face into severity. "For the record, Tony, I never need a hug."

"Oh. Sorry." He straightened himself and stared at the viewing screen, silent as he watched for the Zodiac's return. Every now and again, he took a quick, surreptitious glance at Cara. He noted her unchanging face, her board-straight back, the slight downturn of her mouth. "It's back."

She had been staring at the screen, unseeing. "Oh. Yes." She cleared her throat and brought the control to chest level. "How do you want me to do this?"

"Just aim into empty space and let 'er rip."

Cara did as he instructed, let her mouth drop open as the single burst of Raster fire exploded from the Zodiac and tore through space. "What's the range on these things anyway?"

"How should I know? We never got to fire one before." A smirk dominated his face and he winked.

"Best estimate then?"

Tony shrugged. "Could be a mile. Could be a million miles. Beats me."

Cara blinked and frowned. Her face went through a dozen contortions before coming to rest. "So how do you know that shot didn't tear through space and just slice through some planet."

"I don't. Listen, I had to disable the targeting system in order to test it out. No target, no test. See? Once we enable targeting, the distance and duration of the blast will be calculated before the shot is ever fired."

"But for now, we might have just wiped out an entire planet full of people?"

He looked her dead in the eye and without blinking said, "Naw. There's no way."

"You're sure?"

"Pretty sure."

"Pretty sure?" she said, louder and with more intensity.

"Well, yea. Pretty sure."

She shook her head and looked back at the screen. "So, did she pass the test?"

"Yeah. It's a pass. Go ahead and dock her again."

With a deep sigh, Cara rotated the thumb wheel and pushed the AUTO DOCK button. She waited for the green light to indicate that the Zodiac had arrived safely, shooting an irritated glance at Tony every few seconds. If he noticed, he gave no indication of it.

"Let's go ahead and test the big boys, shall we?" Tony said with a wink and a nod. Start with the Rasters and then we'll test out the Electromagnetic Pulse Cannons."

"Okay." She looked at him suspiciously and frowned. "I'm guessing no targets and no limits."

He shrugged. "No risk, no gain. Fire high, fire low, then aim those cannons in a nice straight shot across the meridian."

"Okay," she said suspiciously. She had a bad feeling about all this. You couldn't just blast a bunch of electro-magnetic pulses into space and expect no casualties.

"Rasters fully charged, Captain. Firing at will." She sensed Tony at her shoulder, felt the heat of his excitement and smelled his sweat. She shrugged it off and focused on her targeting.

She fired a quick burst at a forty-five-degree angle. Then

she fired parallel to her artificial horizon. And the final shot she aimed straight down. The beams of pure energy tore across the space before them, flashing brightly for a second, then seemingly disappearing as they streaked away from the ship.

Cara spun in her chair. "Are they supposed to do that?"

"Yep." Tony made a few notations on his tablet and smiled. "Try the cannons now. Do it! Do it!" With a smug smile, he edged away from her, coming to stand by Hunter, the tablet clutched tightly to his chest.

Cara drew in a deep breath and, with a shrug, adjusted the azimuth and took her shot. Three fast blasts from the cannon zoomed outward from the ship, causing a rumble deep in the bowels of the *Endeavor*. It vibrated through her feet and rattled her nerves a bit.

"Oh my God!" Tony bellowed. "Not that way! Launch the Zodiacs now. Get after them and blast them before they can do any damage."

"What?" Cara's tone was panicked, her voice high-pitched and strained.

"We needed to come about before you fired. Those shots are headed straight for the Kalinski satellite." Tony turned to Hunter, pulled a face and shook his head, indicating that he was having fun with her.

All the color drained from Cara's face as she grabbed the control. She was practiced at functioning in a panic situation. Her hands were steady as she sent the Zodiac racing away from the ship. "On the screen," she growled at Rakhi.

"On the screen, Commander."

Focused on nothing else, the bridge of the *Endeavor* dropped away from her and she saw only what the Zodiac's camera allowed her to see. Carefully, precisely, she guided the little orb toward the first ball of electromagnetic energy. It was touch and go for a while, trying to catch up to the blast.

As she pulled into weapons range, she targeted the energy ball with her Rasters and fired. Luck was with her that day and she scored a direct hit. Then the Zodiac rolled, twisting as it came over the top of the second blast, firing, obliterating it in silent devastation.

The third would not be so easy. She rolled again, but she was too slow. The EMP blast soared under the Zodiac as it rolled and she cursed quietly. A quick boost from the engine and the Zodiac gained on the burst once more. Three thousand kilometers, two thousand, one…and finally within firing range. And then there was nothing but the little Zodiac, racing away from the ship, but slowing steadily, negotiating its first turn.

"And that's how you create a target!" Tony yelled behind her, laughing as she turned and pressed the AUTO DOCK button.

"What?" she screamed, marching on him.

And Tony knew he was dead.

He was still laughing when she stomped up the two steps leading to his level. He stopped laughing when she was toe to toe with him. "Now relax, Bishop. I was just fooling with you. Having a little fun, you know?" He tried on a smile. It felt awkward, even to him, and he let it slide off his face.

"You convinced me that I'd fired a lethal shot at an Earth satellite and panicked me into chasing it down and destroying it?" Her face reddened and her mouth went dry. "For fun?"

"It was just a little joke. Testing you in a combat situation."

"That's what the simulator is for," she answered.

"Grace under fire. You respond really well under pressure."

"But then, we already knew that. Didn't we?" She cocked her head to the side and squinted at him. "And you said that you had shut down the targeting system."

"I turned it back on. See?" Tony held up the tablet and smiled like a kid with his first drawing. "I can do anything from this tablet."

"Can you run?" she spat, eyes flaring.

"Oh damn," he whispered.

He spun on one heel and ran for the elevator. He didn't have to look back to know that she was right on his heels. And it didn't take a genius intellect to know what she would do when she caught him…and catch him she would.

"Commander, freeze!" Hunter bellowed.

Cara froze in place, coming to attention, panting.

Hunter rose slowly from his chair and strode to her position. He looked at her, his hands clasped behind his back and his eyes sparkling. "We'll give Lieutenant Allen this one, single chance. Agreed?"

She looked him dead in the eye, still wanting revenge but too well-trained to disobey even an implied order. Her shoulders slumped imperceptibly and her jaw unclenched. "Aye, Captain."

"Lieutenant Allen," Hunter said more loudly and without taking his eyes from Cara's. "If you pull anything like that again, I'll let her have you. Understood?" With that, he winked at Cara.

Tony softened, his eyes darkening and his face going slack. "Understood, Captain."

"Very good. Now, let's all return to our stations and continue our tests."

Hunter walked slowly to his chair and eased into it, keeping his eyes on Cara and Tony. Tony kept his eyes on Cara, expecting retribution of some kind but slowly relaxing as she made no move toward him. Then, as he passed her on his way to the weapons station, she lunged at him, more as a joke than an actual threat. He jumped, screamed, scrambled backward toward the captain's chair.

Cara merely looked away and grinned but behind her, Rakhi giggled.

CHAPTER 9

They had worked through the morning and into the afternoon before anyone realized that they hadn't eaten since morning chow. He and Tony relieved the women, allowing them to hit the mess hall first. They were operating with a skeleton crew and so had thrown the duty roster to the wind. They ate quickly and then relieved the men, their legs stretched, bellies full, and spirits lifted.

When Hunter and Tony returned, testing resumed, with Rakhi taking center stage this time. Cara admired Rakhi. She was always confident, in charge, brilliant. Cara couldn't help but think that she would have made an excellent pilot, if she hadn't chosen a career in communications and computers.

"I want to test the scanners out first," Hunter was saying. "What is the range on these scanners?"

"Well," Rakhi began, somewhat smugly, "Tony's original specs called for a range of one hundred fifty thousand kilometers. But I tweaked them a bit and now they have nearly two hundred thousand kilometers' range." She turned then and smiled pridefully at Tony, who sneered back.

"Excellent. By my reckoning, we're about that far from Jupiter now. Let's see what those scanners can tell us and how accurate they are. Commander Bishop, would you send out a Zodiac, please? I'd like to compare the readings with those of the scanners."

"Aye, Captain." Cara stepped to the station opposite her and took up the controls. "Sending out a Zodiac now."

"Lieutenant Mitra, what are your scanners showing?"

Rakhi swiped her screen, stabbed at the controls and adjusted for the changing distance. "Life forms: Negative.

Surface temperature: two hundred thirty degrees below zero. Atmosphere: hydrogen, helium, trace amounts of ammonia."

Cara waited, watching as the planet grew larger in her Zodiac's eye. She smiled to herself as she went, impressed by how easily she was able to put herself in the Zodiac's place. It was like she was flying over the planet herself. "Incredible," she muttered.

"What's that, Commander?" Hunter asked.

Cara stared at her controls, clicked through the options. "On the screen, Captain."

Hunter leaned forward, read the data on the screen and smiled. "They match. Exactly. Good job, ladies. Bring the Zodiac home."

Cara brought the Zodiac back to the ship, but not as quickly as she might. She executed a few loops and spins, enjoying herself entirely too much as she watched through its digital eye. When finally it docked, she felt a sadness akin to separation anxiety.

"Thank you, Commander. I'll take your station now. Lieutenant Mitra and I will test the communications systems. I'd like you to take Lieutenant Allen with you. The new Strikers haven't been tested in space. Take one of them out and put it through its paces. But go easy on Allen. I want him back in one piece."

Cara snickered and stood up from her station. "Yes, Captain. In one piece." She relinquished her chair to Hunter and grabbed Tony's arm on her way to the elevator. "This is going to be awesome," she whispered into his ear. "Absolutely awesome."

"Yeah. Awesome." He sighed as he stepped into the elevator, still a bit skittish around Cara and not entirely convinced that she didn't mean him harm.

The doors whooshed open on the launching bay, a cavern of a room that contained the Striker-Zs. Cara smiled at the sight of them. The last time she had been down there, the Strikers hadn't been brought on board yet, so the sight of them all lined up, awaiting a pilot's skilled hands, made her heart soar.

She stepped to the right and grabbed a flight suit off the wall. She tossed it to Tony with a wink. "We're in real space now, not Earth's atmosphere. You'll need to put that on. And grab a helmet. If we have to eject for any reason, you'll need it."

His face paled and his eyes grew large. "Eject?" She had moved on already, leaning against the wall and pulling on her flight suit. "What do you mean, eject? Why would we do that?"

She shot him a quick glance and shrugged one arm into a sleeve. "In case of engine failure or something like that. You know. Probably won't happen but…."

"Probably?" He removed his shoes and shoved each of his feet in turn into a leg of the suit.

"You never know about these things. All kinds of things can go wrong. Come on. Get a move on, Lieutenant."

He shot her a scorching glare and zipped up his suit. He finished just in time to catch the helmet Cara had thrown him. "So, what happens if we eject?" he asked the back of her head. She was striding toward the ship and had already gained three paces on him.

"Well, another Striker will come pick us up. Don't worry. We have a good three hours of oxygen in the suit."

Tony thought for a moment. He shouldn't have been so concerned about it all. After all, she was completely calm about it. Then again, she was the same woman who had flown her Striker into the alien mother ship on a suicide mission. "Three hours? That's all?"

"We'll be close to the ship. That's plenty of time for someone to come get us." She lowered the access ladder on the Striker and stepped onto the first rung.

"Who?" Tony asked.

"Who what?" She turned, hanging onto the rung with one arm and looking down at him.

"Who will come get us? Do we have other pilots on board?"

She smirked at him. "Now that you mention it, we don't. So, we'll try not to eject today, okay?"

With that, she hurried up the remaining four rungs and disappeared into the cockpit.

"Hunter wants me dead. I knew it," Tony grumbled. "Why else would he send me out here with this crazy woman?"

"You coming, Lieutenant?" she asked, peeking her head around the corner.

"Yeah, yeah."

She was already strapped in, flipping switches and running checks when he stepped into the cockpit. "You can strap into the co-pilot's seat if you want. Or if it'll bother you, you can always just sit in the back."

Such an obvious character assassination had to be answered with bravado. "I'll sit here, thanks. There's nothing more thrilling than taking that first exhilarating trip through space."

"Good deal. I'll take it slow at first, until I know how she responds in zero gravity and no atmosphere. Then we can have some fun." She turned and winked at him. "Strap on your helmet. I wouldn't want you to suffer from oxygen deprivation."

She waited until he had secured the helmet on his head, then she pushed the button that started the engines. They hummed with a magnetic vibration and she felt the power surge through her.

"*Endeavor*, this is Striker One, ready for takeoff." She adjusted her helmet and tested the strap on her restraining harness.

"Striker One, opening bay doors. Please wait for the green light. Good luck and Godspeed."

"Thank you, *Endeavor*."

The doors began to slide open, slowly at first, then more quickly. When they were halfway open, she eased back on the yoke to lift the ship off the deck. Then the hangar bay doors clicked into place and the green light switched on. "Here we go," she said, pushing the accelerator and moving the Striker forward.

She would keep the speed low until they had cleared the doors and the doors were shut. Then she could punch it, whatever she wanted. If the doors weren't closed, the blast from the engines would incinerate anything in the hangar, including the other Strikers. Eventually, she would have to finish training the other pilots but for now, it was time for some fun.

Beside her, Tony had a tight grip on the arms of his seat. She couldn't see his face for the helmet, but she was sure his jaws were clenched and that vein in his forehead was standing out. She checked the rear cameras and saw that the doors had closed, so she increased her speed, putting a little more distance between the Striker and the *Endeavor.*

"You ready?"

"I was born ready," he said, filled with horrific expectations and false courage.

"Then here we go."

She shoved the yoke forward, dropping away from the *Endeavor,* then mashed down on the accelerator. The engines roared and the little Striker raced away from its base ship. Within seconds, the *Endeavor* was a mere dot in her rear camera.

Beside her, Tony made a gagging sound.

"Barf bags are on your right. Remember to open your helmet visor."

"I'm fine," he said weakly, and retched again.

She performed a few maneuvers, a hard roll, a loop, stopping, turning, and dropping. She checked Tony's reaction and found him mannequin-still, eyes staring straight ahead and so glazed that she feared he might be dead.

"You okay?"

"I'm good."

At least the retching sounds had stopped. "I'm going to test the weapons, then run it out to full throttle. You up for that?"

He finally turned to glare at her, his face steely, but not quite back to full, normal color. "I can take whatever you dish out, darlin', so bring it."

She shrugged. "Okay, then."

She fired all the Raster banks and then pointed the ship toward the *Endeavor.* With a wicked smile, she sailed off in that direction at top speed, pushing that accelerator to the max and smiling at the speed it gave her. She came in a little under the *Endeavor* and brought the Striker to a halt, slowly letting it rise until the ships were nose to nose. She stopped and waved at them.

"Striker One to *Endeavor.* Are you reading me?"

"Striker One, this is the *Endeavor.* We're reading you loud and clear," Rakhi said with a smile and a wave back. Then she spun her chair away from the others and whispered. "Looking good, Cara. Are you having fun out there?"

"Tons." In a more professional voice, she said, "Request permission for landing."

"Permission granted," Rakhi said. "Hangar bay, prepare for landing. Open hangar doors."

Cara saluted and dropped the Striker below the *Endeavor*'s view, then brought it around to the hangar bay doors, adjusting speed and height so that she could set the ship softly down on the deck inside.

One at a time, she ran through her checks and shut down the systems. Then she opened the access hatch and dropped the ladder.

Tony pushed past her, hurrying down the ladder and stopping some ten feet away, where he bent over, hands on his knees as he gasped for air. Cara came up behind him and slapped him on the back. The helmet was tucked beneath her arm and she was smiling.

"You okay, Lieutenant?" she asked.

"Fine. Fine." He stood up and unfastened the helmet, lifted it carefully from his head.

Cara took two staggering steps backward, putting a hand over her mouth and looking away. "Oh God! What is that smell? Allen! Did you barf? Is that barf in your helmet?"

"Shut up, okay? Don't tell anybody about this. I'm begging you."

"Let me drive your Ferrari when we get back?"

"Yes, yes. Anything."

"Deal. Now, go clean up. Just...clean up."

She walked away in disgust, waiting until she was safely in the elevator before she broke out in raucous laughter. To be honest, she had been pretty hard on him, executing six barrel-rolls at near the speed of light. It had made her a bit queasy if she were to admit it. Still, he had it coming.

"How was the Striker test this afternoon?" Hunter asked later in the mess hall. They had gathered for dinner, occupying only one table since most of the crew wouldn't come on board until they officially launched.

"It went very well, I think. All systems go." Cara winked at him and shoved a forkful of macaroni into her mouth.

Hunter leaned forward and peered down the length of the table at Tony, who sat alone, hunkered over a glass of water. "How about you, Mr. Allen? Did you have fun out there? It's quite a thrill, isn't it?"

Tony pivoted his head and stared at each of them in turn. "If I ate three large pizzas, then swallowed a bag of nails and locked myself in a running clothes dryer for an hour, I could not have had more fun."

Cara let a beat pass and then said, "I might have been a little rough on him."

Hunter snickered and shook his head.

"A little rough?" Tony spat. "A little rough? You put my guts in a blender. I puked up my own toenails, for God's sake." He sipped his water and grimaced.

"Come see me next time," Klein said. "I'll give you an antiemetic and keep you from filling up your flight suit."

Cara giggled into her hand.

Hunter decided to end Tony's torture. "So, we're going to orbit Jupiter for the night. We'll finish our tests and head for home tomorrow. Does anybody have any problems or concerns?"

Heads shook.

"Very good. In that case, I'll see everyone in the morning. David? Join me in a game of chess?"

"I thought you'd never ask," Klein answered as he stood to dispose of his tray.

"I'm going to go take another shower," Tony said with a frown. "My hair still smells like puke."

Cara said nothing but she watched him go, as did Rakhi, who sat across from her. When he had gone, Rakhi leaned forward, her eyes dark and her mouth turned down at the corners.

"You're going to have to make this up to him," she told Cara softly. "You really did hurt his pride and I think you broke his trust."

Cara considered this quietly for a moment, biting into

her lip. "I guess I went too far. Yeah." She sighed heavily. "I'll apologize and find a way to make it up to him."

Rakhi nodded and smiled. "And how about that other little problem?"

"What other problem?" Cara asked, screwing up her face and blinking innocently.

"The one with Captain Hunter?" Rakhi shook her head. "I can hear every word, you know."

Cara sighed deeply and looked to her left. "There is no problem. He's the captain. I work under him. No fraternization, no feelings, all business. Besides, he has absolutely no feelings for me whatsoever."

"You only say that because you can't see the way he looks at you when you're not looking." Rakhi winked and picked up her tray. "If you want to talk, you know where to find me...." And with that she was gone.

Frustrated and more than a little angry, Cara picked up her tray and dumped it into the recycler, slamming the lid closed for good measure. Then she stalked off to her quarters, her face red and her lower lip caught in the vise of her teeth.

"Commander Bishop, report." Hunter said once they were all assembled on the bridge.

"Orbit was consistent within point zero zero two percent. Speed consistent within point one percent. No incidents to report."

"Very good. Only one test remains: the high-speed test. Commander Bishop, set a course for home, maximum speed."

"Aye, Captain. ETA thirty-three minutes." She input the proper coordinates and turned her com on. "Are your engines ready for this, Mr. Allen?" she asked with a smile.

"My engines purr like kittens. Give it your best shot, Bishop."

"Hold onto your hats," she said, and moved the throttle indicator to maximum.

The ship eased away from Jupiter, banked to their left and heeled over a bit. Then it leveled out, straightening until the nose pointed toward Earth. With a push of a button, it bucked forward, speed increasing exponentially until the surrounding stars and celestial bodies were mere smears of light and dust.

"Damn," Hunter muttered, holding onto the arms of his chair.

"Language, Captain," Cara said with a grin.

Half an hour later, Cara felt the knot in the pit of her stomach begin to grow. The most dangerous point of any flight was the landing, and the rapid changes in speed and atmosphere made it most unforgiving. Even the most seasoned of pilots had crashed due to inattentiveness or small error.

"Ready to begin docking procedures, Captain," she said. "Mooring cameras on screen."

"On screen, Commander," Rakhi said.

She had never done this before, not outside the simulator, at least. She drew in a deep breath and swallowed hard, her muscles tight as she concentrated on the screen. The viewing screen had been split, one side showing the fore camera, the other the aft. She could see all four of the magnetic mooring clamps. These would grab onto the ship and first reel it in like a huge fish, then bring it to a halt and stabilize it. First, she had to get them all aligned properly and she had to do so before their altitude decreased too much. If she didn't, the mooring clamps would repel the ship instead of locking it in, sending it careening to one side or another, effectively smashing it to the ground.

"Here we go," she sighed, hoping her lack of confidence hadn't been as obvious as she thought.

Once the ship was near enough to detect the clamps, it would alert her to that fact and then would sound a tone when everything was properly aligned. She had until an altitude of fifty feet to make corrections or abort and try again. Anything below that would mean that she couldn't fire her thrusters. It would incinerate the clamps.

Better safe than dead, she thought, easing back the throttle and letting the thrusters carry the ship gently—and slowly—downward.

"Mooring clamps detected," said the computer in its emotionless voice.

Slowly, Cara reduced the amount of thrust coming from the ship, letting it sink down, adjusting as needed, all the while praying she could get all four clamps lined up. The tone sounded and she cut the thrusters, letting those clamps take over and guide the ship downward, straightening it by infinitesimal degrees. Then she cut all power and shut down the console.

"Done," she said, spinning in her chair and offering up that self-assured, satisfied grin. With any luck, no one would ever know just how terrified she had been mere seconds ago.

"Excellent work, Commander Bishop."

"Thank you, Captain. And to think, I can't even parallel park a car."

He snorted at that and shook his head, then turned on the ship-wide intercom. "Ladies and gentlemen, we are home. Thank you for your excellent work during this trial run. You have liberty until fourteen hundred hours. At that time, we will convene in the onboard conference room for review. Hunter out."

They locked down their consoles and made for the elevator, riding in silence until they reached the cargo bay and its exit ramp. Hunter went down first, disappearing into the far reaches of the facility. Rakhi and Cara followed at a distance.

"I don't mind telling you, I was pretty scared during the docking procedure."

"Me, too," Cara said.

"I know."

Cara looked at her for a moment, then smiled and shook her head. "We really have to do something about that little eavesdropping problem of yours."

Rakhi watched Cara go down the ladder, hanging back and hoping no one would come back for her. The phone was already in her hand and she swiped the screen with her thumb, watching the ladder for signs of intruders.

I need to see you, she texted to Dr. Klein. *ASAP.*

Come to sickbay. I'm still here.

OMW

Thrusting the phone back in her pocket, she turned abruptly and made for sickbay. Her usually bright face was like marble, veins of stress and pain cutting through it. She hurried, listening to the only sound in the ship: her footsteps.

"What can I do for you?" Klein asked as she rounded the open door to the sickbay.

"Are we alone?" She stopped, panting a bit, though not from exertion.

"Yeah, everybody else is gone."

She took two tentative steps toward him, the pain in her face obvious, dark. "I need your help. Desperately."

"Are you in pain? Sick?" Out of instinct, he reached for his clipboard and patted the table.

Rakhi looked at the table, covered in standard-issue paper and stark. On final decision, she climbed up on it. "I'm not sick. The pain is…self-imposed. I guess." She swallowed. It felt like marbles stuck in her throat. "My power…reading minds…it never shuts off. Never."

"I see. And this is suddenly distressing you somehow?" He set down the clipboard and laced his fingers in front of him.

"Recently, yes. I thought I could do it." She hung her head and slowly wagged it back and forth. "With even a skeleton crew…I'm afraid it's too much."

"You hear us all, all the time. It never stops." His face softened as he watched hers.

She looked up then, tears gathering in her eyes. "Yes. Every single moment. I hear everyone's thoughts. I see their daydreams. Their nightmares become mine." Tears spilled onto her cheeks and she brushed at them with the back of her hand. She looked away in shame. "I've tried everything: meditation, medication, even white noise."

"I see." He drew a breath and let it out in a burst. "I can't even imagine how that must be for you. Has it gotten worse recently?"

"No, it has always been like this, ever since I was a girl. It's why I worked in remote locations. The fewer people, the less…noise."

"Okay. I'd like to begin by taking a few scans, an EEG, some other tests. I want to see what effect all this has on your brain. Then we can…."

"Hey, Klein, let's go! We need to take…. Oh! I'm so sorry. I didn't know…" Allen stopped in his tracks and was half-spun by the time the others turned.

"Actually, Tony, I think you could help with this. If that's okay with you, Rakhi."

She nodded her head and met Allen's gaze. "Of course. But, please, we need to keep this between the three of us. I do not want to worry anyone or cause them any guilt. If we cannot find a way to dampen my powers, then I shall have to leave the mission. I cannot be trapped in this ship with a full crew. It will drive me mad."

"None of that!" Allen said, waving his hands furiously. "I haven't met the problem that I can't solve and with Klein's help… we're unstoppable." He smiled that winning playboy smile of his and nodded.

"Very well. I have all the medical scans and tests that were done on me before they sent me on my last assignment. I shall transmit those to you and it will save us some time." She yanked out her phone and began typing, her face slightly softer, less tortured than it had been when she came in. "There."

Klein grabbed his phone from the table nearby and nodded as he looked at the screen. "Got it. Thank you."

Allen stepped in and took both her hands in his, his smile never wavering, his eyes never still. "We are going to go over these with a fine-tooth comb. Then we're going to the lab and work on it. I can't promise anything immediate but I can promise you that we'll work our butts off on it."

"Thank you both, so much." She looked about to cry again but she felt Allen squeeze her hand and it drew a smile.

"In the meantime, I want you to go have a nice lunch. Something you love, something expensive. Eat ten chili dogs if that's what makes you happy. And relax. We got this." Again, the squeeze of her hands and that charming man-boy smile.

"Yes, sir." She slid off the table and straightened her uniform. "Thank you, Dr. Klein. I feel very relieved already."

"We'll have something for you by morning. Don't you worry." Klein waved and smiled and wondered just how he and Allen would pull that off.

"Let's get to work," Allen said, rubbing his hands together voraciously.

CHAPTER 10

Bishop shuffled into the conference room, heavy from a big lunch and a little sleepy to boot. The allotted leave hadn't been enough to actually go anywhere significant, so she had spent her time at a nearby diner, stuffing her face and talking to her father on the phone. Truth be told, she had been full long before she ordered the chocolate cake. She had ordered it just the same and eaten every bite, ordering a brownie and a to-go cup of coffee for the trip back. They made really good coffee.

Now, she was stuffed and dopey and not at all her crisp military self. She regretted nothing.

Captain Hunter came in next, followed by Rakhi, Klein, and Allen some ten minutes later. Benjamin Danforth came in last, his face unreadable.

Danforth adjusted his chair, shuffled some papers, and in general ignored everyone else. Finally, he lifted his head and surveyed the attendants. He smiled.

"That was about the most perfect test flight we could have hoped for. Sure, we uncovered a few tiny glitches. Adjustments have been made. We found needs we didn't know existed. But every single thing worked just as we hoped it would."

"Of course it did," Allen said, arms folded over his chest, rocking slightly in his chair. "I made it." He was stone-cold serious but when he looked up and saw all the raised eyebrows, he cocked one corner of his mouth up and chuckled.

"So, what now?" Captain Hunter asked.

"Now, you say your goodbyes. The powers that be want you back in space before the end of the month. Still, though, we have to keep it on the down-low, as the kids say. We're not announcing anything until you're safely away. Sorry, Mr. Allen, but the world won't start singing your praises until after you've gone."

"And I was so looking forward to all those interviews and endorsements." He laughed again but he was no longer rocking. "I guess I'll just have to be happy with the huge increase in my company's stock. But make sure and let me know if I'm the Time Man of the Year...again."

Danforth shook his head and tittered. "It's not bragging if it's true, I guess," he muttered under his breath. "Seriously, everyone, thank you. You've done an amazing job and I can't begin to tell you how much the service...the entire country, really...appreciates your sacrifices. Now, the rest of your team will be arriving by the end of the week. You have to help them acclimate. I want this to be a real team, so we've added two more simulators to help them train. Let us know if there are any problems, anyone who doesn't fit."

He flashed them a quick smile, then abruptly stood and marched out of the room. Silence followed.

Rakhi awoke the next morning, surprised to find that she had slept. There had been voices in the beginning, as she had introduced her head to the pillow. Then came the dreams. Some were strange, others frightening. None of them were hers. After an hour, though, the dreams had dwindled and, apparently, Rakhi had fallen asleep.

She batted her lashes now and tested the floor, making sure that she wasn't dreaming that as well. It was hard and cool and so she dared to stand. A walk to the bathroom, a quick shower, and she was feeling alert and energized.

She was about to pull on her blouse when the cell phone buzzed, denoting an incoming text. She swiped it, palmed it, squinted at the text.

I have a present for you. Come to sickbay. Klein.

Rakhi smiled in spite of herself and thrust her phone-bearing hand through the sleeve of her blouse. "You are fast, Dr. Klein. I will give you that," she giggled as she thrust her feet into her shoes.

Coming, she texted simply.

The corridor was too long, the elevator too slow. Like a toddler on Christmas morning, she found the wait agonizing. She hurried down that last hall and swung into sickbay by one hand. "Good morning, Dr. Klein."

"Hi, Rakhi. Have a seat." He swept his arm in the direction of the nearest examining table and grinned. "Now, bear in mind that this is the first try. It would be a miracle if we got it right first time out of the gate."

She nodded.

"Except for the fact that I'm involved," came the call from the next room. Tony appeared in the doorway, wiping his hands with a paper towel.

"It shouldn't hurt at all," Klein continued. "It merely generates a field that is identical, but of a different enough frequency, that it literally repels the outside thoughts. Get it?"

"I have several degrees, Doctor. I get it."

"Of course."

Klein held in his hand what appeared to be a hairband. It was about two inches wide and as thin as a tissue. He presented it as one might a crown, smiling as he did so. "Just put it on like you would any other headband," he said.

Rakhi maintained eye contact as she plucked the item from his hands and slipped it over her head. She smoothed back her hair and pulled the band in place, giving her dark locks a quick fluff before letting her hands settle back into her lap. There was, indeed, no pain.

"Now, tell us what you hear...or see...or whatever." Allen had come to stand just behind Klein's right shoulder. He peered at her expectantly.

Rakhi listened. She frowned. "The voices are lower. In volume, I mean. They're still there."

"Okay, we'll adjust the wavelength and the strength. Pass it here."

Rakhi put the device into his waiting hands and watched as he connected it to a computer terminal. A few keystrokes later, he passed it back to her. "Let's see how it is now."

She repeated the procedure, listening intently, frowning, then beaming at him. "Oh my God! I can't hear anything. Not a single voice. Not an image. Oh, Dr. Klein! It is a miracle."

"Yes!" Allen growled from behind him, pumping his fist and smiling.

"Excellent. I'm glad we got it. Now, you have any problems, call one of us. Any questions, same thing. I will caution you, though, not to wear it constantly. You've developed methods of dealing with the voices in your head, ways of coping. If you were to go without hearing them for any extended period, it would be like starting at square one and you wouldn't like that."

"Yes, Doctor." She slid off the table and lunged forward, locking her arms around him and hugging him tightly. "You have no idea what this means to me. It's the solution I've dreamt of my entire life, Doctor." She hugged him again.

"Our pleasure," Allen said, staring at the ceiling. "No thanks necessary."

"Oh, but Mr. Allen…" She threw herself at him next, hugging him as though she might break his spine. Then she thrust him out to arm's length and smiled. "You have saved me. Thank you."

Hunter walked into the dining hall to find Bishop, Klein, and Allen already seated and chatting heatedly. He lifted one hand in recognition and then went straight to the food line. He was a large man with an even larger appetite and for him, this would be only the first of four or five meals he would eat today. Half a dozen eggs, nearly a pound of bacon, toast, and four pancakes filled his tray. Topped off with a large mug of coffee and a tumbler of orange juice, there wasn't an inch of unoccupied tray.

Without reserve, he headed for the table where the others sat and lowered himself into the chair closest to Klein but farthest from Bishop.

"A light meal, Captain?" Tony joked, leaning back in his chair and sipping his coffee. If asked, everyone would wager cold cash that there was alcohol in it.

"I'm a large man." Hunter never looked up, never stopped shoveling food.

"Seriously, though, how can the man eat like that and look like…that." He presented both hands to demonstrate his dismay.

"Alien DNA," Klein explained. "He burns about ten thousand calories a day, even if he never leaves the chair. "And his body will never change. He won't age. He won't get ill. He'll never have a spare tire."

"Yeah, 'cause that's fair!" Allen shook his head and drained his mug. He set it down with a *thunk*.

Hunter's phone buzzed just then and he plucked it from his pocket with his free hand. As he read the text, he smiled. Then he put the phone back in his pocket and continued eating. "We have a launch date," he said around half a pancake. He said no more.

Crickets chirped and tumbleweeds rolled.

"Well?!" Allen shouted at last.

"Twenty-fifth." Hunter's eyes never left his food.

Klein whistled through his teeth. "That's soon."

Allen shot out of his chair and rubbed his hands together, a smile crawling onto his face. "Farewell party at my house on the twenty-third. The hangovers should pass by the twenty-fifth. I think." He paused for a moment, possibly putting together an algorithm to determine how much he could drink and still have the hangover gone by launch time. "Well, gotta go. I have a party to plan, after all."

Allen slapped his hands together, spun, and was gone.

Rakhi handed her keys to the valet and watched her car disappear. Then she turned to face the behemoth standing before her. To say that Allen's house was a mansion would be like saying the *Queen Mary* was a boat. It was huge, sprawling in all directions, a mammoth homage to mid-century modern architecture, a shrine to excess. It covered the top of the mountain and stretched out past the cliffs, over the ocean, as if taunting gravity and defying physics. Everywhere, chrome and glass gleamed in the lights and the moon highlighted its very over-dressed approach. Rakhi smiled in spite of herself and took one step toward the concrete front porch and the multi-windowed door that lay beyond.

"Name, please," said the large man at the door. His face looked like someone had at it with a meat tenderizer, but his suit was immaculate. He was flanked by a larger, better-looking man in an equally crisp suit.

"Rakhi," she said simply.

"Enjoy the party," said the bruiser as he stepped aside.

The door sung open and inside was another world. People milled about the place, some resplendent in their finery, others in nothing more than jeans and a tee. Rakhi swallowed and stepped inside, not at all sure of herself. It was her first American party. It was her first party. She had no idea what to do.

There, at the bar, way at the back of the house, sat Bishop. She was folded over a glass and looking bored. Rakhi drew a bead on her and made her way through the throngs of dancers, drunks, and fellow crew members.

Bishop turned just in time to see her. "Rakhi! You came!" She was off her stool then, hugging Rakhi and laughing. "I was beginning to think you wouldn't."

"I almost did not come. I never go to parties."

"What changed your mind?" Bishop asked, as she reclaimed her seat and patted the stool next to her.

Rakhi tapped her hair and winked. "This did."

"Your hairband?" Bishop laughed.

"Yes, actually. Dr. Klein and Tony made it for me. It blocks out the noise, the voices in my head. So, here I am, at my first party ever."

"Well, then, let me buy you a drink. What's your pleasure?"

"What are you drinking?" Rakhi wanted to know.

"A beer."

Rakhi's nose wrinkled and she shook her head. "I hate beer. I'll have a vodka martini, please."

"You heard the lady," Bishop said to the bartender.

"Where is Tony?"

"He's over in the corner. There. He's been sitting between those two women and holding court for most of the night."

Rakhi nodded, keeping her eye on the bartender. "I can never make up my mind about him. He's either the world's biggest philanthropist, or the biggest show-off."

"Or a little of both."

The bartender delivered Rakhi's drink and she nodded to him, wrapping slender fingers around the stem and taking a short sip of it. It went down smooth; she smiled. "I think I like parties," she told Bishop.

"I like this one." Bishop took another sip of her beer and turned to the window. Just as she came to focus on the ocean beyond the house, beyond the pool, someone or something plummeted through the air and hit the water hard.

"Did someone just jump off the roof and into the pool?" Rakhi asked, alarmed.

"Mm…yes. I think they did. And now I have to stop looking out there because I do not want to end up being the HAIC."

"What is this HAIC?" Rakhi asked, pulling a face.

"Hard Ass In Charge." Bishop checked Rakhi's face and sighed. "Pardon my French. I sometimes forget there are people in the world who are not in the service."

"I understand. But you did not offend me, certainly."

"Good." She took another draw on her beer, gazing over the rim of the glass at the room and its revelers. Her eyes were drawn to the approach of Captain Hunter, he of the incredible physique and handsome face. "Welcome to the party, Captain."

"Commander. Lieutant." He half bowed and smiled, more for Bishop's benefit than Rakhi's.

"Can we buy you a drink?" Bishop wanted to know.

"Thank you, no. It doesn't really do me any good to drink." He looked at his shoes and frowned.

"Ah. That good old alien DNA," Bishop said.

"This is some place, huh?" Hunter said, pocketing his hands and gazing across the room.

"It is indeed," said Rakhi.

"Hunter! Hey, Hunter!" came the call from across the room.

"Excuse me. I'm on Klein duty. He's already three sheets to the wind. I can't leave him alone."

With that, he turned and marched toward Dr. Klein. He seemed sad at that and Bishop shook her head in pity.

"What does this mean, three sheets to the wind?"

"Drunk. It means he's drunk," Bishop explained.

A moment of silence passed between them, during which Bishop registered several things. Something was happening in the west wing that required cheerleaders and a great deal of hollering. Close to the kitchen, someone was crying. The pool jumper had begun a game of limbo out on the patio, apparently without the benefit of a pole.

"Excuse me, Commander Bishop."

The voice behind her startled her and she spun. While that voice had not seemed familiar, the face was even less so. Both belonged to a very young, compact man of African descent. His eyes were wide, his smile even wider, and every single thing about him was high and tight.

"Yes?" she said simply, not knowing what had brought the man there.

He broadened his smile and thrust out his hand. "I'm Lieutenant Jalen Parks, ma'am. I've been hired on as your new helmsman."

Bishop took his hand and pumped it the regulation three times before releasing it back into the wild. "I'm very glad to hear that, Lieutenant. I was about to go mad trying to figure out how I would drive the ship and work the weapons at the same time." She offered what she thought was a whimsical smile.

"Then I've come just in time." The man was genuine and he never stopped smiling. "It's an honor just to meet you, Commander. You've always been a hero of mine. In fact, you're the whole reason I joined the Navy to begin with."

"I'm touched, Lieutenant. And I look forward to working with you." She eased up and back, sliding onto her bar stool, thus signaling that the conversation was over.

It was not.

"Actually, Commander..." Parks cleared his throat, his smile faltering for mere seconds. "My reason for coming over was two-fold. I was also hoping that your friend here..."

"Lieutenant Rakhi Mitra," Bishop tossed out.

Parks bowed and re-energized his smile. "I was hoping that Lieutenant Mitra would dance with me."

Bishop leaned in, half amused, half condescending. "Maybe if you asked her properly..." she muttered.

"Of course." Suddenly, Parks was flustered. He took two steps back and put on what Bishop could only describe as his serious face. "Lieutenant Mitra, would you do me the honor...?"

"Yes!" Rakhi was off the bar stool with a squeal and before Bishop could say a word, the two were skittering across the room, Rakhi waving fingers over her shoulder.

Bishop watched them for a while, happy for her friend. She bored of it quickly, however, and took to tracking Captain Hunter around the room. He was always within reach of Dr. Klein, a wary eye turned to him at all times. Bishop wondered if it had always been that way with them. She wondered if Hunter felt some sort of misplaced familial debt was owed the man, since he had been the Doctor Frankenstein to Hunter's monster, so to speak. She decided, in the end, that it was sweet and showed loyalty and self-sacrifice. Then she wondered if she and Hunter would have spent their time together, maybe dancing, maybe…. She stared into the mirror behind the bar and contemplated this until she could almost see the two of them gliding across the floor in each other's arms. By the time she had snapped out of it, Hunter was nowhere to be found.

For the first five minutes, she thought he had gone to the restroom. When he didn't reappear after fifteen minutes, she became concerned that he had left, so she instituted a search. As she passed by the French doors, which led into the east gardens, she spotted him outside, on the terrace, leaning on the balustrade and staring out at the night. She eased one door open and slipped outside, approaching casually, with her hands in her pockets and her eyes averted.

"Hunter, there you are. Is everything okay?" she asked softly. "I noticed that you'd disappeared. I was afraid you'd left."

He turned to greet her with a small smile. "I'm fine. Just needed some fresh air is all."

She nodded slowly, knowingly, and came to stand beside him, her own elbows leaning on the concrete rail as she stared out at the lights.

"I got a chance to talk to your dad tonight, before he was stolen away by the generals. He's really amazing. He's got a million fascinating stories."

"Yeah, and thankfully none of them have been about my childhood." She gave up a small laugh. It sounded lonely and forced in the quiet of the evening.

"Fathers are like that. They like to tell tales on you and watch you squirm."

"Maybe so. How about your family? Where are they now?"

"They were all killed in the attack on Chicago."

"I'm so sorry," she said softly, placing one hand on his back and frowning. "That damn war cost us so much. So many good people gone."

"Yeah." For a moment, it looked like he didn't want to talk anymore. Then he straightened and forced a grin. "But it gave us things, too. What was it that Tony said in his interview the other day? That the war had forever changed the face of humanity. It was the dawn of a new era for mankind, one of exploration, creation, and cooperation."

"He does have a way with words." She giggled a bit and looked up at him.

He was watching something inside the house and his lips spread into a grin. "Klein is dancing with Maggie. I think he likes her."

Bishop turned to look at the pair, happily gliding across the living room floor. "Aw, that's sweet. Maybe she likes him a little bit, too." Then she turned back to the night.

"How about your mom? Did you lose her in the war, too?"

"No. She died of cancer before the war ever started. That's how Maggie came to live with us. She came to be my nanny and look after the house. And she's been with us ever since."

"Are she and your dad…?"

"Oh no. Maybe she had hopes that they'd get together when she first moved in, but I think she got over that pretty quickly."

"She never got married, had children of her own?"

Bishop shook her head. "Never did. Maybe she didn't want to. Or maybe she just couldn't find a good way to do it. I don't know. I used to think she was waiting for me to grow up, but it's been years since then and she hasn't so much as dated."

"How about you? You ever think of settling down, having a family of your own? Maybe give the admiral there a few little lieutenants?"

Bishop laughed out loud. The sound of it sent echoes across the compound. "Not me. I was always a career girl. The Navy has always been enough for me." She nodded, checked his face. "How about you? You must have to beat the ladies off with a stick."

He laughed too. Perhaps too loudly. "I had a few dates in high school. Not much since. I guess it just wasn't a priority with me. Oh, and then there were the years I spent locked away in the Leavenworth dungeon."

"Not a lot of dating prospects down there, huh?" He didn't answer and she craned her neck to look up at him, only to see a teary smile on his face. "What is it?"

"That song. My mom used to play it all the time." His expression was wistful now, his eyes sparkling with potential tears and his jaw set tight. "She liked to put music on when she cleaned house and then she'd sing along and dance. Sometimes, she'd try to get me to join her. When I was little, I'd get embarrassed and run away and hide. But as I got older, I realized that it was one of the things that really made her happy, so I'd go along. She taught me to dance that way. I got pretty good at it, too."

"No! You can dance?" She feigned surprise, giggled when he made a hurt face at her.

"Oh yes. You wouldn't think that a giant like me could dance very well but I'm really light on my feet." He did a little step to prove himself, ending in a flourish. "Come here. I'll prove it to you."

Bishop looked at the hand he'd held out, then started shaking her head and backing away. "Not me. I'm no dancer."

"Aw, c'mon." He advanced on her, smiling. "You just take my hand. Then put one hand here…" He placed her hand on his waist. "And before you know it, you're dancing."

He pulled her in close then and she felt the blush from her nose to her toes. She tried to find a place to look, other than dead-center on his chest, but the options were limited. Her heart raced and she found herself thinking *left-right-left-left-right* in an attempt to calm herself.

He led her across the patio, holding her a little more tightly than he had a need to. She felt his breath, the tension in his arms, the muscles in his legs as he moved. She felt everything, every single thing in the whole wide world all at once. She thought she would laugh or cry or run away...and did none of them.

Finally, she relaxed, after a fashion, and let him guide her, learned to anticipate his moves, to read the tense-and-release motions of his muscles and instead of pulling away or craving distance, she eased into him.

It occurred to her that she should put her head on his chest. That's how she'd seen other couples—her parents included, back when she was young—dance, but was it too soon for her to do so? Would he think her forward?

"Now you're getting it," he said softly to the top of her head.

She looked up at him with shimmering eyes and smiled. "You're a pretty good teacher. Especially for a giant."

Their gaze lingered, softened, melted into something that was not at all what it had originally been intended to be. Had the song ended? For a frightening moment, Cara thought it might have. Then she heard the chorus swell and she relaxed in his arms once more. For one heart-stopping moment, she thought he might kiss her. Then it was gone as he spun her away with the flick of one wrist, only to reel her in hard with another spin. He caught her in his arms and dipped her, watching her face as he did so and noting the surprise that blossomed there.

She almost squealed as she felt herself drop, but she managed to contain it, morph it into an amused giggle. Then, from the corner of her eye, she spotted movement to her right. She turned her head to see what it was, and nearly toppled to the floor.

"Oh my God!" she spat, virtually climbing up his arm in an effort to gain a standing position.

Hunter pulled her up gently, steadying her on her feet as he looked to see what had so shocked her. There in the doorway stood all of them, Maggie, Tony, Rakhi, Klein, and the admiral. They stood smiling, clapping, whistling and cheering.

Cara made every effort to shake off the embarrassment, but a rabid blush had infected her face and it made the whole process completely impossible. She dusted at her clothes, straightened her hair, cast one tiny quick glance at Hunter. "Have they been standing there the whole time?"

"No. Maybe. I don't think so." If he was embarrassed by it,

he wasn't letting on. He stood there, silent, waiting for her to make the first move. "They're not leaving."

"I know."

"We can't stay out here all night."

"I know." She sighed heavily.

"Let's just go inside. How bad could it be?"

She fixed him with a steely glare and pressed her lips into a tiny slit. "You have no idea."

"After you, m'lady." He swept his arm in the direction of the door, watching her roll her eyes as she passed him.

He held the door for her, which served two purposes at once. First, he was made to look very gallant in front of her father. Second, it forced her to confront their friends first, taking the heat off of him.

She stepped past and not a word was said but as Hunter pulled the door shut, she heard Tony chime in.

"Hunter and Bishop sitting in a tree, k-i-s..."

The rest of it was choked off, presumably by Hunter grabbing Tony's throat. Or at least that was the way it sounded to Cara. She smiled to herself and moved on, fighting yet another blush.

Bishop headed straight for the bar, Rakhi hot on her heels. She slid onto a stool, completely ignoring Rakhi's presence—the presence of everyone there, for that matter—until Rakhi spoke.

"What was that?" Rakhi spat, trying to peer at Bishop's face.

"A dance. Nothing."

"That was not nothing. You are visibly shaken. Cara Bishop, warrior, savior of the planet, has been brought to her knees by...a dance. You cannot tell me that was nothing."

Rakhi reached for her headband, a motion that caught Bishop off-guard. "Don't you dare!" she said, louder than she had intended, loud enough for anyone in a fifty-foot radius to hear. "I mean it."

Rakhi offered her palms in submission. "Okay, okay."

"Just let it go."

The party raged on for most of the night. Bishop, her father, and Maggie escaped around midnight and went to have breakfast and say their goodbyes. Rakhi stayed on another hour, alternately talking and dancing with Jalen Parks, then she, too, made her escape. Captain Hunter walked her to her car, deciding to leave Klein on his own recognizance for once.

No one knew what became of the others but come morning muster, it became obvious that those three were the only survivors.

CHAPTER 11

The mess hall was empty the next morning, save for Hunter, Bishop, and Rakhi. They, alone, had survived Tony Allen's party. Allen, himself, showed up as they were clearing the table. His shirt was buttoned wrong, his hair uncombed. He hid behind sunglasses that obscured most of his face. They all lifted their eyes and watched him come in, half staggering, half shuffling. He was a man in misery as he dropped slowly into a chair at the far table.

"It's alive!" Bishop shouted dramatically.

Allen eased his head into his hands and said, "Shh."

The one thing Bishop loved more than anything else was picking on people with hangovers. She'd never been in that position herself and had little patience for anyone who lost control to that extent. She stood and walked over to where Allen was; he was now trying to rise out of the chair and groaning with each inch he gained.

"Not feeling so good, huh?" she asked quietly.

"Nope." He put one shaky hand on the table to steady himself.

"But you had fun, though, right?"

"Oh, I had so much fun," he groaned. He lifted one leg and leaned forward, crawling onto the table, then sprawling across it, his cheek squished against the Formica and his palms flat.

Bishop stepped over to where he lay and bent over to whisper in his ear. "I want you to remember that I could have been very, very mean to you this morning…but I wasn't." Then she leaned over and kissed him delicately on the cheek. "Bye, bye, Tony," she said and was gone.

Allen's hand came up in a splay-fingered single wave, then fell back to the table with a dull thud.

There were meetings and briefings scheduled for the rest of the day. The compound looked like someone had stepped on an ant hill with people and machines scurrying about, loading the ship, rushing to make refinements and repairs. Once, Bishop was nearly run down by a forklift as it hurried to deliver a load to the ship's cargo hold.

No one was allowed to leave base that night, so a special meal was served up in the mess hall. People had put in requests for their favorites and everything was served buffet style on four tables that stretched across the room. The mood was light but grew heavier and darker as the evening wore on. Talk was centered around family and friends, things people would miss. They shared stories about each of these things, then turned their eyes toward their last day on Earth and the great unknown into which they were headed. There was a lot of conjecture and some trepidation, but in the end, everyone went off to their quarters with smiles on their faces.

The next day dawned bright and the activity level increased. Launch time was thirteen hundred hours and a huge countdown clock in the main hangar reminded them of how much time they had left on Earth. Announcements came every fifteen minutes or so and consisted mainly of reminders. Once lunch was done, they were given the final alarm and made to board the ship through a special gate, which would read their pass keys and make sure everyone was accounted for. Now the mood had become more somber with the face-slap reality that they were about to leave Earth.

"Stations, everyone," Hunter said as he eased into the captain's chair. "It's for real this time so let's keep mistakes to a minimum."

He shifted, trying to find his happy place on the overstuffed and ungiving chair cushion. "Let's get our systems checks underway. Lieutenant Mitra?"

Rakhi scanned her screen and smiled. "Computers fully functional. Communications at one hundred percent."

"Commander Bishop."

"All Zodiacs accounted for. Weapons fully charged."

"Excellent." Hunter pushed a button on the intercom and

straightened. "Mr. Allen, how about your engines?"

"Engines are working perfectly, of course. Life support at a hundred percent. Artificial gravity engaged."

"All right, everyone," he said to the ship-wide intercom, "if anyone forgot anything, speak now or forever hold your peace."

The elevator doors behind them whispered open and Benjamin Danforth stepped out. He looked positively jubilant, his face awash in anticipation. "I just wanted to say goodbye," he began, offering his hand to Hunter and smiling. "It will be a while before we see each other again...if ever."

Hunter nodded. "It's been a pleasure working with you, sir. Rest assured, the ship is in good hands."

"Oh, I have no doubts. No doubts at all. I wish you the best of luck, no matter where you go or what you find out there." The Claxton sounded, signaling five minutes to launch. Outside, people were clearing the hangar. "That's my cue to leave. I'm sorry there couldn't be a parade, media coverage, a band at least. But we're still keeping this on the QT. When you come back, then you'll get your parade. Thank you, everyone, for everything you're doing. Godspeed."

He turned and marched into the elevator then and Hunter watched him go.

When he turned back, everyone was watching him. No one spoke. When the bell rang, signaling launch time, they all turned back to their screens solemnly.

"All right, everyone, let's make history. Mr. Parks, please take us up on my mark."

"Aye, Captain."

The ship was jolted as the lift engaged and the ship ascended toward the sky. It seemed to take forever, but finally the jolt of the lift doors locking shook them. "Mark," said Hunter.

"Thrusters at half," Parks said. Then, leaning toward Bishop, he whispered, "I've never done this in real life. If you see me about to screw up, tell me."

Bishop offered a thin smile and nodded.

"Thrusters at three quarters. Now full. Ground crew, release tethers."

"Tethers released, *Endeavor*. Godspeed."

"Going to one thousand feet, Captain."

"Excellent."

"Altitude: one thousand feet. Engaging planetary drive."

"Take us out of the atmosphere, Mr. Parks."

"Aye, Captain. Engines at half power. Angle set and…there! We're outside the bubble, sir."

"Very nicely done, Mr. Parks." Hunter hit the com again and relaxed at last. "This is *Endeavor* to base. We are away. Hope to see you soon."

"Good luck, Captain Hunter."

"*Endeavor* out."

Parks spun in his seat and looked at Hunter, his youthful face a study in anxiety. "Where do we go first, Captain?"

"Our orders are to go to the nearest star."

"Proxima Centauri," Parks said with a slightly arrogant grin.

"Very, very good, Mr. Parks."

"And the coordinates are in the database." He moved a few things on the screen before him, then expanded the map and tapped the system marked *Proxima Centauri*. "Speed, Captain?"

"Mark Six, Mr. Parks."

Parks turned back to his console, input the speed, and let his finger hover over the button that would set them in motion. The screen showed infinite space, dark and filled with possibilities. He took a moment, perhaps to wonder what was in store for them, then mashed his finger down on that button. "Engaging star drive, Captain."

The screen was still filled with darkness. The ship shuddered as the engines leaped to life. Then they were away, past the orbiting satellites, past the moon, heading for God knew what.

"What's our ETA, Mr. Parks?" Hunter asked quietly.

"Six days, fourteen hours, ten minutes," came his sharp reply.

"Well, I guess we can relax until then, hm?" Hunter said with a smile.

Excitement began to build the moment Proxima Centauri became a tiny dot on the view screen. The first time mankind had cast an eye on a star other than their own. Those on the bridge watched the screen intently; everyone else watched on screens set up throughout the ship. Slowly, that dot grew larger and with it grew the anticipation and, for some, fear. The only aliens they had ever met had nearly destroyed the planet, after all. What if they were all like that? What if, instead of allies, they came away with nothing more than other warring races, bent on destroying mankind and taking the Earth for themselves?

Part of their job included the meticulous study, scanning, and mapping of every celestial body they came across. It was tedious and, at times, incredibly boring. The scientists on board lived for the moment they could actually set foot on an alien planet and place it under their microscopes, as it were. That moment would not come today.

"All engines, stop," said Hunter as they entered the Proxima system. He punched a button on his com and leaned into it. "Lieutenant Allen to the bridge, please."

"On my way," Allen said breathlessly, giving Hunter the mental image of a crazed Tony Allen racing down the corridor. The one thing he had wanted most in life was finally within his grasp.

Allen burst through the elevator doors and drew a bead on Rakhi. "Are we within scanner range yet?"

"We are."

Allen took up the station next to Rakhi's and began typing. "We'll only be within range of the stars for a few minutes, so scan fast. We can't get any closer to it. Stars first, then each planet in succession…."

"I got your memo, Mr. Allen. To quote the vernacular, I have this."

"I got this."

"What?"

"The saying is, 'I got this.' Not, 'I have this.'" He never looked up.

"I see."

Allen watched the data stream past on his screen, turning occasionally to peer at the red dwarf star and its larger brethren.

There were several planets within that belt of habitability, and hopes were high that they would find some sign of life, whatever that life may be.

"Anything of interest, Mr. Allen?" Hunter asked.

"God yes!" Allen replied, clearly enraptured by the data he was receiving.

"Any sign of life?"

"Not so far."

"Let me know if you find anything." Hunter settled in for a long wait.

The scanning and mapping process took more than a day and in the end, they had scanned all three stars, each of their six planets, and a small asteroid that passed close enough to come under their scrutiny. The end result was that they found no breathable atmosphere, no signs of life, not even a single habitable planet. The only one not upset over this was Tony Allen, who was so fascinated and elated with his newly collected data that he studied it for three days without sleeping.

Having found nothing significant, they moved on to Barnard's Star and Ross. If those yielded no results, then they would move on and would keep moving until that elusive first sign of life finally presented itself.

They had been gone for over three months by now. Bishop had grown used to the noise of the engines, the sound and sense of two hundred other people being so near to her. She had lived her life that way, though that time had been spent on different ships, on Earth. Now, she was so far from Earth that she couldn't even see it, a concept which she found disconcerting to the point of distraction. She was a veteran of space, a warrior, brave and adventurous. She had not expected such a reaction from herself.

As so often happened when things preyed on her mind, she found it hard to sleep. The tedium of each day made her weary but sleep was elusive and so she found herself once again wandering to the gardens. It was late and the ship was fairly quiet, so she didn't expect to see anyone there. She walked in and headed straight for the fish pond, breathing deeply as she passed the rose bushes and gardenia clusters. There, sitting on a flat rock next to the pond, sat the captain himself.

"Hunter. I didn't expect to find you here."

"I thought I'd take a page from your book and come to visit the fish. They're actually doing quite well."

"They are, yes. Then again, nothing's changed for them. They still swim around the same pond, eat the same food pellets, sleep in the same reeds. They have no idea that they're hurtling through space at three times the speed of light."

"Is that what's been keeping you up? I notice that you've been having a bit more insomnia than usual."

She smirked. "I wasn't aware that you were studying my sleep habits."

"Well, what affects one crew member affects us all. I make it my business to know when something's bothering one of my crew members."

A moment of silence stretched out and Cara actually heard crickets. "Do you think we'll find anything out here? I mean, we've been out here for three and a half months and we haven't seen a single sign of life. What if it's just us and the Denarans, and nothing more?"

"That's what's bothering you?"

"The thought did cross my mind that we might have come out here for nothing. Maybe there is no other life. Just the Denarans and us. Maybe we just came out here to die."

"That's not at all morbid." He chuckled.

"Sleeping only three hours a night gives you a lot of time to think."

"Well—and I'm no expert, so don't quote me—but I think the fact that there are two of us out here means that there's a damn good chance that there's more. We just haven't found them yet."

"'For the universe is vast and I am small…'"

"A million miles behind me before I fall…"

"And the ocean is dark and deadly deep…"

"A hundred fathoms down before I sleep."

"I didn't know you liked poetry."

"Never sleeping gives you a lot of time to read." He looked

at his feet and sighed. "Are we ever going to talk about the elephant in the room?"

She looked at him, her face betraying nothing. She thought she knew what he was talking about but she sure wasn't going to admit it. "What do you mean?"

"You. Me. Us."

"There is no you, me, us. So, nothing to talk about." She slapped her knees and stood up. Quickly, as if she could leave the conversation behind, she walked to the overlook and leaned on the railing.

Hunter came to stand next to her, just close enough for discomfort, but not actually touching her. "Come on, Cara. You can't say you haven't felt it. It started the minute we met and it's been growing ever since. We have feelings for each other and we can't ignore it."

"I can ignore anything that interferes with my job."

He leaned toward her just a bit and drew the tips of two fingers slowly over the back of her hand. "Tell me you can ignore this." Sparks chased his fingertips and gooseflesh preceded them. She gasped audibly and drew away.

"Look, Captain Hunter, I know that we're out here in space, trapped in this little ship. And I get that men have needs...."

"Is that what you think this is?" He straightened, seeming taller and making him look down at her. "Just a physical need? Some sort of pressure valve?" He ran a hand through his hair. "I thought you knew me better than that."

She merely blinked at him, a thousand words running through her head and unwilling to give voice to any of them.

"I've been with a woman exactly one time in my life and that was just a date. And at the end of it, I kissed her on the cheek. So, I don't even know anything about *that*. What I do know about is affection. Caring. Devotion. And I know that whenever we get close to one another, you feel it as strongly as I do. Why won't you admit it?"

She was red in the face, though whether from anger or embarrassment, she couldn't be sure. She swallowed hard and fought tears. Good soldiers never cried. They never showed weakness. They never admitted they were wrong. "Because to admit it," she said softly, "would mean to give in to it. And to give in to it would mean to be devoured by it. I've run through every scenario in my head and it always comes out the same. We split up in the end, become the laughing stocks of the whole ship. It costs me my career, my dignity. It negates everything I've fought for my entire life. No. You are my captain and we are on a mission. And as long as we are on that mission, we can be nothing more."

He nodded, slowly, sadly. "All right. And after the mission is over?"

She looked at him long and hard. It hurt her to do so. In the end, she merely shrugged.

He nodded. "Cara Bishop, I will love you for all time. Even if we're never together. Even if you don't love me. I will love you… always. And there's nothing you can do about it. But if it's not what you want, then nothing will happen. And we will forever wonder. Unless…." He stepped closer, placing one palm against her cheek and gazing into her eyes. She didn't pull away and it gave him hope. "Just one kiss. One kiss to last for all time and then…never more."

The heat ran through her, her heart hammering and her breath taken in huge gulps. "One kiss…and never more."

He leaned in and down…so far down…her body stretched out as she reached up to meet him. It was a tentative move, her hands trembling as they smoothed over his sides and around his back. His breath danced over her cheek and then he hesitated. Drawing it out? A second thought?

She trembled harder. She wouldn't be the one to complete the act. She wouldn't. But her body ached to share his breath and she thought her heart might stop from the anticipation. Was that what he wanted? To make her beg? To make her desperate?

Then his lips found hers, resting gently upon them, warm and soft and filled with promises. She melted. God help her, she sunk right into the embrace. The entirety of her being lost itself in that one, single, desperate kiss. Surprise struck as she realized that she was clutching at him, forcing her body against his as though the two could become one. It went on forever, always, until her breath threatened to leave her and her heart threatened to stop.

Then he pulled back. So reluctantly, so delicately that she almost didn't realize it was happening. They separated, she now alone and wanting, he now resolute. She looked up at him, wanting to kiss him again, to ask what was next, anything. He took a step back.

"Good night, Commander," he whispered.

Just like that, he walked away.

She stood shaking, flushed, her head spinning and her heart skipping every other beat. Then she spun, grabbing onto the railing and holding it in both hands with white-hot desperation. Eventually, the dizziness would pass and she could function again.

"Damn him," she muttered, and a tear slipped free to roll down her cheek.

That night, that kiss, both were the stuff of dreams and nightmares. They would come back to haunt her sleep and stalk her mind and every time it happened, a cold gray blanket would fold over her heart.

The crew had settled into a rhythm, going about their orbits with practiced ease and an economy of emotion that some would find admirable. The most exciting thing in the world, being in space, had been overlaid with the most tedious of tasks and mundane chores of staying alive. They had learned how to live in space but they had forgotten what it was to be alive. Every day was the same, every meal, every shift, every greeting, every wall, in short, every single detail of their day was the same as the last.

So, on it went for three months more, until the fire had nearly gone out of them and the dreams of their sleep and the dreams of their days had become one. The diligent scanning of space for some sign of life had become a prayer, cast up or out or over to a God who seemed to respond only with, "You are alone."

At last, the day came when Bishop and Hunter and Allen and Parks awoke knowing, just knowing, that something would happen. Hunter sat in his big captain's chair, staring at the blankness of space with an equally blank expression. Bishop fancied that he was staring at the back of her head and, if she had turned at just the right moment, she would have known it was so.

"Captain," Rakhi said, breaking the silence, the mood, and everything that could be broken, "we'll be nearing our point of transmission in thirty minutes."

"Good." He wanted to say no more than that, felt it was too pretentious not to. "Send all packets, especially the maps and scans."

"Yes, Captain."

No more was said and the ship moved on, gliding or zooming or whatever you prefer through space. At the predetermined time, Rakhi sent her packets, transmitting the whole of their newfound information back to Earth.

"Done," she said, and settled back in her seat.

"Thank you." Hunter shifted again and cast a longing glance at Bishop's blonde hair.

Moments passed, as though nothing whatever would infect the monotony of the day. Then, "Captain! We have two ships approaching from the stern."

"Put it on screen and scan them."

The screen flickered and shifted to the aft camera. The view was of two small dots, approaching quickly and growing in size. Everyone leaned forward and squinted in unison, trying to see more than they could.

"The ship in front has a single passenger, humanoid. The second ship has a full crew. Over a hundred...men. Unknown origins. Not humanoid."

"Are we on a collision course?" Hunter wanted to know.

"Negative, Captain. They will pass close, though."

The ships grew until details were visible. The first, slightly larger than a Striker-Z, was white and very streamlined. The second was about the size of the *Endeavor*, but dark, covered in what appeared to be armor and weapons. They passed by the *Endeavor* as though she wasn't even there, coming within twenty kilometers of her position.

"Are you picking up any transmissions?" Hunter wanted to know.

"No, Captain. None at all." Rakhi paused, watching her

scanners and stealing glances at the view screen. Then an alarm sounded, making her jump. "Captain, we have an intruder on Deck Three."

Hunter slammed his hand down on the com button and leaned in. "Security to Deck Three. We have an intruder. Proceed with extreme caution."

"Captain, intruder on Deck Five. Now Deck Two. Captain, we've lost control of Deck Three." Panic stripped Rakhi of her usually calm voice and she had begun to gasp for air to feed her oxygen starved lungs. "Captain, Deck Two reports a hostile entity has simply appeared in engineering." Rakhi listened for a moment. "Deck Five also reports hostile on board. Decks Six and Four now...."

"General quarters. Dispatch with extreme prejudice," barked Captain Hunter.

"More reports coming in now, Captain. Security has lost Deck Two...."

Bishop shot out of her chair, eyes targeting Rakhi. "Set ship's Rasters to continuous charge. Prepare for self-destruct."

Hunter spun, scorching her with his gaze, his jaw set. "Step down, Commander."

"Sir, regulations clearly state..." She met his gaze for a moment, never blinking, her heart pounding in her chest and her mouth dry. Then she exhaled and stepped back, bowing her head before coming to attention. "Captain," she said, relinquishing all power to him.

"You are concerned only with regulations and following orders, Commander. I am the captain. I am concerned with this ship, the crew, the future of this mission. We can rid this ship of the invaders. And we will. Grab a raster and come with me. Lieutenant, once we leave, seal this door behind us and don't let anyone come through it."

"Aye. Captain."

Bishop rushed to the weapons cabinet and grabbed two Rasters, shoving one out to the captain. "Here," she said.

"You take them both."

"But you need a weapon, sir."

"Commander, I *am* the weapon."

It took about three seconds for the enormity of that to sink in. Then she nodded and was through the door.

Hunter stepped into the elevator behind her, tapped his earpiece, and said, "Rakhi, are you reading me?"

"Loud and clear, Captain."

"Good. Use the ship's internal scanners. Tell us where they are."

Rakhi seemed to have calmed some, but her voice still had a razor's edge to it. "First stop, Deck Two. It's overrun. There are two in the corridor, right outside the elevator."

"Deck Two," Hunter told the elevator's computer control. "Ready your weapon to fire when the doors open."

Bishop nodded.

Ten seconds later, the doors opened on the promised intruders. Bishop managed to shoot them both before Hunter could get fully clear of the doors. They paused for a moment, gazing down at them. The aliens appeared nearly humanoid, with two arms and two legs, but there was the hint of a tail at their backside and their bodies appeared covered in some sort of armor. Perhaps it was scales. They couldn't really tell. Their faces were nearly Cro-Magnon in appearance, with broad brows and thrust-out chins. Bishop shuddered inwardly.

Around the corner, at a plodding pace, came one of their fellows. Hunter was quick, so quick that Bishop didn't see him move at first. He lunged forward and to the side, grabbing the thing by its thick neck. He hoisted it from the ground with the ease of one lifting a child and in two fast movements, bashed it, club-like, against each wall of the corridor. Bishop fancied that she heard something snap and then the thing was dead.

The beasts, for Bishop could think of nothing else to call them, were lumbering and large, easily Hunter's size, but without the muscles of an altered human. No sooner had the third one hit the ground than Rakhi was barking in their ears.

"Two more coming your way. One left, one right."

"Got it."

Bishop dove into the intersecting hallway and fired fast and hard at the alien. She spun just in time to see Hunter fling down the lifeless body of his opponent.

"Nice work," Bishop said.

"Really? I thought it was kind of slow, myself."

She shook her head and chuckled a bit. "Where to now, Rakhi?"

"Move toward engineering. There are four of them in the hall outside engineering. Mr. Allen reports that they have dispatched the intruder there and have sealed the doors."

"On our way."

They hurried toward engineering, taking two turns and counting on Rakhi to warn them of any impending danger. As they rounded that third turn, they spotted the group of four. They were just outside the doors to engineering, pounding at them and trying to breach them. Bishop took one by surprise, shooting it in the head before it could finish turning. Then Hunter was on the second, a third grabbing him from behind as he twisted to break the second's neck. Bishop shot the third and then drew a bead on the fourth. He went down with some sort of a yell, part scream of pain, part battle cry.

"Thanks for the assist," Hunter said with a smile.

"Any time."

"Rakhi?"

"Deck three next. There are four of them near the crew's quarters."

"Got it."

They ran back to the elevator and darted in, still panting from the adrenalin overload. They stepped into the hallway and moved toward the starboard side, where the crew was quartered. They had just reached the long hall that bisected the deck when Rakhi cried out to them.

"Stop! You've got three coming at you from behind. Two from in front."

"We're on it," Bishop said, drawing her second weapon and standing at the intersection of the hallways. Feet firmly planted, arms raised to each side, she relied on her peripheral vision to know where her foes were.

First came the two and she fired on instinct. The three appeared immediately, seeming faster than their lumbering predecessors had been. She shot one, then held her fire as she saw Hunter race down the hall toward them.

Hunter grabbed one low, by the thighs, then used him as a battering ram to knock another off his feet. Switching his stance and his grip, he swung the alien like a club, smashing his compatriot against the wall, then eventually beating the two of them together until they were bloody heaps. He turned and walked down the hall toward Bishop.

"Did you just beat that guy to death with another guy?"

"Yeah." He shrugged.

Bishop snorted. "Awesome!"

Rakhi was screaming at them now. "They're coming at you. All directions. Ten. Twenty. I can't count. Get out of there!"

Hunter shot a look at Bishop. She had paled a bit but stood her ground. She gave a slight nod.

"We got this," they said in unison.

Rakhi had not downplayed the situation at all. A hoard of yelling beasts ran at them from down the hall, easily a dozen, maybe more. Bishop heard the yells of even more coming at her from the other direction and from her left. She pulled both her weapons, stood strong, waited.

The sight of it was a video gamer's worst nightmare, a first-person shooter gone mad. As Bishop opened fire to her left, she caught a last glimpse of Hunter. With a crowd of aliens rushing at him, he ran to meet them, repelling off the wall and diving into the mass, arm cocked, fist clenched, battle face on.

Bishop managed to take out five of them but she was missing an unacceptable number of shots. Perhaps it was the panic, perhaps the desperation, but she was firing blindly almost. She grabbed a deep gulp of air, clung to it, and calmed herself. As she shot the last man, clearing the hall to her left, she spun to the right, firing and yelling and firing some more as she backed away. They continued to rush at her, the final man a mere three feet from her when he dropped.

She hadn't realized where she was going, had merely executed a strategic retreat. Her back was to the elevator door now and as she registered the coolness of its metal, the door whooshed open and something—someone—grabbed hold of her with steel hands and claws like daggers. She yelped and tried to spin but the grip was too tight. Her arms had limited movement but she managed to cross them in front of her, firing both weapons behind her. They went wide, pinged off the walls.

It had been a long while since she had engaged in mortal combat. Sparring was a different beast and it didn't offer the urgency that a life and death battle would. A calm overtook her, though, and she realized that it was all just like riding that proverbial bike.

With the monster locked onto her, she raised her feet and kicked out against the wall, sending them both backward and smashing the beast against the wall. Then she raised her feet high and kicked down and back, hitting that same wall with all her might and tucking as she felt them rocket forward. It cost the alien his balance and as he stumbled forward, she completed the movement, bringing him to the floor and breaking his grip.

She was on him then, one weapon still in her hand, the other dangerously in her belt. What he lacked in speed, he made up for in strength, and it took him no longer than a few seconds to throw her off. To say he threw her off was a gross understatement, as he catapulted her through the air, slamming her against the wall near the ceiling. Just before warm flesh met cold metal, Bishop drew her second weapon and fired, repeatedly, with both.

As she slid to the floor, she smiled.

Slowly, she pulled herself to her feet and went to find Hunter. He was superhuman, for sure. Strong and fast, he was a literal killing machine. For all of that, she couldn't be completely certain that he had survived. After all, he had thrown himself headlong into an army of armored aliens.

She dashed to the intersection of the hallways, ready for nearly anything. Her weapons were still drawn and she had every intention of offering her assistance. Yet, there stood Hunter, the hall floor littered with aliens and gore, holding an arm in one hand while clutching an alien's throat in another. All the while, he was beating the alien about the head and body with that severed arm.

When at long last the alien dropped, dead, onto the floor, Hunter turned to face Bishop. His uniform was covered in green gore, torn, and spoiled with bits of…something. Still, he held the alien's arm in his hand and as his eyes fell on Bishop, he let it slip, almost comically, to the floor.

Bishop cocked her head to one side and sighed. "Tell me you didn't just rip off that guy's arm and beat him to death with it."

He had the smile of a kid who'd been caught with his hand in the cookie jar and he shrugged. "Of course not." A breath. "No." Another breath. "Maybe."

Bishop laughed. "You're a berserker, that's what you are."

"Is that bad?"

"Not today, Captain. Not today." A beat passed and she said, "Rakhi, are we all clear?"

"All clear, Commander."

"Good. We're heading your way."

"Not quite yet," Hunter said, stooping to grab an intact body by one arm. He walked a short way toward the elevator, dragging the body with him.

"What are you doing?"

"A little present for Dr. Klein. I want to know everything there is about these aliens."

Into the elevator and down to the medical deck, he dragged the body all the way to sickbay, leaving a smear of alien blood all the way. When he reached the outer office of sickbay, he called out, "Dr. Klein, I have a present for you."

"What's that?" came the call from inside his personal office. Then he appeared around the corner.

"This." Hunter hoisted the alien up onto one arm and slammed him hard onto the table. "Find out everything there is to know."

"Good God, man! Are you insane? You can't just…."

"I can and I did. Now get with the autopsy. I need to know who we're fighting."

Klein's mouth was still gaping as they left, marching down the corridor toward the elevator.

"*Now*, we go to the bridge," Hunter said.

CHAPTER 12

"Thank God you're okay!" Rakhi said as Hunter and Bishop stepped out of the elevator. "But what is that all over you?"

Hunter looked down like he didn't have any idea in the world what she was talking about. "Oh, that's alien blood. I think." He walked over to the console and leaned one hand on it, looming over Rakhi. "The computer has a record of all crew-members' signatures. Scan the ship and see if there's anyone who doesn't belong."

"Yes, Captain."

Bishop came to stand at Hunter's back. She was tired and anxious and more than anything she wanted to just take a shower and lie down. Even if all was well and she'd had the chance, the adrenalin pumping through her body wouldn't have let her.

"I have one, Captain." Rakhi tilted her chin upward and met his gaze.

"Where?"

There came a sound like a huge puff of air and Bishop at once drew her weapon and stepped backward. "Behind you!" she yelled. "Freeze!"

Hunter spun to see what she had targeted and there stood a perfectly ordinary-looking man, tall and thin, with the white complexion of bleached linen and light brown hair. He wore a white jumpsuit and white shoes. Every inch of him shimmered as though it were dusted in glitter.

"Who are you and how did you get on my ship?" Hunter spat, his face pressed into service as a weapon.

"I am Kimdihr, First Ambassador of the Oden-Rha and I

ported onto your ship." His voice was quiet and calm. If he felt any fear, he didn't display it.

"What does that mean?" Bishop wanted to know, her weapon still trained on him.

"I used this…." Kimdihr tapped a thing on his wrist that looked like a watch but clearly was not.

Bishop raised the raster to target his head, her grip steady and her eyes narrowed.

"Relax," Kimdihr said. "This is not a weapon. It's a teleporter. It opens a portal which, when I step through it, will take me to whatever coordinates I enter."

"Hand it over," Hunter demanded, holding out one large hand.

"I assure you, Captain, I have no intention of escaping. Even if I did, I have nowhere to go. One cannot port through space."

"You came from one of those ships, did you not?"

"Yes, Captain. And quite honestly, I didn't know it would work. But I had to try. The Oden-Khaar were almost on me."

Hunter stepped forward and grabbed a handful of Kimdihr's jumpsuit, yanking his face to within millimeters of his own. "And that's why they invaded my ship? They were looking for you?" His voice was loud and deep, threatening in a way that even he had not thought possible.

"I'm afraid so, Captain, and for that, I am truly sorry."

"Why do they want you so bad anyway? What did you do to them?"

"I did nothing. They claim that I killed their prince but I assure you, I did not."

Hunter studied his face for a moment, finding no change in it whatsoever. Then, without looking away, he said, "Rakhi, can you tell if he's lying?"

Rakhi stood and removed her headband, immediately assaulted with the thoughts and dreams of nearly everyone on the ship. When she stepped in and took Kimdihr's hand, however, all those thoughts quieted. She could see only Kimdihr's thoughts and memories then, those and nothing more. She sorted them, watched them almost scroll by like a filmstrip in slow motion, and Hunter and Bishop watched her face shift as she did so. Then she released Kimdihr's hand and put her headband back on.

"He is telling the truth, sir. I find no memory of the deed, nor of covering it up."

Hunter released him then, suddenly and with a slight shove backward. It was satisfying. "Very well. But watch him," he said to Bishop.

She nodded and lowered her weapon, but did not holster it.

An alarm sounded just then, causing them all to jump. No one moved faster than Rakhi, who turned and threw herself into her seat. "Ships incoming. Three. Same as..."

"The Oden-Khaar. They've come for me." If it was possible for something to fade to a lighter shade of white, that's what Kimdihr's face did and he took two steps backward.

"Well, this can't possibly be bad," Bishop sighed. "I mean, we only just killed half their crew."

"Captain, there is an incoming message from the alien ship."

"Put it on the screen." Hunter sat in his chair, glad for the chance to get off his feet. This was more excitement than he had ever counted on and he found himself longing for the Leavenworth dungeon. "This is Captain Hunter of the Earth ship *Endeavor*. To whom am I speaking?"

"I am Benom, Admiral of the Oden-Khaar Imperial Fleet and Minister of War. You have something I want and if you give it to me immediately, I will overlook the fact that you have killed over fifty of my best men."

Bishop looked at Hunter, realizing as she did so that Kimdihr had shrunk from view. He was pressed to the wall, just outside the periphery of the viewing screen camera. She lifted her weapon slightly, keeping it hidden from the screen. Then she tilted her chin downward and tapped the raster. Kimdihr nodded his acknowledgment.

"Your men invaded my ship!" Hunter barked, hands gripping the arms of his chair so tightly that even his wrists had gone white. Bishop thought he might just snap the arms off the chair. "What could I possibly have that you would want anyway?"

"You have that Oden-Rha pig, Kimdihr, who murdered our

prince, stole a ship and is, even now, hiding aboard your ship."

"Exactly what proof do you have that he committed this crime?" Hunter had calmed somewhat, but his entire body was still on high alert and he hadn't released the chair arms or even eased his grip on them.

"We have video of the murder, Captain Hunter. See for yourself."

A video took possession of the screen as the bridge crew watched. It showed an ostentatious sleeping chamber, dripping in heavy, dark fabrics and gilt with silver. Upon the bed lay a thin young man, apparently asleep. Another man entered the periphery of the camera, creeping along the edge of the room and making his way toward the bed. In the soft light, he was hardly visible, that is, until he reached the bed. As he stood over the young man—Hunter assumed it was the prince—he raised a long, wavy-bladed dagger. The light glinted off the blade and flared at the camera. The blade plunged into the prince's body once, twice, three times. Then, the man turned, his face now clearly visible. Beyond all possible doubt, it was the face of Kimdihr.

The video ended and Benom's face reappeared on the screen.

"Irrefutable proof of his guilt. You will give Kimdihr to us within sixty of your Earth minutes, or we will destroy him and your ship along with him."

The screen went dead for a second, the blackness replaced with a view of the Oden-Khaar ships that lay before them.

"Fantastic," Hunter growled. He took a moment to compose himself, drawing a deep breath and forcibly releasing the chair arms from his grip. He stood slowly and walked at a measured pace toward Kimdihr. Nose to nose, with barely an inch to spare between them, Hunter said, "Explain yourself."

"I swear to you, Captain, I am innocent."

"Rakhi, are you completely sure there's no way he could have done this?"

"Yes, Captain. I am one hundred percent certain."

"How do you explain the video they have?" Hunter wanted to know.

"Captain Hunter, on my world, all people have the same

face. We call it The Face of Rha. It is why we have been at war with the Oden-Khaar for so long."

Hunter blinked and his brow furrowed. "Everyone?"

"Every single person. They are all identical in every way."

Hunter shook off the hundred questions he wanted to ask of Kimdihr and opted, instead, for something that might save them. "Bishop, do you see any way we can beat them in battle?"

"Not a chance, Captain. Sorry."

"Mr. Parks, can we outrun them?"

Parks' head spun and he looked down at his screen for a second as though studying something. "Doubtful. Their engines are twice as fast as ours. They'll be on us like…."

Hunter spun on Kimdihr, targeting him with his crocodile stare.

"How large is the portal this thing makes?" he asked, tapping the device on Kimdihr's wrist.

"About the size of an average man."

"Can it be made larger?"

"I'm a diplomat, Captain. I've no knowledge of these things."

To Rakhi, Hunter said, "I need Mr. Allen here now." He heard Rakhi calling for Allen but kept his attention on Kimdihr. "Have you ever heard of someone transporting a large thing…a ship, perhaps."

"Not ever."

"You need me?" came the call from behind Hunter. Allen stepped onto the bridge in a rush, his face slightly red from running and his breath coming in short gulps.

Hunter stepped away from Kimdihr, shoving out the man's wrist as he did. "This thing opens portals through which you can travel. Problem is, the portal is too small for a ship. I need you to make this thing larger. And we'll need a remote trigger. It has to be activated from outside the ship, see? You've got…." Hunter took a quick glance at the chronometer on the console. "Fifty-four minutes."

"No problem. Have this ready in a jiffy." Allen reached out his hand and waited anxiously as Kimdihr removed the device from his arm and placed it in Allen's hand. Then he was gone, rushing off the bridge and down to his lab.

Tony Allen ran through the door to his lab almost before it opened. The edge of one side of the door smacked lightly into his shoulder as he passed through. He hit the wall intercom hard as he passed, hollering into it. "Klein! My lab! Now! Emergency!"

"Coming," was the response.

Against the back wall stood all manner of equipment, the purpose of which was known only to Tony. He hit several buttons in sequence, letting the hum wash over him as he watched their lights all come on. Then he opened a large glass case, sliding the teleporter into it and closing it tightly.

"Computer, scan."

"Scanning."

Tony hit another, larger button and a light shone down from the ceiling. Trapped within its beams were particles of something. They shimmered and winked, drifting around as though they had no real purpose. Tony didn't hear the door open, nor acknowledge Klein as he came to stand beside him.

"Okay, computer, give me the 3D model."

"What are we doing?" Klein wanted to know.

"This little gem produces a portal. You input coordinates, step through the portal and…voila!...you're there. We need a portal big enough to drive a ship through, activated from outside the ship, and we need it in…." He paused to let the computer finish.

"…forty-seven minutes."

"Or what?" Klein studied his face, not amused in the least.

"We all get destroyed."

"Oh. Is that all?"

A model of the teleporter rotated slowly before them, enlarged and reproduced in vivid detail. Tony placed his hands at the center of it, suddenly jerking his hands outward. The teleporter hologram exploded in an instant, giving him a clear view of every mechanism, every circuit, every single detail inside.

"This is where you enter the coordinates," Tony said, speaking more to himself than to Klein. "This must generate the portal, here. There's the power source…interesting."

"The software must regulate the size and placement of the portal."

"Download the software onto console four," Tony said, never looking away. "Okay, so touch screen dealy. Coordinates in, set, go. But what the heck is this?"

"Not sure." Klein stepped over to console number four and sat down. Programming code streamed across the screen but it was nothing he had ever seen before. "I don't know how to tell you this, but this isn't English. Or any other programming language I've ever seen."

Tony moved to look over his shoulder, frowning. He punched the console button and said, "Rakhi, my lab. Fast."

Moments later, Rakhi rushed through the door, coming to a stop behind Klein. "What do we have?"

"The program that runs the damn thing." Klein sighed. "It's not English. Not binary...."

"Do not panic. Let's look at it logically. There's going to be a portion for running the power source, a diagnostic, variables for parameters like portal size and distance. Then a set of if-this-then-that for coordinate entries and such. There!" She stabbed her finger at the screen. "Their alphabet and numbers are different, just like ours. They have a sequence. May I sit down?"

"Bingo!" Tony said from behind them. "I can expand the power source, increase the size. Now the trigger...ah, the trigger. Got it!" He rushed to another console and began typing furiously, pausing every now and again to perform calculations in his head. The large replicator in the corner began to hum and Tony smiled.

"While we await our fate, why don't you explain to me just how and why all your people have the exact same face." Hunter eased into his chair, still tense, but not quite on the verge of snapping chair arms. "Bishop, I think you can put down the weapon now."

Bishop gave a curt nod and holstered the raster.

"Captain, thousands of years ago, the Oden-Khaar and the Oden-Rha shared the same planet. We were—are—the same race. We believed that by removing our individuality and becoming more like our god, Rha, we would become gods ourselves. It would remove the baser emotions like hatred, jealousy, envy, and lust. And it did. It eliminated crime. Our scientists genetically engineered future generations, altering our own DNA, over a period of hundreds of years, until we all came to be alike. We all came to be like Rha. Some of our people wanted to hold on to their individuality. They were against tampering with nature.

"There was a great deal of strife on our planet. Wars were fought, millions died. And then we reached a decision. Followers of Rha would stay on our home world while those who had broken from our beliefs would seek a new planet to make their home. Thus, we became the Oden-Rha, or Children of Rha, and the Oden-Khaar, or Children of Fate. Our two worlds have been at war ever since. My trip to the home world of the Oden-Khaar was a peacemaking mission. We were to sign an accord which would end this war, share in trade and knowledge, and bring peace to us all. I had not even arrived on the planet at the time when the prince was killed. My ship suffered a malfunction shortly after launch and I was forced to turn back and board another ship."

"I suppose you have a log that backs this up?"

"I do."

"Then why not just explain that to the Oden-Khaar, rather than run?"

"They wanted only to kill me. They were not interested in hearing evidence."

Bishop stepped in, her brow furrowed and her eyes dark. "Maybe I'm missing something, but...two-part questions here... how do you tell each other apart, and how did the Oden-Khaar prove that was your face on the screen?"

Kimdihr looked at his feet for a moment, then sighed. "My uniform. We all have different badges in the form of a triskelion. One part bears our rank, one bears our birthplace, and one bears our name. See?" He pointed to the sewn-on patch on the left side of his chest. "It is clearly visible in the video, if you noticed."

"That provides a simple answer, then," Bishop said, offering up her open palms. "Someone else was simply wearing one of your uniforms. Do you have no other means of identification? Fingerprints? DNA scans?"

Kimdihr shook his head. "Our genetics were engineered to all be identical. Anything that marked us as individual was engineered out."

"Wow," Bishop said simply and took a step back.

"Then we have to look at who had motive to frame you," Hunter said simply. "Who wanted this treaty to fail most?"

Kimdihr screwed up his face in thought and was about to reply when the communications console beeped, signaling an incoming message. Hunter stabbed at the button on his own console and looked askance at the view screen.

"Captain Hunter here."

Benom's grim face appeared on the screen and Hunter frowned. "You have twenty of your Earth minutes left to you. I suggest you reach a decision and make your final arrangements. Give Kimdihr to us now, and all will end well for you and your people. Refuse, and you will all die at my hand."

The screen went dark.

Bishop turned a sullen face to Hunter, staring a bit as a range of emotions passed over his usually calm façade. "What do we do, Captain?"

"Let's just hope Mr. Allen comes through for us."

"And if he doesn't?"

Hunter looked from Kimdihr to Bishop, then back again. His face was once more at peace. "Then, Commander, we die."

Seconds ticked away like hours until the bridge doors finally slid open. Tony and Rakhi burst through, their faces awash in stress. They were panting and even as Rakhi took a seat at her console, she looked as though she might collapse.

"Got it!" Tony held out a small gray box and smiled. "You owe me big-time for this. One portal generator, size, distance, and destination variable. Sorry. No time for remote activation. I'll have to mount it on the front...."

"...Bow...." Bishop corrected.

Tony shot her a sneer and continued, "...on the bow of the ship and activate it manually. How much time do we have?"

"Eleven minutes," Rakhi interjected.

"I better suit up, then." Tony passed the box to Hunter

and rummaged in his pocket for a second, finally producing Kimdihr's teleporter.

"You didn't destroy it." The man was incredulous over this, his smile tilting off at a jaunty angle and his eyes sparkling.

"You're not dealing with rank amateurs, here. I scanned it and worked from a model. Captain, what coordinates should we use?"

"My home world," Kimdihr said quickly. "We'll be safe there."

"Might as well." Hunter passed the box to Kimdihr with a shrug.

Tony made for the starboard wall of the bridge, yanking open a compartment and pulling out a protective suit. He pulled it over his feet and shimmied the rest of the way into it, grabbing a pair of magnetic boots and a helmet for good measure.

"So, you're actually going to sit on the bow of our ship and activate this thing."

"Uh-huh," Tony said, struggling with the latches of the boots. He flipped a switch and activated them, testing the large magnets inside. He would depend on them to keep from floating off into space. Then he eased the helmet over his head and activated the console. The suit filled with oxygen at once and he smiled and gave a thumbs-up. "Testing com. One, two, three...."

"Loud and clear," Rakhi said, turning to give Tony a thumbs-up.

"Once they see you outside the ship, they're going to get suspicious," Hunter whispered to Tony. "They might come after you."

"Then, I hope they don't see me." Tony winked and moved toward the access ladder. "Wish me luck."

He switched off the boots and mounted the ladder, making it upward three rungs before Kimdihr approached, lifting the box to the full extent of his arm. "Perhaps this might help."

Inside the suit, Tony blushed, though none of them could see it through the polarized faceplate. He took the box under one arm and began his ascent once more.

Once he had successfully sealed himself into the airlock, he activated his boots again. Instead of weights to compensate for a lack of gravity, the boots had strong electromagnets in them. They remained active until one turned them off, and each one worked independently of the other. It did not allow for a normal gait, however. Walking was slow and cumbersome. Each time a foot was lifted, a switch turned off the magnet in that boot until such time as the foot was pressed downward again. Running was an impossibility.

In this slow, foot-up-foot-down manner, Tony made his way to the very front of the ship's bow. He placed the box carefully, switching it on only after it was mounted. Inside the ship, the crew watched his progress through the view screen, eyes riveted to it, breath held.

"I'm ready when you are," Tony said with a wave.

"Very good, Mr. Allen. On my command, then." Hunter muted the console and leaned toward Rakhi. "I don't suppose you guys tested this."

"How could we possibly? Just open a portal in the middle of the ship? God knows what would have happened."

Hunter held her gaze for a moment longer, then righted himself and sighed. "Well, then. We shall all hope for the best." He switched the console back on. "Mr. Parks, on my command, hard to port and give her every ounce of speed she's got. Mr. Allen, stand by."

"Aye, sir," said Mr. Parks.

"Damn," Tony yelled into his com. "Damn, damn, damn. I've got company."

"How many?" Hunter wanted to know.

"One. Big dude."

Bishop dove for the weapons console, snatching up the Zodiac control as she collided with the chair. "I've got this," she yelled, her voice pitched with adrenalin but her hands steady.

In seconds, a Zodiac flew onto the screen, angling so as to take a shot at the intruder without risk of hitting the ship. Bishop watched through her eyepiece as the Oden-Khaar grabbed Tony about the neck, seemingly bent on unfastening his helmet and putting an end to him. Tony threw a slow-motion punch, having very little effect on his opponent, but managing to tilt himself backward in the process.

Targets popped onto Bishop's eyepiece and she fired, one quick burst striking the Oden-Khaar in the center of the chest. Without gravity, the body simply floated there, motionless but dead. It gave Bishop the creeps and she spun the eyepiece away from her face.

"Thanks, Bishop. I owe you one." Tony waved and moved toward the box.

"My pleasure, Mr. Allen."

"That was quick thinking, Commander." Hunter smiled and offered a nod. "If you're ready, Mr. Allen...."

"Ready." Tony squatted down next to the box, his hand poised over the screen. With his other hand, he gave a thumbs-up.

At that moment, with Tony ready to open the portal and Captain Hunter's mouth open, ready to give Lieutenant Parks the go-ahead, the Zodiac that had saved Tony's life simply exploded.

CHAPTER 13

The second the Zodiac exploded, things shifted into slow motion for Tony. He spun in place to see the debris from the Zodiac spin out and away in slow-motion clarity. Behind that, and coming on far more quickly than his perception allowed him to realize, was another Oden-Khaar. This one was shorter and bulkier, appeared to have muscles on his muscles and a singularity of purpose that Tony could only strive for.

Through his communicator, Tony heard everything that was happening on the bridge.

He heard Captain Hunter give the command for Mr. Parks to begin his maneuver.

He heard the furious yelling and threats of Benom.

He could not hear the *thunk-clunk* of the Oden-Khaar warrior as he made his way toward Tony's position.

The ship banked hard to starboard but Tony's boots held fast. The additional motion of the ship gaining speed worked against him, but he managed to keep his position steady. It was the first time he had ever been grateful that there was no air and no gravity in space.

His hand shook hard as it hovered over the portal generator's screen, awaiting further orders. Squatted down, half turned, he kept an eye on his would-be attacker.

And in turn, the bridge crew heard Tony's desperate prayers and panting.

"Now, Tony!" Hunter yelled into his com.

Tony's hand slammed down on the button and he held his frantic breath, awaiting the appearance of the portal. What seemed to take days and actually took only seconds was a personal triumph for Tony. He was rich and handsome and brilliant, but he was not brave. Yet, in the past five minutes, he had defeated a foe, clung to the hull of a ship that he, himself, had built, and activated the portal that would save the entire crew. The way he had it figured, if he died right then, all his arrogance would be vindicated. He would die a hero.

Once the portal opened, Tony had about a second to stand and spin to face his opponent. The brute already had his weapon in hand and for a brief second, Tony wondered why he hadn't just fired it and killed him on the spot. If his calculations were correct, he had about ten seconds before the ship went through the portal. He had ten seconds to rid himself of his attacker or else risk being killed by him.

He took a chance.

Maybe their anatomy was the same and maybe it wasn't, but Tony only knew of one sure-fire way to drop an opponent. He had used the method only once before, in the only fight he had ever been in in his life. It had saved him from a huge beating at the hands of a bully and had also been the sole reason he had never been involved in another fight.

Tony grabbed the attacker's wrist and twisted the weapon away from himself, at the same time releasing his right boot and kicking it upward, bringing it to bear on a spot directly between the warrior's legs. It was a sissy move, as any schoolyard boy will tell you, and even though his leg never gained the momentum or force that he had hoped, it did manage to stun and confuse his opponent long enough for his only other move to come into play.

In his confusion, the soldier accidentally released his left boot, tilting him to the side and throwing him off balance. Instantly, Tony followed with a right cross, and stomped on his right foot, thus releasing his right boot. Untethered from the ship as he was, the Oden-Khaar warrior simply floated off into space, arms and legs pinwheeling.

Smiling, Tony turned to face the portal, which was now mere feet away. Arms in the air in a triumphant gesture, Tony rode the hull of the *Endeavor* straight into the portal.

The bridge crew watched with fascination as Tony's drama played out. White-knuckled and wide-eyed, they felt every moment of it as if it were their own. They saw Tony's fight take place against the backdrop of the shimmering portal as they zoomed toward it. The Oden-Khaar took up the chase, closing fast and firing frantically. At the last possible second, Tony won his personal battle and they won theirs, the hitchhiker sailing off into space only seconds before the ship hit the portal.

One moment, they were streaking through empty space, headed for a rip in that space's fabric and with no idea where they would end up or if they would even be alive when they got there. The next moment, they were staring at a planet and cheering.

"Mr. Parks, reduce speed and establish an orbit." Hunter turned his chair and smiled. "Kimdihr, welcome home."

Outside, Tony threw himself dramatically against the view screen, arms and legs splayed, helmet resting against the screen. "Request permission to come inside and clean out my suit, Captain."

Hunter laughed at that, the sound of it booming out across the bridge. "Permission granted, Lieutenant Allen."

A few seconds later, Tony made his way down the ladder, dropping the last two rungs to land on the deck. He unbuckled his helmet and set it down, clearly still a bit shaken. He pulled off both gloves and began massaging his right hand with his left. "You know, it really hurts to hit a guy in the face. I think I might have broken something."

"Funny, I never noticed," said Hunter smugly.

"Oh no! You do not get to do that," Tony chided, marching on Hunter and shaking his head. "You are not the hero today. Not today. You have to admit, what I did out there was the single bravest, most self-sacrificing thing you've ever seen in your life." And he stabbed a finger into Hunter's chest, targeting him with his narrow gaze.

"You're right," Hunter said, stepping closer to Tony and peering down the end of his nose at him. "You saved us all. You stepped up, you risked your life to save us, and in the face of great personal peril, you took the steps necessary to ensure the safety of this ship and her crew first, and yourself second. This will appear in my report and I hazard to guess that you might even garner an accommodation from it."

Tony nodded slowly and turned. "Thank you. It was the proudest moment of my life and I only ask that it be acknowledged." He took a few steps toward the elevator, then spun on his heels. "But did you see that? I totally kicked that guy's ass and then surfed my way through a space portal. Hanging ten in space! Oh yeah!" He pumped his fist once and then stepped backward into the elevator.

"There's no living with him now," Bishop giggled.

"No, and we'll never hear the end of it." Hunter slid into his chair with a sigh. "Rakhi, please open a channel to the planet below.

"Yes, Captain."

The screen lit up and Hunter straightened himself. He was greeted by Kimdihr's face staring back at him, though the uniform differed slightly. "This is Captain Steven Hunter of the Earth ship *Endeavor*. We have someone here who wishes to speak to you." He motioned for Kimdihr to step within viewing range.

"Ambassador Kimdihr, is that you? You're alive?"

"I am alive, yes. I request permission to meet with the prime minister at once."

"One moment, please." With a slight tilt of his head, the man pushed a button and the screen was graced with a still image of his face. Moments later, the screen reactivated and the man smiled. "The prime minister requests your presence immediately. She also requests that Captain Hunter accompany you."

"By the grace of Rha," Kimdihr responded.

"By the grace of Rha," was the answer and the screen went blank.

"Commander Bishop, you're with us." Hunter pressed a button on his console and leaned in. "Lieutenant Allen to the bridge. Lieutenant Allen to the bridge."

"We'll use my teleporter," Kimdihr announced, fiddling with the screen and smiling. "It will be good to be home again."

The elevator doors opened and Tony stepped out, his face still flush but his uniform clean and his hair neat. "You wanted to see me, Captain?"

Hunter spun his chair around and smiled. "How would you like to meet some friendly aliens for once?"

"You mean it? I can go down there with you?"

"Yep. That's what I mean."

"All right!" Tony rubbed his hands together and beamed.

With a wave of his hand and a smile, Hunter said, "Whenever you're ready, Kimdihr."

Kimdihr pushed a button on his teleporter. There was a slight delay, but finally a portal opened. It very much resembled the one they had flown through but smaller and less bright. Through it, they saw a city, all gleaming white and gold.

"After you, Captain."

Hunter stepped through the portal, followed by Tony, Kimdihr, and finally Bishop, who brought up the rear. As soon as they were through, the portal closed. It was like nothing had ever happened.

The landing party stood in the middle of a small street. People passed around them, wary, curious, staring. All of them had Kimdihr's face and manner of dress and as with Kimdihr, their skin glowed as though from a coating of gold. The buildings were all white stucco, painted in a gloss finish and topped with brilliant gold roofs. They were very much in a Russian style, with onion-shaped roofs and shiny gold doors. Towering above them all, ornate and shining with captured light, was the church. The landing party stood gawking, spinning slowly around as they fought to take it all in. It was like standing in the middle of a jewelry box.

"Kimdihr, your city is beautiful," Bishop said in awe.

"Thank you. But if you think this is beautiful, you should see the valley when the blood cherries bloom. It's like a sea of pink blossoms as far as the eye can see."

"Sounds amazing."

Tony bent and ran his hand along the bricks of the road. "Is this real?" he asked, almost reverently.

"I assure you it is." Kimdihr smiled, patient and calm.

Tony stood. "The streets here are literally paved in gold."

"Back home, they'd be stealing these bricks right and left," Hunter sighed.

"Back home, just a one-mile stretch of this road would make me the richest man in the world." Tony chuckled.

Bishop smacked Tony's shoulder lightly and scowled. "You're already the richest man in the world."

"Oh yeah!" Tony laughed and winked at her.

Kimdihr finally moved away, headed for a large building to the east, though he walked slowly and seemed to be in no hurry to get there. "Here, gold is the most common substance on the planet. It is literally everywhere. We use it in our construction, in our technology, even in our clothing."

"I have to say," Hunter began, "I don't see any of the usual trappings of war."

"We are a peaceful people, Captain. The word of Rha tells us that we should never take a life, even if it means we have to sacrifice our own. We have no weapons, only defenses. The entire planet is protected by an impenetrable shield, thus the delay in opening any portal. A signal must be sent for a portion of the shield to be dropped before the portal can be activated. The Oden-Khaar have launched many an attack on our planet but, so far, none have managed to breach our shields. However, in the event that the shield is breached, we have many underground shelters in which our people will be safe."

"So, basically, you have a run-and-hide approach to war." Hunter found this fact confusing.

"Exactly, Captain." Kimdihr fairly beamed, obviously proud of his people's strategy.

"Forgive me if I'm being indelicate," Tony said, "but all your people appear to be males. Don't you have any females?"

"We are all non-gendered. We lack sex organs of any kind."

Silence filled the space around and between them and only Tony had the audacity to press on. "So, then, how do you…do you even…?"

"Procreate?" Kimdihr smiled that beatific smile of his and nodded slowly. "We do not, in fact. We have almost no disease, no crime. The rare deaths that occur are usually the result of accidents. When that happens, the council will create a replacement in the lab."

"So, no children?" Bishop asked.

"No love," Hunter said, stunned.

"You don't have sex?" Tony spat. "At *all*?" His face was that comical mixture of terror and shock usually reserved for teenagers who have their cell phones taken away.

They mounted the steps of the building slowly, though Tony remained planted where he stood. After a few beats, he threw up his hands in disgust and trotted after them. "Seriously? No sex? Ever. Like, not even once?"

"No," Kimdihr said simply. He seemed more amused at their incredulity than irritated.

He led them down the hall and into an elevator, which took them quickly up to the twentieth floor. Once there, they walked down a corridor lined with gold doors, until they reached the end, where two large doors stood open, showing the enormous office inside.

"Prime Minister," Kimdihr said with a deep bow. Behind the desk sat Kimdihr's identical twin, who rose and stepped forward to meet them as they approached. He grasped Kimdihr by the neck and Kimdihr followed suit, each pulling the other in until their foreheads briefly touched. Then they took a step backward.

"It is so good to see you again, my friend. By the grace of Rha, I thought you were dead. And you bring friends with you. We haven't had visitors in over a hundred years. This is truly a special day."

"Prime Minister, I would like you to meet Captain Hunter, Commander Bishop, and Lieutenant Allen. It was they who rescued me. Everyone, this is Prime Minister Sansa."

The prime minister stepped to each of them in turn and greeted them in the same way that he had greeted Kimdihr. Then he stood back and waved his arm in the direction of a bank of chairs. "Please, sit. Do you have needs?"

Taken slightly aback by the phrasing of it, Hunter's mouth worked for a second but produced no sound. Tony opened his mouth, no doubt to say something offensive or at least questionable. Bishop elbowed him hard, then smiled at the prime minister. "Thank you. We're all fine."

Kimdihr wrung his hands and frowned, his back

straightening by degrees and his shimmering face growing paler by the second. "I'm so very sorry, Prime Minister. I failed in my mission. I've failed our people." His voice was low and reverent, a church whisper.

"Let's not worry over the treaty now, Kimdihr. I know that you did not kill the prince. No Oden-Rha is capable of murder. But how did you ever escape the Oden-Khaar prison?"

"When they were transferring me from the holding cell, Minister. I slipped their grip and, when they fired upon me, I held my cuffs up so that they were broken by the beam. Then I simply ran, back to my ship and toward home. That's when I came across the *Endeavor*. It was a terrible risk, I know. And I'm afraid that I put our new friends in jeopardy. I could think of no other way…."

"Captain Hunter, we are very grateful to you and your people for seeing Kimdihr safely home. Your ship could easily have been destroyed." Sansa took a beat, staring briefly out the window before continuing. "How did you manage to avoid the Oden-Khaar's wrath?"

"That's where I come in," Tony said with a sheepish grin. Uncharacteristic humility lit his eyes and he bowed his head. "I took Kimdihr's teleporter and made a modified version of it. Then we simply ported the ship to your planet."

Sansa's face dropped, his eyes bulged and he let loose an audible gasp. "You made a portal large enough to fit an entire ship through? That quickly? However…?"

"I had a lot of help." Tony beamed at them all, his chest swelling with pride, and not for the first time that day.

"Oh, you must speak with our minister of science, Mr. Emok. I'm sure he would love to see your design."

"And I would love to dissect your planetary shields. I can think of a hundred uses for that, I'll tell you."

"Very good." Sansa clapped his hands and waited. Presently, a gentleman bowed into the room, his hands clasped at his waist and his eyes lowered. "Daimor, please take Mr. Allen here to visit with the Ministry of Science. He has much to teach them."

Tony rose and checked Hunter's expression for signs of worry. "Is it all right, Captain?"

"By all means, Lieutenant," Hunter said with a wink. "Have fun."

Tony was alight with joy as he followed Daimor out of the room.

"Now then, Captain Hunter, you may stay with us as long as you wish. If you have need of something, simply ask any citizen and they will give freely of whatever you need. When you return to your ship, there are portal stations located throughout the city which you may use." Sansa bowed deeply, smiled, and turned to Kimdihr. "Now then, my friend, we need to discuss how we can salvage this all and complete the treaty with the Oden-Khaar."

Feeling dismissed, Hunter took Bishop's arm and turned toward the door. They walked in silence until they reached the front entrance of the building. Then Hunter turned and looked back, seemingly puzzled. With a sigh, he spun and marched through the door and into the clear, bright, shimmering sunlight

.

Tony hurried along behind Daimor until they reached a large building at the end of the block. It was all made of white marble and capped in gold, just like the other buildings in town. But this building had an air of reverence to it, a sophistication which shone out every bit as much as the gold that comprised its roof. Very nearly gothic in style, it stretched out and back and up far enough to make Tony dizzy as he tried to see the top of it.

By the time he looked back, Daimor had already crested the steps and was holding the door open. Tony hurried again, anxious to meet what he considered his new best friend. Sharing ideas with a fellow scientist was pretty much at the top of Tony's list of favorite things.

Daimor pulled the door shut once they were inside and, with a slight bow to a passerby, he guided Tony toward the back of the building, where a circular desk stood vigil, lorded over by another Kimdihr lookalike. He smiled as they approached and leaned forward as he spoke.

"How may I help you?" His voice was somehow softer and richer than Daimor's, Sansa's, or Kimdihr's.

"Where might we find Mr. Emok just now?"

The man consulted a small screen set into his desk and nodded as he stabbed a finger at it. "There he is. Lab thirty-four. The molecular imaging lab."

"We thank you."

A quick bow and they were moving again. Tony felt the man's eyes on him as they left. If he were to hazard a guess, he would say that they did not often see people who looked different from themselves. No doubt, he would attract attention wherever he went. Whether that was good or bad—for Tony or for the citizenry—was anybody's guess.

He was herded into an elevator by Daimor, he of few words, and a button was pushed. Tony thought it archaic, the use of buttons when your voice could do all the work. He did not say so.

They exited on the thirty-fourth floor and hurried along two intersecting corridors until they came to a door covered in labels and stickers. They proclaimed such ominous things as "Stop! Danger! Sterile Lab!" Next to the door was a sort of intercom with a single white button and a single speaker. If there was a microphone, Tony couldn't spot it.

"I have brought a visitor from the alien ship," Daimor said as he pressed that button. "Prime Minister Sansa wishes for you to confer with him."

"Yes, yes. That's wonderful. We're not sterile today. Come in." The man spoke quickly, his words sloppy and stinted.

Daimor pushed open the door and air rushed past them into the room. What Tony saw inside almost made him giggle. Everyone on the planet looked exactly alike, perfect carbon copies of each other. This man stood out. His size and shape were the same as everyone else's and even his eyes and smile matched his fellow citizens'. But his hair was snow white and long, flying carelessly about his head as he moved. His skin lacked the golden sheen of the others and he was disheveled. His lab coat bulged here and wrinkled there, and on his face he wore safety goggles that enlarged his eyes comically. Tony stifled a laugh and pinched his lips together in a tight little smile.

"I'm Mr. Emok, the minister of science. Pleased to meet you, sir. Very pleased to meet you." He marched at Tony with both arms open wide and Tony nearly bolted.

Steeling himself, Tony accepted the man's traditional greeting, then stepped back. "I'm Lieutenant Tony Allen. It is my very great pleasure to speak with you."

"If you have no more need...." Daimor said, bowing.

"Yes, yes," Mr. Emok responded with a wave of each hand in turn. "You may go. Thank you. Thank you."

They watched Daimor go, then turned back to each other with matching grins. "You have an amazing lab here. And I understand this is just one of them?"

"Oh, my, yes. We have over a hundred labs in this one building alone."

"It's like Heaven," Tony muttered as he gawked at the equipment. His head snapped back around to Mr. Emok and he smiled. "If you don't mind me asking, why is it that you look so different from everyone else?"

"I look different because I *am* different." Here, he giggled. "I was the product of an accident, you see. An explosion in the lab immediately following my conception caused a chemical leak. They did not discover it until after I had become fully formed and by then it was too late. Ah, but I am so wonderfully different for I am the smartest man on the entire planet!" He stabbed a finger into the air for emphasis, his eyes sparkling.

"Me too!" Tony laughed. "Well, on my planet anyway. I'm the smartest and the richest."

"What does this mean...richest?"

"I have more money than anyone else."

"And what is this money?"

Tony took a beat, considered his options. "Never mind. It's not important. Now, tell me about these goggles you're wearing. They magnify things, do they?"

"Oh, yes. Yes, indeed. The micro-optics can magnify a thing right down to the atomic level. Here! You should see." He removed the goggles and slipped them over Tony's face, adjusting the strap. "You turn this little dial on the side and... see?"

Tony watched through the goggles as his hand grew larger, closer, the cells more defined. Soon, it was as though he were looking through a microscope. And then things got really interesting. He was able to dial all the way down to the molecular level, isolating a single cell, then going beyond. "Amazing," he sighed with all the reverence he could muster.

"I know. I'm constantly astounded by it. Constantly. Now, over here…."

Mr. Emok was already crossing the room when Tony removed the goggles. He shook his head to get his vision to clear. "What is it we have here?" Tony asked as he came to stand behind Mr. Emok, staring over his shoulder.

"This machine…I invented it, by the way…is the basis for our planetary shields."

"Wonderful! That's exactly what I wanted to talk to you about. I was thinking that I could adapt this technology and apply it to our ship. Sort of like adding a protective layer over the hull. I have such a thing installed on one of my cars back home but I was never able to stabilize it enough to be viable on the ship."

Mr. Emok turned his head to smile at Tony. "I've already done that. I'll give you a prototype, if you'd like."

"Are you kidding?" Tony's face lit up and he nearly squealed, he was so excited.

"I am not kidding. I would just give it to you. Honestly."

Tony laughed then. It was the first time he had laughed since leaving the ship and the first laughter he had heard here. "It's a saying we have on my planet. But I thank you. I could reproduce one and give every ship in our fleet a shield to protect them."

"You have a fleet, eh?"

"Well, not yet we don't. But we will. We are making the maiden voyage for our planet. We're kind of like guinea pigs." He noticed Mr. Emok's confused frown and he grinned in the face of it. "I mean, we're like test subjects."

"Ah! I see. So, you built your planet's first interplanetary vessel and you came to see us. I feel most honored."

"I wish it were true. Honestly, the whole thing was an accident. Kimdihr teleported onto our ship and the Oden-Khaar wanted him back. So, I turned his wrist teleporter into a ship-wide teleporter and we came here to bring him home."

"Just wait a minute!" Mr. Emok said, holding up one hand. "Do you mean to say that you took a simple teleporter and adapted it so that the portal would allow an entire space vessel to pass through it? Without losing integrity?" He watched as Tony nodded. Then his arms shot out and clutched at Tony, dragging him into a bear hug. "Oh, you are my brother!" He shoved Tony out to arm's length and smiled. "At long last! I finally meet a man who is as smart as I am. Come! You must show me how you accomplished this. Oh! And I will give you a shield generator to take home with you."

"Fantastic! We can pick each other's brains. I have so much to show you."

Mr. Emok stopped, looking confused and a little scared. "This is another of your colorful sayings, yes?"

Tony laughed. "Yes. It just means that we can have a total sharing of information, a collaboration, if you will."

"Yes. Oh yes! Yes-yes-yes-yes! We can swap technology. I will impart the collective knowledge of the Oden-Rha to you… you do have computers, do you not?"

"Yes, we have them."

"Most excellent. Then I shall have our knowledge base sent to your computer. Provided, that is, that your computers have the storage space."

"Bring it on, my genius friend. We can handle anything you send our way."

"Then I will send it all!" Mr. Emok yelled, throwing his arms wide into the air.

"You will send it all!"

Tony threw his arms into the air as well and suddenly, they were laughing and hugging again.

Hunter and Bishop had been strolling along the streets for about an hour, taking in the sights, greeting those who bowed at them. The sun was high overhead but the day wasn't terribly hot. A light breeze tousled their hair every now and again and the gold silt, which seemed to be everywhere, shimmered in that breeze.

"It's a beautiful city," Bishop noted.

"It is, indeed. And quite different from any city on Earth. There are a few things missing."

"Yes. Like police stations and libraries."

"And schools and hospitals."

"I haven't seen a single mall or theater. Not even a TV." Bishop sighed

"Matter of fact, I don't see any towers or antennae. And I haven't heard a sound since we got here. No loud muttering from crowds, no music, no traffic noise."

"It's kind of unnerving." Bishop tittered nervously. "And we are attracting a lot of attention."

"We're different. In a world where everything is the same…." Hunter said in his best announcer voice.

"Two people stand out," Bishop mimicked. Then she laughed.

"Let's go into this restaurant here and talk to some people. Maybe it will give us a better feel for the lives of these people."

Bishop nodded and followed Hunter across the street. Each building bore a sign declaring that building's purpose, though Hunter and Bishop didn't need a sign to pick out the restaurant. People inside sat at large tables, dining in large groups. Heavenly smells filled the air surrounding the place, making Bishop's mouth water. It became painfully obvious, just then, that she hadn't eaten in quite a while.

"Welcome to our visitors from another world," said the man standing vigil at the door. He clutched a stack of menus to his chest and smiled warmly as they entered. "There is space at the table with Galifred, if that is all right."

"That will be great," said Hunter with a nod.

The gentleman led the way to a table at the back of the room, waiting until they were situated on the long bench before handing them menus. "Would you care for something to drink? We have yet some tea. It's very good, steeped all night in cold water. Our tea is prized throughout the city."

"Two teas, then," Bishop said with a smile.

All heads had turned and Bishop felt dozens of pairs of eyes staring at her. She glanced briefly around the room, her eyes finally settling on the gentleman seated across from her. "Hello," she said gently. "I am Cara Bishop and this is Steve Hunter. We're…."

"Off-worlders. You are the ones who rescued Kimdihr. Greetings! I am the one known as Galifred."

The waiter returned just then, sliding two glasses of tea in front of them with a smile. Bishop took a sip and smiled. It was warm and soothing, mellow with just a hint of sweet aftertaste. She sighed as she sat the glass down. "It is delicious."

"I'm afraid we have no money," Hunter said. "Perhaps we can work out some sort of trade."

"I do not know what money is," said the waiter with a smile, "but I'm very sure you do not need it to eat. You choose what you would like to eat and I will bring it to you."

Bishop and Hunter looked over the menu. There was nothing even remotely recognizable on it and Hunter frowned. "What do you recommend, Galifred?"

"By far, their best dish is the filet. They cook it over an open flame and it is spiced to perfection. You will not be disappointed."

Hunter smiled in return and nodded to Bishop. "Two filets, please," she said, passing the menu back to the waiter.

"How do you find our planet?" Galifred asked, clasping his hands together and easing forward to rest his elbow on the table.

"It's a beautiful place," Bishop said quickly. "And very peaceful. Are all your cities like this?"

"My, yes. Not all are this large, though."

"I see," said Hunter. "It's very different from our world. For instance, you have no police, no army."

"We have no crime." Galifred smiled.

"And I haven't seen a single library or school," Bishop added.

"Our people are educated from the moment they are born. They begin learning the scrolls and move on to their science and history and mathematics. All learning happens at home, on their Books."

"Books?" Bishop asked, confused.

The waiter arrived with their food: huge steaks dominated the large plates and were festooned with some sort of beans and a large portion of what looked like potatoes.

"Books. Like this." Galifred produced a tablet-like computer. "In ancient times, books were stored in libraries, which were also places of learning. Now, all books are electronic. This one, and all the others, contained the collected knowledge of the Oden-Rha. Paper volumes are stored in museums."

"I see," said Hunter. No knife had been brought with his steak, so he took a chance and cut off a piece with his fork. The meat was tender and surrendered easily to his fork. The flavor exploded in his mouth, making him shut his eyes and moan with delight.

Satisfied, Bishop took a bite of her own steak and had a similar reaction. "Oh, this is delicious," she said around the remains in her mouth. "It's a thousand times better than the beef steaks we get back home. What sort of animal is it from?"

"No animal. Worm." He watched in amusement as Bishop and Hunter both stopped chewing, midbite. "It is filet of gillworm."

Bishop shot a look at Hunter and he shrugged. "Well, it's delicious, so I don't care what it's from." She swallowed hard and took a sip of her tea.

"You say that all books and educational materials are kept on your books. Do you also keep your entertainment there?" Hunter downed the last bite of his filet and pushed a few beans around the plate, hoping they would reveal themselves.

"I do not know what entertainment is," offered Galifred.

"Back home, we perform plays…or skits…dramas…." Bishop began awkwardly. "We record them and then broadcast them around the world so that people can watch them on their own computers…or books, if you will. We have theaters where we perform live stage plays and we record plays, which we call movies, that we showed in different theaters." She felt as though she weren't explaining things properly. It was painfully hard to put something with which you'd lived your whole life into words that a stranger could understand.

"I do not think I've ever heard of such a thing." Galifred seemed very confused.

"Well, what do you do for fun?" Hunter asked. "Sports games? Dancing? Music?"

"We do not compete in any form," Galifred answered, rather disdainfully. "We are all equal, so none would win. And I am not sure what dancing and music are."

Hunter pulled out his communicator and switched it on. It looked like a cellular phone, though the screen was larger. He swiped the screen and tapped an icon. Suddenly, the room was filled with the snappy opening song to some old movie or other. It had a quick tempo and catchy lyrics. A strong beat rounded things out.

Galifred half-stood and leaned forward to peer over the phone at the screen. "This is music?" He smiled broadly. "I like music. Is there more?"

"Sure," Hunter said and dialed up a new song. Suddenly, he became aware that everyone in the place had gathered around them. They were smiling and tapping their feet. Several of them swayed or bounced to the beat. "I'd be happy to share it with you. There's a lot of different music. Here. Do you have a cord or something? I'll give you all the music."

"No need," said Galifred. He pulled out his Book and tapped a few icons. Suddenly, his head was bobbing to the beat of a sock-hop classic.

And so it began. Galifred shared with the man next to him, who shared with the two people behind him. And they shared, and they passed it on, and so it went until music was coming out of every Book in the place.

It spread like the plague, creating a cacophony of sound out in the street. Hunter was certain that if he had a map and each red dot on the map stood for one person with the music, that the red dots would splay out across the globe in a matter of minutes. It was unnerving to say the least, scary at best.

Bishop and Hunter thanked Galifred for his help, thanked the waiter for the fine food. Then they stepped into the street, the formerly quiet and peaceful street, where a chaos of sound now terrorized their ears and shook their brains.

"What have you done?" Bishop asked.

"I'm not sure, but I think this might be a good time to say our goodbyes and get the heck out of Dodge, if you know what I mean." Hunter chuckled uneasily, tugging her back across the street and toward the center of town where the government buildings were located. "And an even better time to teach them about earbuds."

CHAPTER 14

"Rakhi, hey!" Tony said into his communicator. He stood in the middle of Mr. Emok's lab, cables draped over his shoulder, things tucked under his arms, and the phone barely clutched in his right hand, between thumb and forefinger. "Have I got a present for you!"

"A present?" The cheer in her voice bubbled out from the speaker. "What is it?"

"Oh, it's just a little something to remember the Oden-Rha by. A tiny gift really...."

"Stop toying with me. Tell me what it is. Please?"

"Okay. Get your download and upload speeds on steroids, because I'm about to hook you up with the collected knowledge of a civilization that has been traveling space for thousands of years."

"You are what now?"

"Basically, they will download the entire contents of our ship's computer and we will download theirs. There are star maps, details about tons of other races, science that you wouldn't dream of in a million years."

"I'll need to set a dedicated connection for this. Otherwise, it will take months."

"Yep."

"It will take me a few minutes but it should be a piece of pie."

"Cake, Rakhi. Piece of cake."

"Yes, that." She giggled. "Hold on just a minute while I parse out the data stream." She moved from captain's chair to her own, heaving a sigh of relief at being set to a familiar task. She scanned and typed, always keeping a watchful eye on the screen before her. "Okay. This type of connection will only provide a one thousand terabyte per second download but the upload should be at least ten times that."

"Nice work, Rakhi. I'm coming back in a few minutes and I'll be bringing Mr. Emok with me. He's the minister of science here. He's providing us with a shield generator and we're giving him the larger teleporter."

"It sounds like you're having a lot of fun down there." His voice sang with excitement and she pictured his face, all lit from within and child-like.

"Oh, you have no idea. I have finally met someone who is as smart as I am and I really wish I didn't have to leave."

"I'm happy for you, Tony, but have you heard from the captain and Bishop? They haven't checked in."

"Not a word. I'll check in with them and let the captain know that I'm headed back to the ship with Mr. Emok."

"Good. And you can establish the computer link whenever you are ready. Everything here is set. *Endeavor* out."

Tony turned off his communicator and smiled at Mr. Emok. "You can make the link now, sir. Everything is ready."

"Excellent!" Mr. Emok flipped a switch, typed a few commands, and then stood back, watching proudly as the two huge computer systems exchanged data. "That is a much faster connection than I would have expected from such primitive equipment."

"Hey now! Don't insult my baby. I built that ship and everything on it with nothing to go on but an idea and a few small ion engines. You act like we're still working with stone tablets or something."

"So, you don't want me to teach you about quantum memory?" Mr. Emok's face toyed with a smile.

"Oh, yes, my friend," Tony said, looping an arm over his shoulder. "Yes, I do. And I'm going to teach you about a little something called Scotch."

"That was Tony," Hunter said, tucking the communicator into his belt and sweeping back an errant lock of blond hair. "He's back on the ship with the minister of science. They're playing with big boy toys and inventing things."

"Well, at least somebody's having fun."

"I suppose we should get back, too. Rakhi's been in charge for too long and I know she isn't comfortable in a position of power. Besides, I could use a shower. All this gold is making my skin itch."

"There's a teleporter on the corner there."

They made for it together, both anxious to be home. The street porter was a simple device, consisting of no more than two tall poles with a keypad on side of the left pole. When Hunter pushed what he assumed was the ON button, the two poles hummed to life, giving no other sign that it had been activated. The screen on the keypad showed them a short list of previous and potential destinations and their coordinates, each with a small icon next to it. As luck would have it, the third choice down was their ship and so Hunter selected that one. The poles buzzed louder and suddenly a portal appeared between them, affording them a clear view of the *Endeavor*'s bridge.

"After you," Hunter said with a gallant sweep of his hand.

Bishop stepped through, then Hunter, and the shock that registered on Rakhi's face as she saw them step out of nowhere made each of them laugh in turn.

"Welcome home, Captain Hunter. Commander Bishop." Rakhi stepped out of the chair, assuming Hunter would take command again.

"Everything good?" Hunter asked.

"Yes, sir."

"Excellent. I'm going to take a shower, then you can catch me up on everything."

"Very good, Captain." Rakhi eased back into the chair, looking forlorn.

"So," Bishop began, leaning on the arm of the chair and smiling at Rakhi. "How was your first command?"

Rakhi turned to make sure Hunter had already gotten into the lift and couldn't hear her, then leaned in to Bishop and whispered. "Terrifying! I mean, nothing went wrong, but I kept sitting here and thinking of all the things that could go wrong and what I would do if they did...."

"I know this isn't exactly your thing but there's a chain of command we have to follow and since you're the ranking bridge officer...." Bishop shrugged.

"I understand. But could you just promote someone else? Then they could be in charge instead of me."

Bishop giggled and patted Rakhi's shoulder. "We'll try not to leave you too often, okay?"

Rakhi nodded and sighed.

Captain Steve Hunter had the sort of job that you just couldn't train for. There were no text books, no simulations broad-reaching enough, and no mentors that could have prepared him for the diverse situations that would be hurled at him at lightning speed. He didn't doubt his abilities for one second. Insecurity had never been one of his failings. If anything, he was guilty of caring too much and trying too hard.

To that end, he began his sleepless evening by reading a few tech manuals. Quickly tiring of the dry writing style, he moved to his computer console and started poring over some of the data that Tony had already downloaded from the Oden-Rha. This contained the entire history of the Oden-Rha people, from their caveman beginnings to present day, including their literature, art, and even the most basic and yet forgotten piece of their culture: music.

He found it increasingly hard to focus, though. Something was nagging at the back of his mind, something that just wouldn't let go of him. He needed answers. A series of unforeseen events had led them to be in orbit around this planet, embroiled with Kimdihr and his people and he needed to know why.

"Computer, play back the bridge recording from yesterday. Start when the Oden-Rha ship first showed up on the sensors."

"Playing."

He watched carefully, leaning forward and squinting a bit, more from stress and concentration than anything else. It was odd watching a video of his own actions, hearing words that had long ago left his mouth.

The alert from Rakhi, telling him that a ship was

approaching. The sound of the intruder alert siren. "Computer, pause." The video stopped playing. "How much time elapsed between the first intruder and the second?"

"Five seconds, Captain."

"Hmm," he said. "Continue playing the video."

He watched carefully and counted. Less than a minute had elapsed between Kimdihr's arrival and the total invasion of his ship.

"Computer, stop." He leaned back and stared at the screen, his lips tightly pursed and his brow knit. "Show me a star chart of the area in which we were located on that day. Zoom in. Zoom again. Now, show me where the *Endeavor* was. And now, trace the path that Kimdihr's ship took from the time it appeared on our scanners until it disappeared."

Kimdihr's ship came from the upper right of the chart, bearing directly toward the *Endeavor*. It passed within a hundred yards of them—the point at which Kimdihr boarded their ship—then made an abrupt course change and arced away toward the upper right of the chart.

"So, an unmanned ship made a quick course change," Hunter said to himself.

"It would appear so, Captain," the computer responded.

"Computer off."

Hunter was halfway to the door when the screen shut down and went black.

With any luck, Mr. Emok would still be on board, working with Tony. Hunter went first to engineering to see if they were there, and when he found no one but the night crew, he went to Tony's lab.

There, amongst a mile-long tangle of cables and piles of parts and tools and things even Hunter couldn't identify, sat Tony and Mr. Emok. They looked tired but exhilarated. They might have been a little drunk.

"Mr. Emok, I'm glad you're still here," Hunter said as he came through the door, his hand thrust out in greeting before he remembered that their culture didn't use handshakes. He pulled his hand back and thrust it into his pocket. "I have a quick question for you."

"Everything okay, Cap?" Tony asked. He didn't bother to stand.

"Yeah, fine," he said to Tony. Then to Mr. Emok, "Do you have an autopilot on any of your ships? Something that would bring the ship back to your planet, should the pilot be lost?"

"No, nothing like that," Mr. Emok said with a hard shake of his head. It sent his wild hair flying and morphed him into the proverbial mad scientist.

"You couldn't pre-program a series of courses into the ship? You couldn't tell it where to go and then send it off autonomously?"

"I'm afraid our smaller ships are very simple. We would have no way of doing that."

"Then there was someone on that ship, even after Kimdihr ported off. Thank you, Mr. Emok." Hunter turned on his heel to leave, then thought better of it and spun about to target Tony with a glare. "Do I even want to know what's going on in here?"

"We're installing shields on the ship, Cap." Tony's face lit up. Clearly, he was in his element now.

Hunter took a glance around the room at all the parts, then looked back to Tony. "Just don't screw it up."

With that, he marched out, leaving the two men to whatever madness had gripped them, to their piles of parts and schematics and dreams.

"Commander Bishop, reported to the Captain's quarters. Commander Bishop to the Captain's quarters."

Bishop was only half dressed when the call came through over the intercom. She made fast work of pulling on her shirt and shoving her feet into the regulation boots that she hated so much. Then she pulled her hair into a sloppy ponytail and hurried out the door.

She had no idea what Hunter wanted with her, but it must be urgent if he was willing to call for her over the ship-wide intercom. She rushed down the hall to his door, then pushed the buzzer and waited.

"Come!" was the response and the door slid open.

"You wanted to see me, Captain?"

"Yes, Bishop. Have a seat. I have something to show you."

She slid uneasily into the chair and waited as he turned the computer monitor to face her.

"I spent the night reviewing the bridge recordings from the day we met Kimdihr. I found some very interesting details. Look at this star chart...." He leaned in and braced himself on the desk. "Computer, bring up the star chart with the ship overlays."

"On screen, Captain."

"There. You see. If you follow the path of Kimdihr's ship, it headed one direction first, then veered away to pass close enough to our ship. After that, the ship completely changes course. I checked it and that course was set for Kimdihr's home planet. So, where did it go?"

Bishop's mouth worked, she shook her head and offered up her open palms. "I don't know."

"It went out of sensor range and we lost it. But...and here's the important thing...I asked Mr. Emok and he says that the ship could not have changed course unless someone on board changed it. That means that someone was on board even after Kimdihr ported onto the *Endeavor*."

"Who do you think it was?"

"I'm not sure. More importantly, though, where did that ship go? It's a small ship and her speed isn't half of ours. Besides, we went through the portal. There's no way that ship beat us here. So, either it's floating dead in space, it went back to the Oden-Khaar, or it was picked up by another ship."

"Reasonable."

"We know it's not floating around in space somewhere. That would be suicide. So, if it got picked up, it had to have been picked up by one of the Oden-Khaar ships."

"And if he returned to the Oden-Khaar home world, that means that he's one of theirs. Or working for them."

"Precisely. So, that brings me to my next question: Where did those three Oden-Khaar ships go after we went through the portal?" Hunter smiled smugly.

"I just figured they would go back home. Once we got away from them, I really didn't give it any thought."

"You follow my logic, though, right? I'm not crazy?" Hunter's lips twitched up into a grin.

"Not crazy at all. Kimdihr had a stowaway from the minute he escaped the Oden-Khaar. And that means that the stowaway was working for the Oden-Khaar. The question is…why?"

"What I need is a scan of Kimdihr's ship. And I need to know where it went."

"We scanned his ship when we first spotted his approach. There should be…."

"I already checked. It passed so quickly that we only managed to scan for life forms. Besides, that doesn't tell us where it went. For that matter, we don't know where Benom's ships went after we escaped through the portal."

"I assume they went back home. They sure didn't come here or we would have picked them up on our scanners." Bishop thought for a moment, unsure of how to ask her next question. Finally, she just dove in and hoped for the best. "What if I took a Stryker back to…?"

"Absolutely not. If they went after you, you'd be dead."

"Oh, please! I took out that entire mother ship with just a Stryker…."

"And a nuke. Commander, I absolutely forbid you to go anywhere near that planet. That's an order."

Bishop sighed heavily, her face darkened. "Aye, Captain."

"Besides, I have a better idea. We'll take the *Endeavor*."

"With all due respect, Captain, it's better to risk one life than the entire crew."

"There's no risk at all. We'll take the *Endeavor* just close enough to stay out of scanner range. Then we'll send in a Zodiac. With any luck, they won't even spot it."

"Captain, that borders on genius. Let's do it."

Hunter propped his chin up on one fist and smiled. "Lieutenant Allen, has Mr. Emok returned home yet?"

Tony slid out from under Rakhi's console and lifted his head. "Yeah, he went back about an hour ago. But I'm supposed to go back down…."

"It'll have to wait. I assume everything is fully functional, despite the mess you've made out of Lieutenant Mitra's console there."

"Fully functional. I'm just installing a few relays that I can connect later in order to...."

"I don't care. Mr. Parks, take the ship out of orbit and bring her to bear on the coordinates I gave you."

"Aye, Captain." Parks steepened the angle of the orbit and slid the speed lever upward, angling the *Endeavor* upward and away from the planet's atmosphere. "Speed, sir?"

"Mark seven."

Parks whipped his head around and stared. His mouth fell open.

"You heard me. Do it."

"Engaged."

"It is essential that we stay out of scanner range of the planet, Mr. Parks. So, bring the ship to a full stop well before that."

"Aye, sir."

"Bishop, the rest's on you. Just remember that if the first Zodiac fails, we've got a lot more. For that matter, Lieutenant Allen can just keep cranking them out, so don't worry if a few get destroyed."

"Hey!" Tony said from his position under the console. "Those things take time and resources to produce, you know. Don't just go around blowing them up all willy-nilly!"

Hunter cocked a grin at Bishop and winked. She snickered in response.

"Now approaching the Oden-Khaar home world, Captain. Still well out of scanner range."

"Full stop, Mr. Parks. Commander Bishop, you're up."

Bishop nodded and took her position at the Zodiac console. She fit the headset and controls to herself and turned on the panels. "I'm going to go for a long-range scan first. From Kimdihr's description of what happened, I can approximate the location of their base...within a couple of miles, of course. Can't do any better than that."

"Very good, Commander. We already have a scan of the Oden-Rha's ships, so we know what the energy signature should look like. Try that first."

"Aye, Captain."

Bishop focused in on the view from the Zodiac as it eased out of its dock and left the ship. She pointed it toward the planet's surface, just north of the equator, and approached from behind the moon. The little Zodiac moved at almost a crawl, making steady but slow progress toward its target.

"Why so slow, Commander?"

"An object streaking toward the planet is bound to raise some red flags, Captain. This way, it at least stands a chance of being mistaken for space junk or a small meteorite." She never looked up, spoke in a dream-like voice. "There. I'm within scanning range now."

"Good thinking, Bishop." Hunter watched the screen and the data that streamed across it. He hoped that they wouldn't spot the *Endeavor* before they found what they were looking for.

"I've found the base. Going in a little bit closer...there! At the south end of the base are nine Oden-Khaar ships, in a hangar. Inside one of those ships is an Oden-Rha ship. I assume it's the one Kimdihr abandoned."

"Can't be too many more Oden-Rha ships in the area, I wouldn't think. Very good, Bishop. Bring the Zodiac home, please."

"Aye, sir. But Captain, this ship has weapons."

Hunter paused, obviously stunned. "The Oden-Rha don't use weapons."

"I know." Her expression was intense, worried. She held his gaze for a long time, watching his expression change several times as he considered the ramifications of that last.

"Mr. Parks, make ready to head for...."

"Captain, we have three ships incoming. Oden-Khaar. Same configuration as before...." Rakhi took a breath. "They're headed straight for us."

"Bishop, get that Zodiac back here. Mr. Allen, I don't suppose you've finished installing those shields."

"Sorry, no. But I have something even better." Tony crawled across the floor on his hands and knees, rising to kneel before the weapons console. "Where shall we port to this time?"

Hunter grinned. "Same as before. Kimdihr's home world. Post haste. Bishop, the Zodiac?"

She watched through her headset as the Zodiac approach

the ship, then docked aggressively. "Back home, sir." She tore the headset off and tossed it onto the console.

"Excellent. Mr. Allen, engage the portal. Mr. Parks, take us through."

"Captain! The Oden-Khaar ships…." Rakhi yelled, her eyes wide.

The view screen showed the aft end of the three ships as they streaked past, headed for God knew where.

"Just passed us by," Hunter mused, staring. "They blew past us like we weren't even here. Something's wrong."

"You think they're headed toward the Oden-Rha?"

"Mr. Parks, take us into that portal. Now."

"Aye."

The ship lurched forward, the bow of it barely grazing the portal before it was pulled in, appearing on the other side, very nearly in orbit around the Oden-Rha's planet.

"Nice work, everyone. Rakhi, open a channel to the prime minister."

"Prime minister is coming online…now." Rakhi sat back and watched, eager for any glimpse of the alien world she could get.

"Captain Hunter, how nice to hear from you again."

"Prime Minister, I'm afraid I come bearing bad news. There are three Oden-Khaar ships headed your way at high speeds. I can only assume they have ill intentions."

"I appreciate your concern, friend, but I am aware. I called them here."

"You did? Why?"

"There is still the matter of our peace treaty. The Oden-Rha are most anxious to see it signed and put into action."

"I see." Hunter muted the transmission and turned to Tony. "Any chance you have one of those small teleporters left?"

"No, but I have the prototype of the onboard teleporter. It should get you down there. Of course, it hasn't been tested and you could end up a pile of banana pudding…."

"Good enough." He punched the button on his console and smiled at the screen. "If it's all right with you, Prime Minister, Commander Bishop and I would like to come down. I know who really killed the Oden-Khaar prince. And I'm pretty sure I know why."

"But of course, Captain. You are welcome any time."

"Thank you. We'll be there presently. Hunter out."

"You know who killed the prince? How?"

"Something just occurred to me, Bishop. Come on. I'll tell you about it in the lift. Mr. Allen, with me."

By the time the trio had geared up and set the coordinates into the teleporter, the Oden-Khaar ships had already arrived. They established an orbit, shields down. Hunter took that as a good sign, one that meant there would be no violence.

Bishop, Tony, and Hunter ported to the station just outside the ministry building, then walked the short distance through the building and into the lift. People bowed politely and smiled as they passed, apparently happy to see the strangers visit their planet once more.

As they rounded the corner and stepped into the doorway, Hunter stopped, putting one hand on Tony's chest and one on Bishop's in order to halt their progress. Inside Prime Minister Sansa's office sat Kimdihr and four Oden-Khaar soldiers. Hunter couldn't be certain, but he thought one of them to be Benom.

He adjusted his demeanor accordingly and strode into the room, rubbing his hands together and smiling. "Oh, good! We're all here. That will make this a lot easier."

A very large, very angry Oden-Khaar stood up from his seat on the dais and growled into Hunter's face. "What is the meaning of this interruption, Captain Hunter? You have no place here."

"Ah, Admiral Benom, I presume. Excellent because this mostly has to do with you, sir. Now, sit back down and I'll explain."

Slowly, grudgingly, Benom regained his seat. His face was set in fury and his eyes stared daggers through Hunter.

Hunter paced as he spoke, in true detective-uncovering-the-killer fashion. Truth be told, he felt a little like Sherlock Holmes, if Sherlock Holmes had been a super soldier and had traveled through space.

"Kimdihr didn't really kill your prince, did he? I mean, we know he didn't because of what Rakhi saw in his thoughts. You know that, too. In fact, you know who did kill the prince, don't you? It was all part of an elaborate plan to get inside the Oden-Rha's defense shields."

Benom shot up from his seat and gestured wildly. "Prime Minister, I must protest this interference. Surely you cannot believe this madman's rantings...."

"Please, sit down, Admiral Benom. It is our way to listen to others. Captain, please continue."

Hunter watched as Benom dropped onto his seat and turned his head, hiding his gritted teeth and tightly clenched fists. "You faked the video to give your people a credible reason to arrest Kimdihr when he arrived. It was a very good fake, but you were lacking one key bit of information that would have made it one hundred percent authentic-looking. You see, when I visited his home world, I realized that it was covered in gold. They didn't just use gold to decorate their buildings or make jewelry from. Gold is everywhere down here. So much so that their skin is even coated in it. I noticed that right off. The image of Kimdihr in your video had no such shine to his skin. You'd never been on his home world, so you didn't know until you met his aide. You just hoped that no one would notice it when the time came to show that video you'd mocked up.

"The prince's murder and Kimdihr's guilt were key to your plan, weren't they? You knew that Kimdihr would fear for his life at your hands and so, given a chance to escape, he would run for home as fast as he could. You gave him that chance. You let him escape and make it all the way to his ship, a feat which, had he thought about it at the time, should never have been possible. You'd already had your hands on that ship for nearly a day by that point, easily enough time to fit it with the weapons you needed and to plant your stowaway. The plan was that Kimdihr would take his ship straight home and be welcomed with open arms. Once they opened that shield to let him in, your stowaway would pop out and take control. He would use those weapons to disable as many shield generators as he could, allowing the rest of your force to wipe out all the Oden-Rha. Then the gold would be all yours."

"Preposterous!" Benom sprang up from his seat once more, spittle flying from his mouth as he yelled out that one word.

"Admiral Benom! Sit down at once!" Sansa said in a tone that carried far more anger than Hunter would ever have thought possible. "Continue, Captain. Please."

"You didn't count on the *Endeavor* being here, though, and once you lost Kimdihr, you knew you had to get him back at any cost. So, when he changed course and headed for our ship, you panicked. He was so scared at that point that he did the only thing he could. He risked his life porting onto my ship, even though he had no idea if it was possible to port through empty space. You knew, though. You didn't even hesitate. You ported your men onto my ship mere moments after Kimdihr arrived. And you did it again while my man was rigging the teleporter onto the hull of the ship. Thinking back on it, when Kimdihr ported onto the *Endeavor,* his ship went straight back to a course for his home. Almost like someone was piloting it. Someone was piloting it. I see that now. It was your stowaway.

"The only question that remains is: who did kill the prince? I mean, he was the driving force behind the peace treaty. A treaty, I might add, which would have cost you your job. There's not much need for a minister of war if there is no war. And with the treaty in place, you would have had to trade for the gold you wanted. Or pay for it. A man like you doesn't like to pay for things or be at the mercy of his trading partner. He prefers the spoils of war. So, I think you either killed the prince yourself or you had it done. Since you're an admiral, I lean more toward you had it done. I wonder what they do to assassins on your world. Especially assassins who murder the crown prince. I'm betting it's not pretty. Which makes me wonder why you don't look more worried."

The door behind Sansa opened just then and someone stepped in, though he had begun to speak before he could even be seen.

"Perhaps he doesn't look worried, Captain, because he knows that I was not killed."

"Your Highness! You're alive!" Hunter beamed.

"Yes. My servant is a member of a group of people who, much like myself, want peace between our two worlds. They uncovered this plot and warned me. I was not the man who was sleeping in my bed that night. It was the assassin instead. He was caught by my bodyguard, sneaking into my room. We drugged him and placed him into bed in my place. When he didn't report in, another was sent. And even when they were altering the video they stole, they did not realize the deception. Kimdihr was allowed to escape and only one ship chased him. However, when he ported onto your ship, the general sent three other ships, the ones who accosted you, to retrieve him at all costs. Only there were four ships that left the dock that day and not just three. Three came after you. The fourth whisked me away to safety. Because my people could never get the assassin to talk, I was just waiting to make my return until I knew who had constructed this plot. I was waiting on Kimdihr's planet. The peace treaty was signed yesterday by myself and the prime minister. So, you see, Admiral, all of this was for nothing. Our two worlds are at peace once more. An equitable arrangement will be reached for the trade of their goods, including the gold that you so coveted. And hopefully, we will never again have need of a man like you."

"What will happen to him?"

"He is a traitor. He and everyone who worked for him will be put to death for treason."

Hunter nodded solemnly, though he thought the punishment quite fitting. "As soon as Mr. Emok and Lieutenant Allen have finished their exchange, we will be on our way. And might I say, it has been a pleasure meeting you all. We could not have hoped for a better first contact."

They exchanged the traditional Oden-Rha greeting/farewell and then Bishop followed Hunter out of the building and into the street. They were quiet as they walked, mulling over everything that had happened in the past three days.

"Captain Hunter! Wait!" came the call from behind them.

Hunter turned to see who had called to them, and smiled as he spotted Kimdihr's name and rank badge. "Kimdihr, is there something you need?"

"No, Captain. I need nothing more. You saved my life back there. If you hadn't uncovered the real killer, I would have faced death for a crime I did not commit. So, I owe you my life. I am yours, to do with as you choose."

Hunter clapped a hand on the man's shoulder and smiled warmly. "My wish for you, Kimdihr, is to stay here. Your people need you. Help them through the difficult times ahead, as you and the Oden-Khaar adjust to the peace treaty and move forward as allies."

Kimdihr nodded and looked down at the ground. He looked as though he were about to cry. "Will you come back one day?"

"I'm sure we will."

"Mr. Emok tells me this is a traditional human farewell. I hope I am not acting inappropriately." Kimdihr threw himself, arms wide open, at Hunter and grabbed him into a huge bear hug, slapping his back for good measure.

"It is indeed. And quite nicely done. Thank you, my friend." Hunter shook his hand for good measure.

"Goodbye, Kimdihr." Bishop shook his hand as well, then turned to program the teleporter.

Hunter nestled into his chair with a sigh, staring out at the planet below them. It was true: As first encounters went, they had had a very good one. And they had made several invaluable trades in the process. His console buzzed and he pressed the button. "Hunter," he said blandly.

"Captain, I thought you'd like to know that all updates to the ship have been completed. The shields are in place, the teleporter has been incorporated into the bow, and we have a new teleporter room now."

"Excellent, Mr. Allen. I do appreciate all the hard work you've put in on this."

"It was a true pleasure, Captain. We even have a huge new database to work from. So, we can shove off any time you're ready. Like the way I used the term 'shove off?' Real nautical. I learned if from the captain of my yacht when we sailed...."

Hunter hit the button and Bishop snickered. "What?" he asked with a smirk.

"You just cut him off mid-sentence," she giggled.

"He's brilliant, but there's only so much of that man I can take."

"So, where to next, Captain?" Lieutenant Parks wanted to know.

"Oh, I don't know. The closest friendly planet on Kimdihr's database perhaps?"

"That would be...this one." Parks put up the star chart and stabbed his finger in the direction of a small, blue-green planet.

"Are we in a hurry?" He turned to look at Hunter.

Hunter shrugged. "Not really."

"Mark three it is, then." Parks dramatically extended one arm, index finger pointed downward, and stabbed at the star drive ignition.

Bishop leaned back in her chair and spun to face Hunter. "You know, it was pretty impressive the way you solved that murder back there. I think you missed your calling. You should have been a detective."

"Steve Hunter, Space Detective. That's me. I'll consider it for my retirement." He laughed.

"But you don't age. You never have to retire."

"Now, you're getting it."

"So, you'll just travel through space for all of eternity?" She cocked a mocking grin at him.

"Unless I get a better offer. Do you have a better offer, Bishop?"

His tone had been just this side of flirtatious and she shut him down by pulling a face at him. A light flashed on Rakhi's console and Bishop caught it from the corner of her eye. "No, I don't. But I'll bet whoever is on that ship does." She switched from star chart to view screen. An enormous ship loomed just off the starboard bow, filling most of the view screen and gleaming as though it were made of marble.

Hunter glanced up and sighed. "I'll bet they do." Another sigh, heavier this time and with a hint of dread. "Let's go find out."

ABOUT THE AUTHOR

Patricia Lee Macomber is the former editor-in-chief of ChiZine. She has been published in "Cemetery Dance" magazine and such anthologies as "Shadows Over Baker Street," "Little Red Riding Hood In the Big Bad City," and "Dark Arts." Currently, she lives in North Carolina with her husband, David, and their children.

BOOK LIST

Stargate Altlantis: SGA-15 BRIMSTONE with David Niall Wilson
Intermusings with David Niall Wilson
An Unkindness of Ravens with David Niall Wilson
Casual Casualties
Zombie - A Love Story
Love Lost

The Jason Callahan Mysteries

Book 1: *Murder, Sometimes*
Book 2: *Dead, Sometimes*
Book 3: *Scarlet, Sometimes*

Curious about other Crossroad Press books?
Stop by our site:
http://store.crossroadpress.com
We offer quality writing
in digital, audio, and print formats.

Enter the code FIRSTBOOK
to get 20% off your first order from our store!
Stop by today!

www.ingramcontent.com/pod-product-compliance
Lightning Source LLC
Chambersburg PA
CBHW060434180626
46817CB00007B/2814